Strong Enough

by

Jana Richards

The Masonville Series, Book 4

Strong Enough

Cover Art by *Rae Monet, Inc. Designs*

The Wild Rose Press, Inc.
PO Box 708
Adams Basin, NY 14410-0708
Visit us at www.thewildrosepress.com

Publishing History
First Edition, 2022
Trade Paperback ISBN 978-1-5092-4247-4
Digital ISBN 978-1-5092-4248-1

The Masonville Series, Book 4
Published in the United States of America

He slowly lowered his head, his breath mingling with hers. But he held back, as if waiting for her permission.

Charlotte stood toe to toe with him, her lips mere inches from his, their only connection his hand holding hers. Her senses filled with him, with his scent, with the look in his eyes, and the sound of his ragged breathing. She trembled, but she wasn't sure if it was with excitement or fear. Perhaps it was both.

All she knew was that right now she wanted to kiss Damon Greyson more than she'd wanted her next breath. She stretched up on her tiptoes and touched her lips to his.

Damon's arms came around her and crushed her against his broad chest. Somehow her arms wound themselves around his neck and hung on tight. Every part of his body seemed to fit perfectly with hers, as if they were puzzle pieces made only for each other.

And his mouth. Oh, his clever, wonderful mouth. His kiss was demanding, and yet so utterly tender it made her want to weep. It had been a long time since she'd been kissed like this.

No, she corrected. *I've never been kissed like this.*

Dedication

To my critique partners and friends,
Who help make my writing so much better:
Ishbel M., Judy S., Helen N.,
Kathy S., and Alison L.
Thank you!

Chapter One

The incessant ringing of his phone woke Damon Greyson from a deep sleep. He groped blindly for the annoying device, trying to silence it before it woke everyone in the house. Finally, he got his hands on it.

"Hello?"

"Damon…Damon, son, you need to be careful… please."

"Dad?" He hadn't spoken to his father in months.

"Son, be careful." Peter Greyson's voice was a whisper. "She's planning something."

"She? You mean Mother?" Damon sat up, now completely awake.

"I've heard Victoria talking to someone, saying your name. I don't know who."

Damon rubbed his forehead. Was Peter drunk? He didn't sound drunk, though God knew he often was.

"Why are you telling me this? Why call in the middle of the night?"

"Because she watches me. I have to be careful."

He made it sound like Victoria was holding him prisoner. What the hell was going on?

Damon hardened his heart. Why should he care? Peter did nothing while unspeakable things were done to Damon in childhood. He'd never tried to protect him then, so why should Damon care what happened to the man now? Peter had been too drunk most of the time to be a real father to him and his siblings. He saved his rare sober periods for his work as a state senator in the Minnesota legislature.

Damon pushed a tired hand through his hair. As a counselor, he knew alcoholism was a disease, not a character flaw. But when the chaos of the disease happened close to home, finding empathy was difficult.

"I'll be careful. Watch out for yourself, too. Okay?"

"I will. I'll call you again if I learn something."

The line went dead. Damon checked the time on his phone. Three-thirty-five a.m. He set his phone on the night table once more and hung his head. Every time he believed his childhood nightmare was over, something dragged him back in.

He wouldn't let it happen this time. He couldn't.

Damon swung his legs over the side of the bed. Despite the time, he was far too keyed up to go back to sleep. He dressed and straightened his bedcovers, then quietly descended the stairs of his sister's farmhouse. Blair had inherited the farm and everything in it from their grandfather, and in typical, generous Blair fashion, she had opened her home to him while he waited for renovations to be completed on his own home.

He walked across the dark farmyard to the barn where he'd set up a heavy bag in one of the empty stalls. After wrapping his hands and shoving them into his boxing gloves, he took out his frustrations on the bag, pounding it over and over until he was exhausted. And then he hit it some more.

He'd be damned if he let his mother take away the peace he'd worked so hard for.

****

The next afternoon, Damon made his way across the Masonville, North Dakota elementary school grounds, looking for his brother Ben among the many other adults assembled there. His five-year-old niece Sophie was playing her first ever tee-ball game today, and Damon wanted to be there to witness the momentous occasion.

Apparently, Sophie's game wasn't the only one scheduled today. Kids a few years older than Sophie were warming up for their own games. They fielded grounders and tossed balls to each other on two of the softball diamonds on the school grounds. He headed toward the third diamond, the one nearest the school, and saw adults chatting amiably as they set up folding chairs behind the backstop in preparation to watch the game.

And then it started, as it often did when he found himself in a public place. The hypervigilance, the suspicion. He scanned the crowd, trying to decipher the reason every adult male was in attendance. *That man standing off to the side by himself. Is he a parent? Had he seen him before? Are those kids playing by themselves on the playground equipment being supervised by their parents? Is the coach standing too close to that group of children as he talks to them? Did that touch on the shoulder look normal?*

Stop! Everything's fine. He had to constantly remind himself that not every adult meant harm to a defenseless child. But the eight-year-old boy inside him who'd been on the receiving end of sexual abuse didn't always believe it.

Finally, he spotted Ben standing behind his wife's folding chair. Damon joined them, leaning over to kiss his sister-in-law's cheek.

"How are you, Jamie?"

She rubbed the rounded bump of her pregnant belly. "I'm great. How about you? How are the renovations on your building coming along?"

Damon straightened and shrugged. "It's slow going. At this rate, it'll be months before we can open our veterans' retreat."

When Damon inherited a large, three-story building in downtown Masonville from his grandfather, Everett Branson, his first thought had been to turn it into something useful. As an army veteran and now a professional counselor, he understood the high toll of operational injuries, more commonly known as Post Traumatic Stress Disorder or PTSD. His plan was to turn the second and third floors of his building into living quarters for veterans and himself, with space for group counseling sessions and recreational activities. He'd teamed up with his sister Blair on the farm. There, veterans would help care for Blair's rescue horses and, in doing so, receive some healing themselves.

But none of that work could happen if the damn renovations didn't get done. Damon bit back his frustration.

"What is it this time?" Ben asked.

"A plugged sewer line. We may have to dig up the street in front of the building to replace the line. If we do, it'll cost thousands of dollars."

"If you need help with money, let me know," Ben said.

It was typical of his big brother to look after everyone in his life. Like him and Blair, Ben had received an inheritance from Granddad Everett. His consisted of a house in Masonville, a partnership in a law firm, and cash to secure the futures of his stepdaughters. Damon nodded to make him happy, but he'd never take money from him. Ben was starting a new life with Jamie, and they were about to have a baby. Soon he'd have three kids to care for. For the first time, Ben was truly happy, and Damon didn't want to cause him even one second of worry.

"Where's Bella?" he asked.

"She's over at the playground with a friend." When Damon turned in the direction of the playground to search for her, Ben put a hand on his shoulder. "We can see her from here. She's fine, Damon."

He nodded again, though he wasn't exactly reassured. Ben was a protective father, but he had no idea what could happen to an unattended child, the horrible things—

Stop. Damon made himself take a breath.

He considered telling Ben about the phone call he'd received from their father, Peter. The strange call had haunted him, nibbling on the edges of his peace of mind, ever since he'd received it. He had no idea what it meant that Victoria was talking about him. For all he knew, Peter could be making the whole thing up. He decided to keep the conversation to himself. Ben didn't need the aggravation.

Sophie's tee-ball game began, and conversation between the adults ended. One kid sat cross-legged in right field and made a bouquet with the dandelions surrounding him. The girl on second base stood on the bag and picked her nose. Damon grinned and shook his head. *Should be an interesting game.*

Sophie came to bat. A coach set the ball on top of

the tee and stepped away in the nick of time as Sophie swung her bat with all the might she could muster. To everyone's surprise, the bat connected with the ball. The ball rolled past the infield as several players on the opposing side swarmed toward it. Sophie stood immobile, the bat still in her hands.

"Go, Sophie!" Jamie yelled. "Run!"

Ben clapped. "Run!"

Sophie took off toward first base, taking the bat with her. Through a series of overthrows and players not being where they were supposed to be, she rounded the bases. Reaching home, she jumped triumphantly on the home plate, tossing her bat to the ground at last.

"Yay, Sophie!" Jamie jumped to her feet, her arms stretched over her head. "Did you see that?"

Ben clapped madly. "She was amazing!"

Damon laughed at the proud parents. "She's a regular Babe Ruth."

The next couple of innings weren't nearly as exciting, and Damon's attention wandered. He saw two adults approach the playground where eight-year-old Bella was playing with a friend. He touched Ben's arm.

"I'm going to say hi to Bella."

Ben looked toward the playground. "Okay. You coming back?"

"I'll be back later to congratulate Sophie on her home run."

Damon headed toward the playground, his eyes on the two adults, a man and a woman. As he got closer, he saw that they had a small child with them, maybe two or three years old, and they were trying to convince him to go down the slide. The boy wanted nothing to do with the slide and clung to his mother's leg. Damon relaxed. Just a couple of parents minding their own business. No threat here.

"Uncle Damon!" Bella raced over to him. "Can you push us on the swings?"

"Sure."

The girls hopped on the swings, and Damon pushed them high enough to give them a thrill, but not so high that they were out of control. Their excited giggles made him smile.

"Hey, look at you being the cool uncle."

Damon turned at the sound of the familiar female voice. Charlotte Saunders stood a few feet away from the playground equipment, holding the leashes of her two dogs. In one glance he took in her smile, the long blonde hair pulled into a ponytail, and the gorgeous legs that went on forever. He couldn't help but stare.

"You might want to be careful, Damon." Charlotte's gaze was on something behind him.

He turned and ducked in time to avoid being brained by an incoming swing. *That's what I get for staring*. After giving each child one more push, he stepped away from the swings.

"I'll be over here talking to Charlotte, Bella. I'll be back to give you a couple more pushes before I go back to Sophie's game."

"Okay, Uncle Damon."

Damon joined Charlotte on the grass surrounding the play equipment. Her beagle Daisy sat obediently at her feet, while the younger River, a Shepherd/Lab cross of some kind, strained at the leash to continue their walk.

"How's it going?" he asked.

"It's going good. We had our last fittings for our

bridesmaid dresses today."

Charlotte's brother Garrett was marrying Damon's sister Blair, and Damon and Charlotte were paired in the bridal party. "I look forward to seeing them. Only ten days to the big day. Have you been practicing your dance steps? No pressure, but I don't want you to embarrass me."

"I haven't been practicing, but I did buy steel-toed high heels to protect my feet."

Damon put his hand over his heart. "Ouch. You wound me, Charlotte. I've been told I'm very light on my feet."

She grinned. "As long as you're light on *my* feet."

He grinned back. "Don't worry. We'll shuffle around the floor for the obligatory bridal dance, and then your feet are safe from me."

"Sounds like a plan." She lowered her gaze as she stroked Daisy. "Garrett and Blair are good together. I haven't seen Garrett this happy in a very long time."

Damon heard the wistfulness in her voice. "I feel the same about Blair. I think she's truly happy for the first time in her life. She finally has the home she's always wanted."

Charlotte lifted her head and smiled, but there was a forced quality to it. "I'm glad they found each other."

He was usually pretty good at reading people, but Charlotte Saunders held her cards close to her heart. He wondered, not for the first time since he'd moved to Masonville and gotten to know her again, what was going on inside that beautiful head of hers. She was no longer the open girl he used to know. What secrets was she hiding?

He leaned over to scratch Daisy's head. River came

close for his share of attention, and Damon obliged with some scratches behind his ears.

"You're not fooling me, Damon Greyson. You're an old softy when it comes to dogs. So it totally baffles me why you won't include them in your veterans' retreat." Charlotte gave her dogs a command, and they obediently sat.

Damon grinned at the irritation in her voice. They'd sparred over this question almost from the moment Damon announced his plans for the veterans' retreat using Blair's rescue horses for equine therapy. He'd decided long ago there would be a place for dogs in his program, but he hadn't yet told Charlotte. It was too much fun getting a rise out of her.

Or maybe, if he was honest with himself, he wanted to keep their relationship light. He was afraid to feel too much for her, like he had as a teenager, back when he and his siblings spent summers at their grandparents' farm and Charlotte Saunders lived just down the road.

"I've told you before, Charlotte. We're emphasizing equine therapy."

Her hazel eyes flashed. "And I've told you not everyone is comfortable with horses. They're big and scary. Some people might like the comfort of a dog, an animal they can play with and love and even take to bed with them. I sleep with my dogs every night."

At the mention of her bed, Damon allowed his imagination a moment to go on a wild, erotic ride. Lately he'd found himself having more and more erotic thoughts, with Charlotte Saunders in the starring role. But he'd never act on those thoughts, knowing she didn't have the same feelings for him. Besides,

Charlotte was his future brother-in-law's sister, and he didn't want any awkwardness between him and Charlotte to affect his relationship with Garrett.

Also, he sensed a vulnerability in Charlotte he didn't yet understand and wouldn't exploit. Something had changed since they were teenagers. So he contented himself with light banter and teasing.

Charlotte's face flushed. "You know what I mean. Dogs can give support and comfort anywhere, not just in the barn."

"I'll admit dogs have some advantages."

"And?" she prompted.

"And I'll think about it."

Charlotte made a sound of frustration. "Dammit, Damon, you make me crazy." To Damon's surprise her mouth twisted as if she were struggling to hold back tears. "If you knew how many unwanted dogs are languishing at the shelter in Bismarck right now, if you knew how many were euthanized…"

She didn't finish. She looked away and pulled on the dogs' leashes. "I should go."

Damon grasped her elbow. "Charlotte, wait. I'm sorry. I didn't mean to upset you. I think there'll be a place for dogs at the retreat. But I don't know yet what their role will be or how many we can use. Maybe we can figure it out together."

She lifted her head and her eyes met Damon's. He had the feeling she held back her tears by sheer will. He certainly had no wish to make her cry and felt like an ass for teasing her. He'd misjudged how much this meant to her.

"Do you mean it?" There was more than a touch of suspicion in her voice.

"I mean it."

She looked away. "I'm sorry. I hate women who use tears to get what they want. It's just that yesterday the shelter had to put down three dogs. There was this one old dog, Shep…" She shook her head, unable to finish.

He squeezed her elbow before letting her go. "I'm sorry."

She nodded, and again Damon sensed her vulnerability. Charlotte tried to give off an aura of strength. She was the caregiving nurse, the person others looked to for help. But who helped Charlotte?

After a few breaths, she straightened her shoulders and faced him, her composure once more back in place. "How long do you think it will be?"

"You mean until the retreat is up and running?" When she nodded, he blew out a breath. "I don't know. My building's in worse shape than I first thought."

"If there's anything I can do to speed up the process, let me know."

"You know anything about unplugging sewer lines?"

She made a face. "You're on your own, Greyson."

Don't I know it. "Hey, you asked. From now on, I'll only request your help when it comes to dogs."

She chuckled. "Good plan."

This time Charlotte's smile was genuine, and for a moment Damon couldn't breathe. He found himself wondering what it would be like to have the full force of her smile directed at him and to know there was real affection for him behind the smile. The longing he experienced at that thought shocked him.

Better not to allow such notions to take root.

Despite all the work he'd done over the years to overcome the harm done to him in the past, he still had questions. Would it ever be possible for him to have a normal, loving, long-term sexual relationship with a woman? The longest relationship he'd had lasted six months.

Maybe he'd always be damaged goods.

Chapter Two

After her shift at the hospital, Charlotte changed into street clothes and headed to Best Friends Haven for Dogs, the shelter where she was a regular volunteer. The sound of barking dogs greeted her as she walked into the building, muffled somewhat by the door separating the front office area from the back where the dogs were housed. She smiled at Best Friends' long-time receptionist.

"Hi, Michelle. How's your day going?"

The older woman smiled. "We had two adoptions completed today and three people came by who seemed very interested in getting a new pet, so all in all, it's been a good day."

"That's wonderful news."

In a perfect world, every dog in the shelter would find a loving, safe, forever home. Charlotte amended that opinion. In a perfect world, shelters wouldn't be necessary. Too many dogs were housed at Best Friends, and though volunteers like her did the best they could to make their lives happy, the sad fact was, they couldn't save them all. The truth of that statement had been brought home to her with stark clarity four days ago when they'd had to euthanize three dogs.

Including Shep.

Her heart ached when she thought of the German Shepherd. He was over thirteen years old and had been surrendered to the shelter when his elderly owner had to go into a nursing home. Because of his age, no one was willing to adopt him. Charlotte had thought about taking Shep home, but she already had two dogs, and her busy work and volunteer schedule meant she often had to hire a neighborhood kid to walk and feed them. She simply didn't have time to adequately care for an old dog.

When Shep developed a serious heart problem, he became unadoptable, and the decision was made to euthanize him and end his suffering. In her head, Charlotte knew it was the right thing to do. But in her heart, it was a difficult, bitter pill to swallow. She'd attended Shep's euthanasia, gently stroking him as the shelter's veterinarian administrated the drugs that would quietly end his life.

And then she'd gone home and cried for an hour.

"Is Gina in?" she asked.

"Yeah. She's in her office."

Gina Watson, Executive Director of Best Friends Haven, had been a close friend since Charlotte started volunteering there. She headed for the door separating the reception area from the rest of the shelter. "Make sure you say goodbye before you leave for the day."

Michelle gave her a wave. "I will. Have fun."

"As much fun as I can have cleaning kennels." Charlotte heard Michelle's chuckle as she opened the door.

As soon as she entered the shelter area, the familiar smell hit her—part disinfectant, part urine, part wet dog. She made her way to Gina's small, crowded office. Empty wire crates were stacked against one wall of the office and second-hand, dented filing cabinets lined the opposite wall. In between was Gina's desk with its ancient computer and stacks of papers taking up most of the surface space. Gina smacked the side of her computer monitor, making her "Executive Directors Get It Done" sign fall to the floor.

"Dammit all to hell."

Charlotte stepped inside the office and sat in the chair across from her friend. "Whoa. What did the computer do to make you so mad?"

Gina looked up at her with a frown. "It told me the truth. We have too many dogs and not enough budget. Or space."

Charlotte understood what she meant. Animal protection officers had recently shut down a puppy mill and brought more than a hundred dogs to the shelter. Overnight, the shelter had swelled to 150 animals, fifty over the number it had been designed to house. By using some temporary kennels and asking their foster families to look after several puppies from the mill, they'd been able to cope, but it was a struggle.

Gina sighed and removed her glasses. "I'm confident most of these dogs will be adopted. But it will take time. Did you hear one of the bulldogs bit a volunteer? Jenny Howell only started volunteering a few weeks ago."

"Oh, no! Is she okay?"

"She will be, but it was pretty traumatic for her. She had to get antibiotics and a tetanus shot. It goes to show how messed up these puppy mill dogs are. Bulldogs are usually so laid-back and friendly."

Charlotte sighed. The puppy mill dogs were a combination of popular breeds like pugs, French bulldogs, and American bulldogs. But obviously they had not been well socialized. How could they be, when they'd been confined to cages all their lives, in overcrowded, unsanitary conditions.

"Almost all the new arrivals have parasites or eye infections. Some of the older dogs need dental work."

"That doesn't sound good."

"It isn't. It's going to cost a fortune in veterinary fees."

"Don't you have a big fundraiser coming up?"

"That's not till September, and the money we expect to raise is earmarked for operating costs in the coming year. We always have a contingency fund for emergencies such as this, but this influx will tax all our resources. The board and I have already made the decision not to accept a group of dogs we were planning to bring in from Kentucky."

Charlotte knew that Best Friends Haven for Dogs was part of a network of shelters and volunteers that transported dogs from overcrowded shelters to facilities better able to find homes for them. For the past several years, Best Friends had brought in dogs from shelters in Kentucky.

"Maybe you can transport some of these dogs to another shelter," Charlotte said.

Gina shook her head. "Transporting is a stressful proposition. Dogs have to be healthy and well-socialized before we can put them in a vehicle for several hours and move them to a less crowded shelter. Right now, very few of our dogs fit either of those qualifications."

Charlotte sat back in her chair, her heart sinking. If the shelter was strapped for money, did that mean more dogs would have to be euthanized? The thought saddened her.

"Hey, I'm sorry. I didn't mean to infect you with my bad mood," Gina said.

"It's okay. We're all in this together, right? You shouldn't have to worry alone. I'll worry with you, and we'll be twice as depressed."

Gina chuckled. "Right. Thanks for listening. Sometimes I just need to vent, you know?"

"Yeah, I know." Charlotte sat up straighter. "I almost forgot. Damon Greyson finally agreed to use dogs at his veterans' retreat. We don't know how many yet, but maybe it will help ease the burden here a little."

"That's great news. Thanks, I really needed some today." Gina grinned across the desk at her. "So. Damon Greyson. What's he like?"

"He's…." Charlotte tried to come up with a word to best describe Damon. *Enigmatic*, *secretive*, *annoying, funny* came to mind. *Handsome*, *sexy*, and *great butt* followed closely, but she ignored them. Sort of. "Interesting. He's an interesting person."

"Interesting?" Gina made a face. "You've talked about him every day for weeks, and interesting is the best you can come up with?"

"Come on. I have not talked about him every day." When Gina only raised an eyebrow at her, Charlotte frowned. "Well, if I have, it's only because I've been trying to get him to commit to adopting dogs from the shelter. He drove me crazy with his excuses."

"Isn't that…interesting?" Gina tapped her pen against the desk. "In the six years I've known you, I've never heard you talk about any man as much as you talk about him. Actually, I don't think I've ever heard you talk about anyone you're interested in."

17

"Don't read anything into it, Gina. There's nothing there." Sometimes her friend could be very annoying. Maybe that was because she knew her so well.

Gina sighed and leaned back against her chair. "If there isn't, I wish there were. I've never known you to have a romantic relationship with anyone. I don't get it. You're beautiful, funny, smart, and you've got the best heart of anyone I know. You have so much to give. Guys hit on you when we go out together, and it's as if you don't even notice. So if you're finally noticing Damon Greyson, I say it's about time."

Charlotte rose to her feet, growing too uncomfortable with the conversation to listen any longer. "Well, this has been fun, but those kennels aren't going to clean themselves."

Gina gave her a knowing smile. She knew avoidance when she saw it. "Knock yourself out."

In the back room, Charlotte geared up with ear protection, rubber gloves, and a face mask. Unfortunately, the pressure washer was broken, so she had to clean kennels by hand. She mulled over Gina's words as she scrubbed and disinfected. Her friend was wrong. She'd only spoken about Damon because of his decision to open a retreat for veterans and to use Blair and Garrett's farm as part of it. But Gina had been right about one thing. She *had* noticed Damon.

She'd seen him again for the first time in years at his grandfather's funeral last summer, when he'd arrived with his brother Ben. Ben Grayson's movie-star good looks had caused a stir among the women of Masonville.

But Damon was the one who'd stood out for Charlotte that day. Though grieving his grandfather's death, he'd exuded a sense of calm. He was solicitous of his siblings, especially Blair, who'd taken Everett Branson's death very hard. There was a strength about him that told her she could depend on him. Lean on him. That he would understand.

Charlotte scrubbed hard at a plastic kennel. She didn't want to notice Damon, not in the way Gina meant. And she sure as hell didn't want to lean on him.

She especially didn't want him to understand her. He wouldn't like what he discovered.

****

Damon's heart sank as he stared at the water covering the flat roof of the Fletcher Building. He knew next to nothing about construction and building maintenance, but even he knew there shouldn't be water up here. He and his contractor, Clayton Brown, had come up to the roof through the staircase access on the third floor after Clayton informed him there was a serious problem he needed to see.

"The roof's shot," Clayton told him. "It's supposed to be sloped enough so that water can drain off, but obviously that's not happening. The waterproof coating is failing. Remember that stain I showed you on the ceiling on the third floor? It means there's been some leakage already, and it's only going to get worse."

Damon suppressed a groan. It was one thing after another with this building. The plumbing, and now the roof. What else could go wrong?

He didn't want to tempt fate with an answer to that question.

"Cut to the chase, Clayton. What are we talking moneywise, and how long is it going to take to fix?"

Clayton named a sum of money, and Damon

pressed his lips together to keep from swearing.

"My crew will get it done as soon as possible. It's a pretty big job because it means we have to build a slope into the roof and then completely reseal the entire thing. I may have to bring in more men on this project so we can get back on schedule."

More workers meant more money. At this rate it would be weeks, maybe months, until he could house veterans. The only bit of good news lately was that they didn't have to dig up the street to unclog the sewer line. The blockage was discovered in the basement of his building. But the good news was only marginal since the crew had had to break the concrete floor and dig down to replace the old pipes. It had still been expensive, though not as expensive as digging up the street would have been.

There was a distinct possibility he would run through the money Granddad left him plus his entire life savings before the renovations were completed. Even worse, the Veterans Administration had let him know they had veterans who needed help *now*. He'd been forced to turn them away.

The frustration burned in his gut, but there was nothing he could do. The renovations had to be done right.

"Fine. Make it happen. Keep in touch."

"Will do," Clayton said.

Damon left his truck on Main near his building and headed down the street on foot, needing to walk and blow off some steam. Maybe later he'd go for a run. Long runs through the pasture at Blair's farm soothed him, probably because it was the place he felt his grandparents' spirits the strongest. He wished he could ask for Granddad's counsel right now. He'd always depended on Everett to steer him in the right direction.

He walked the six blocks to his brother's law office and found both Ben and his law partner Morley Walker at work there. Ben met him in the reception area.

"Hi. I didn't expect to see you today."

"I didn't mean to interrupt your work. I was at the Fletcher Building, and…" Damon shook his head, his frustration cutting off his words. "I needed to walk. So here I am."

Morley stepped out of his office and joined them in the reception area. "What's going on with your building that's got you all riled up?"

"The building's in bad shape, far worse than I first imagined. The cost overruns and delays are hitting hard." He told them about the latest setback. "At this rate, I'm going to run out of money before I run out of renovations."

"Granddad was a shrewd investor. It seems odd that he would purchase a building with so many issues, especially since he was planning to leave it to you. He wouldn't want to saddle you with problems. It's unfortunate he didn't have it inspected," Ben said.

"Everett bought the Fletcher Building from George Armstrong," Morley said. "We knew him for years, and he assured us the building was sound. We had no reason to doubt him."

"Either George Armstrong didn't know the extent of his building's problems, or he hid the truth from you and Granddad," Ben said. "An inspection might have revealed some of the difficulties Damon is finding now."

"An inspection can only catch so much. It can't go

behind the walls or beneath the concrete floor," Damon countered.

"True, but if an inspector got up on the roof, he might have at least found the trouble there," Ben argued. "Maybe George Armstrong was less than honest."

Morley shook his head. "I find it hard to believe George knowingly deceived us. But I can't rule it out entirely. If Everett had known there were so many issues, he could have negotiated a better price. Or maybe he wouldn't have bought it at all. I'll speak to George, see what he has to say."

Damon sighed. "I appreciate that, Morley, but what's done is done. I can't change the past. I can only look to the future and try to do better." It was the creed by which he lived his life, the mantra he whispered to himself every day. "The important thing is that my contractor is fixing the issues as they come up. It's just taking a lot of time and money."

"Are you happy with your contractor's work? Brown Construction came highly recommended, and I checked out his references myself," Morley said. "I'm going to feel really bad if both the building and the contractor I recommended turn out to be duds."

Damon had checked out Brown Construction's references as well and found them to be impeccable. The company had been around for a long time and had a reputation for quality and integrity. Clayton Brown had taken over the running of the company from his grandfather in the last couple of years, but he'd heard no reports that workmanship had suffered since the changeover.

"No need to beat yourself up, Morley. The work

that's been completed so far has been good, but it's behind schedule. The VA is breathing down my neck to begin our program now. If we continue to be delayed, I'm afraid they may cancel my contract."

Ben clapped him on the shoulder. "Remember what I told you. If you need more money, come to me."

Once again, Damon nodded in agreement, though he couldn't, in good conscience, take money away from Ben's family.

If he had to, he'd borrow money from a bank. He'd work through this setback on his own, the same way he handled every aspect of his life.

The thought of being alone with his problems elicited a melancholy he was unprepared for. He was used to being on his own. Why was it suddenly bothering him now?

Chapter Three

"Blair and Garrett are two very special people."

Emotion overcame Charlotte as she neared the end of her short speech to the bride and groom. Her throat closed, and her eyes burned. It embarrassed her to get weepy at her brother's wedding. She could usually hide her feelings under a cover of humor, but jokes weren't working for her today. Garrett and Blair's happiness felt too important to kid about.

As she struggled for composure, her gaze locked with Damon's. He gave her an encouraging nod as if to tell her he had faith in her, that she could do it. Charlotte nodded back, and calmness spread over her like a warm blanket. Taking a deep breath, she faced the seventy-five invited guests once again.

"You meet thousands of people in your life, but most don't touch you deep inside. And then you meet one person and your life is changed forever. That's what happened when Blair and Garrett met. They touched each other's souls, and their lives will forever be changed for the better."

She lifted her wine glass and turned toward the newly married couple. "Blair and Garrett, may you always have patience, good humor, peace, love, and joy in your life together. To the bride and groom."

"To the bride and groom," the guests repeated.

Charlotte sipped sparkling grape juice from her

wine glass. Blair had been an easygoing bride, but the one thing she'd insisted on was that no alcohol be served at her wedding. Charlotte knew Garrett had abused alcohol in the months following the explosion in Afghanistan that resulted in the amputation of his right leg below the knee. The first few months after his retirement from the Marines and return home to North Dakota had been rough. Fortunately, his problems with alcohol appeared to be over. But perhaps Blair didn't want to put temptation in his way.

She met Damon's gaze once more over the rim of her glass. Charlotte nodded in thanks, and to her surprise he gave her an exaggerated wink and a goofy smile. She couldn't help but laugh. He was right. Today was a time to celebrate and to put away worry. At least for a few hours.

Soon the caterers cleared away the dishes, and tables were moved against the wall. A DJ began to play music, mostly country tunes that Blair and Garrett both liked. The bridal party assembled in front of the head table, and the song chosen for the ceremonial first dance began to play. Charlotte listened to the bluesy opening strains of "Blessed." The lyrics spoke of being blessed to find the person they loved, about it being so much more than luck.

Her heart ached at the sentiment. Most days she could accept that love like that wasn't in the cards for her. But today, with all the trappings of love and marriage on full display, the knowledge tasted bitter.

The master of ceremonies, Hank Dawson, a fellow veteran and friend of Garrett's, wheeled his chair onto the dance floor and spoke into the mic.

"Mr. and Mrs. Garrett Saunders will now have

their first dance together as husband and wife."

The crowd clapped wildly as Blair stepped into Garrett's open arms. They made a slow circle around the floor, smiling at each other as they shuffled along. Charlotte choked up at the sight of her brother dancing, despite his amputation. Perhaps it wasn't the most elegant dance, but to her it was beautiful.

"And now joining them, the best man and matron of honor, Chris and Alison Redwick."

Alison grasped Chris's hand with a smile and they joined Garrett and Blair. Over the music, Charlotte heard a young voice.

"Go Mom and Dad!"

Everyone laughed at the enthusiastic cheer from Chris and Alison's daughter. Chris was another of Garrett's friends from his military days. He struggled with PTSD, but he and his family had come a long way since they first arrived in Masonville.

"And now the rest of the bridal party. Sister of the groom, the lovely Lauren Walsh with brother of the bride, Ben Greyson. Following them is Charlotte Saunders, another beautiful sister of the groom, along with Blair's brother, Damon Greyson. And now I know who got all the looks in the Saunders family. Will Garrett's parents, Grace and Robert Saunders, please also join the happy couple on the floor."

As their names were called, Charlotte reached for Damon's outstretched hand and stepped into his arms. They glided effortlessly across the floor as if they'd been dancing together all their lives. As if they were perfectly in sync.

"You've been holding out on me, Greyson. You never told me you could dance."

He appeared uncomfortable with her compliment. "My school had obligatory ballroom dance classes. To be honest, I haven't danced in years, but apparently it's like riding a bike. You never forget."

"Those classes were time well spent, I'd say."

To her surprise, his mouth twisted in distaste. "My mother would likely agree with you. She'd be the only one."

Charlotte heard the bitterness in his voice. Last summer at Everett Branson's funeral, she'd sensed a deep tension between the three Greyson children and their parents. Blair had refused to invite her parents to the wedding. It seemed very important to her, so despite the odd request, Charlotte hadn't questioned it. Now, as she stared up at the tight line of Damon's pursed lips, she wondered at the reason.

"In any case, you make even someone like me with two left feet look good."

To Charlotte's relief, the tension eased from his face.

"Glad the classes weren't a total waste of time."

With that, he pressed Charlotte close and spun her into a tight, fast spin. She let out a squeak of surprise and hung onto to his broad shoulders. As he straightened their steps, she laughed in pure delight.

"Maybe I don't have two left feet after all."

"Maybe you just needed the right partner."

Charlotte stared at him, her heart doing a panicked two-step as she tried to interpret what he was saying. Did he want a different, more serious relationship with her? She needed to keep their relationship light because she didn't think she could deal with a totally serious Damon Greyson.

"Anytime you want dance lessons, give me a call," he said, a teasing light in his eyes.

She relaxed again, relieved their relationship remained in the friendly, playful zone.

"Get over yourself, Greyson. You're not *that* good."

Damon laughed and spun her again. This time Charlotte was more prepared, matching his steps. He held her close, and she was suddenly aware of her breasts pressed against the hard wall of his chest, of his chiseled chin, of the smell of his cologne. As he gazed down at her, all teasing gone from his dark brown eyes, Charlotte found it hard to breathe.

He leaned forward to whisper in her ear. "I think you make *me* look good."

Charlotte could only stare back at him. Soon the dance floor grew crowded as many of the guests joined them. When the first set finished, she breathed a sigh of relief. They switched partners, and she danced with Ben while Damon danced with her sister Lauren. After that Charlotte partnered with her dad, then Morley Walker, and Chris Redwick. The joyous mood in the room was infectious, making it easy to have a good time. Everyone was delighted Garrett and Blair had found happiness together.

After her dance with Chris ended, Charlotte made her way to the refreshments table and poured herself a glass of lemonade. She sat in an empty seat at the back of the hall and slipped off her shoes, sighing with relief. Smiling, she watched her sister Lauren dance with her husband Cole. They looked at each other as if they were the only two people in the room. They'd been through hell, but their love for each other got them through the hard times. And now they had a beautiful baby, her niece Piper. Charlotte was glad for them.

She watched other joyful couples dance by. Chris and Alison. Ben and Jamie. Even her parents, Grace and Robert. And now she could add Blair and Garrett to the list of happy couples.

At one time she'd believed she'd be part of a happy couple someday, too. But those dreams had died a long time ago.

"Mind if I join you?"

Charlotte startled at the sound of the deep male voice. She looked up to see Damon standing next to her, a glass in his hand.

"No, of course not. I was just resting my feet for a minute. These new shoes are killing me."

"Yeah. I needed to get away from the crowd for a few minutes, too."

"Speak for yourself, Greyson. I wasn't being antisocial."

"Just anti-shoes?"

He always managed to make her laugh, even when she was annoyed with him. "Yes. Anti-shoes. I may start a new support group."

For a few moments they silently sipped their drinks and watched the dancers. All the happy couples. The group to which she'd never belong.

"Okay, that's enough. Put your shoes back on."

"What?"

"Enough brooding. Let's get back out there."

"I wasn't brooding." Where did he get off telling her what to feel? What did he know about her?

"All right. Wallowing then. Call it whatever you like, but we're putting a stop to it right now."

29

He stood and held out his hand. Charlotte looked away, anger and petulance welling in her chest. And fear. Why was she afraid?

"Go annoy someone else, Greyson."

Damon sat beside her once more. "When I get in one of these moods, I've learned it's best for me to get out of my own head. I need to be with people, to change my thoughts before I'm that little boy once more, the one whose parents have repeatedly left him with a family friend who's touched him in places no adult should ever touch a child. I need to change the channel, Charlotte. Will you come with me?"

Dear God. Emotions swirled in her head—shock, compassion, despair, anger. She wanted to say something to take away the pain he must have gone through. But what could she say?

He rose once more and held out his hand to her.

Charlotte stared at it, her heart racing. She cried inside for the little boy he'd been, for the child whose parents had failed him so miserably. She had a strong urge to follow that child, to find out everything about him.

"Okay, but I'm not wearing those shoes. I'd rather go barefoot." Her voice was surprisingly steady considering the turmoil inside her.

"Suit yourself."

She looked up into his face and saw calm acceptance there. Charlotte placed her hand in his and rose to her feet. Damon tightly squeezed her hand.

She squeezed back. After what he'd just told her, Charlotte was overcome with the need to comfort him. "It'll be okay."

He grinned at her. "Yeah. It will. I promise."

As they walked to the dance floor together, she had the disorienting thought that he was the one comforting her.

Chapter Four

The Monday after the wedding, Charlotte allowed herself to be lazy. Sunday had been busy with clean-up at the community hall where the reception had been held and then helping her mother get ready for the gift opening celebration and dinner at her parents' farm. It had been a hectic, whirlwind weekend.

She lounged in her robe until nearly noon, indulging in a rare morning of reading, drinking coffee and simply relaxing. Or at least she tried to relax. Damon's words kept playing in her head, disturbing her peace.

I'm that little boy once more, the one whose parents have repeatedly left him with a family friend who's touched him in places no adult should ever touch a child.

After he'd dropped that bombshell on her at the wedding, they'd danced. Neither of them spoke again about what he'd told her. But she couldn't stop thinking about it.

How could his parents have let this happen? Why didn't they protect him? He'd been a little boy. An innocent child.

And why had Damon told her about the abuse on the night of the wedding? Why had he told her at all?

Beside her on the couch, River whimpered, and Daisy looked up at her with sad eyes. She sighed, knowing her lazy morning was about to come to an end. The dogs needed to go out for a walk. Charlotte put down her book. She couldn't remember what she'd read anyway.

"Okay, guys. I'll get changed, and we'll go."

When she stood, they jumped off the couch and followed her to the bedroom. Charlotte had just finished zipping up her shorts when her phone rang. She saw Gina's name on the screen.

"Hey, Gina. What's up?"

"Total craziness, that's what's up. Animal protection officers apprehended thirty-three dogs at a hoarder house over the weekend." Charlotte heard the stress in her friend's voice. "There's a variety of breeds, most of them large, all of them hungry, and each in need of some level of veterinary care. Three of the dogs were too far gone and we had to put them down immediately. We're swamped, Char."

"Oh, my gosh." *Thirty more dogs?* With the recent addition of the puppy mill dogs, this couldn't have happened at a worse time. The shelter now had nearly twice as many dogs as it was designed to house. Charlotte grabbed a pad of paper and a pen to take some notes. "You think they all need veterinary care?"

"Yes. Most are malnourished, some dehydrated, and several have skin infections and hair loss. Our volunteer vets have been working flat out." Gina paused, and Charlotte heard her take in a breath and blow it out slowly. "There's four pregnant females, and three of them are in bad shape. They have sores on their skin and one has diarrhea. The fourth pregnant dog is a Border Collie cross, maybe three to five years old. She's in better shape, or at least she doesn't have skin problems. We think she'll be the first to give birth. I'd like to get her out of here before the babies come, so they don't get any of the mites or skin diseases. And frankly, we don't have the room."

"What about our usual foster families? Can they handle any of them?"

"Most of our families are already fostering dogs and simply can't take more."

Charlotte wrote the statistics on the pad of paper. *Thirty dogs, four pregnant, all sick.* Somehow, looking at the words in black and white made the situation feel even more dire. "Are all the apprehended dogs at the shelter right now?"

Right on cue, a cacophony of barking began in the background. "Yep. They sure are. I've had to isolate the hoarder dogs from the rest by turning our storage closet and the reception area into kennels. We're full to the gills here. Honestly, Char, I'm at my wit's end. We were already stretched, but now…" Gina gave a deep sigh. "The animal protection officers said the conditions were some of the worst they'd seen. Feces and urine everywhere and the stench of ammonia so strong they had to use masks. Neighbors have been complaining about the smell and the deterioration of the house for a while. But the owner insisted her dogs were well cared for and healthy."

Charlotte paced her bedroom, her dogs following her. She knew such assertions were common in cases of animal hoarding. "Listen, I'll come to the shelter as soon as I can, and we'll figure this thing out, okay?"

"Yeah, okay." Gina sounded relieved. "I'm sorry to dump this on you."

"Don't be silly. You should have called me

yesterday."

"I wasn't going to call you the day after your brother's wedding, Char. How did it go?"

"The wedding was beautiful, and everything went according to plan." Except perhaps for what Damon had told her. That bit of news wasn't in any of her plans.

They signed off, and Charlotte clipped the dogs' leashes to their collars and took them outside. As they walked, Charlotte called Cole and explained the situation. He offered his veterinary services without her even asking. Charlotte thanked her lucky stars he was the kind of guy his family could always depend on.

After getting off the phone with Cole, she called Blair. Fortunately, she and Garrett had decided they'd rather stay home on the farm instead of going on a honeymoon.

"Hey, Blair. I'm sorry to bother you so soon after the wedding, but there's a serious situation at the Best Friends shelter."

Blair didn't hesitate. "Tell me what you need."

****

Damon returned to the farmyard after his run through the pasture, his body sweaty and tired, but his mind at ease. He'd gone over and over his decision to tell Charlotte about the abuse that had been inflicted on him as a child. It hadn't been a conscious decision so much as a truth working its way up from his soul and out through his mouth.

He was at peace with what he'd told her. As they'd watched the dancers, he'd sensed her unhappiness, and though he didn't fully understand the reason, his gut told him she would relate to the traumas of his past.

Perhaps it was one damaged soul recognizing another.

He had no idea what made him believe that. It wasn't like Charlotte had ever shared intimate secrets of her life with him. But there was a connection between them. At times, when he looked into her eyes, he'd see a flash of panic or pain and he knew something had happened to her in the years since he'd first known her. Something bad.

Damon opened the door to the farmhouse and entered the kitchen. Blair paced the floor, her phone to her ear.

"Thanks, Jamie. I'm glad you're able to help. This is a definite emergency, but please don't overdo. Okay?"

Damon's heart began to pound at the word "emergency." He waited for Blair to say goodbye to Jamie.

"What happened?" he asked.

Blair blew out a breath. "Charlotte called. We've got a situation with some hoarder dogs." She filled him in on the shelter's problem. "Jamie and Cole and Dr. Waverley are going to assist the other vets from Bismarck who donate their services to the shelter. I told Jamie I'd help her as much as I can. The shelter is overcrowded with sick, homeless dogs—at least eighty dogs over capacity. What are we going to do?"

"We?"

"I've been thinking—"

"Stop right there." Damon held up his hand. It was never good when his sister began a sentence with that phrase. "There's no way you can bring eighty dogs here to the farm."

Blair gave him an indignant glare. "Of course not.

I'm not an idiot. I thought we could foster one dog who's about to have a litter. That seems doable, and it would help take a bit of pressure off the shelter. I told Charlotte we'd take her in."

Damon relaxed. Blair had a compassionate heart, especially when it came to animals. It was why she'd chosen a career as a veterinary technician and rescued horses in need of a home. Her compassion also meant she sometimes spread herself too thin, but at least she was being practical this time.

"Yeah. That sounds doable. I'll help you look after her."

She smiled. "Thanks. I appreciate that."

"When are we getting the dog?"

"Soon. I spoke to Charlotte over an hour ago, and she said she'd bring her from the shelter right away."

Blair had no sooner spoken when they heard a vehicle drive into the yard. They stepped out onto the porch just as Charlotte parked her Jeep in front of the farmhouse. When she got out of the vehicle and walked toward them, Damon could see the anxiety on her face, though she tried to cover it with a smile.

"Thanks so much, Blair. I can't tell you how much this means to me."

Blair ran down the steps of the porch and enveloped Charlotte in a hug. "You're very welcome."

Damon's eyes locked with Charlotte's over his sister's shoulder. He'd come to understand that the dog shelter was more than a volunteer opportunity to her. It was her heart and soul, and right now her heart was breaking.

Blair released Charlotte from her embrace. "Can I see her?"

"Sure."

Charlotte leaned into the back seat and pulled out a plastic kennel with a carrying handle on the top. She set the kennel on the ground, and Blair peered inside through the wire door. Her dog Frisco walked around the kennel, giving it a thorough sniff.

"Hey there, sweetie," Blair cooed. "She looks stressed. And scared."

"She's experienced a lot of upheaval in the last forty-eight hours."

Blair rose to her feet. "We'll make sure she has some calm from now on, so she can give birth in peace. Garrett's getting a stall in the barn ready for her right now."

"When is she supposed to deliver?" Damon asked.

"Jamie thinks it will be in the next week or two. She x-rayed her at the clinic and says there's six puppies." Charlotte turned back to Blair. "The mother is underweight, but at least she's not dehydrated. Jamie wants you to give her plenty of water, and for the first few days you're to feed her small amounts of dog food several times a day." Charlotte retrieved a plastic bag from her vehicle and handed it to Blair. "It's only a couple of cans. We didn't have enough at the shelter to go around."

"That's okay. We carry this brand at the clinic. I'll get more tomorrow."

"Jamie said if you had any concerns to let her know and she'll stop by to examine the mother-to-be. And she said it's probably a good idea to keep Frisco away from her. This dog looks all right, but we don't know what parasites she might have. We don't want anything passing to Frisco."

"Okay. Let's get her into the barn."

Damon picked up the kennel and heard the dog's plaintive cries as he carried her to the barn. Charlotte greeted her brother with a hug as Blair shooed Frisco away when he tried to get inside the stall Garrett had prepared. Fresh hay covered the concrete floor of the stall, and a low-sided cardboard box filled with blankets had been placed in a corner. Damon set the kennel near the box and opened its door. With some urging from Blair and Charlotte, the dog emerged from the kennel, sniffed at her surroundings, and then with a wary glance at the humans in the room, curled up on the blankets inside the box.

"She's very thin," Garrett said.

"She sure is." Blair handed Charlotte a stainless-steel dog bowl. "If you fill this with water for her, I'll go to the house and open a can of the dog food."

"Is there a tap in the barn?" Charlotte asked.

Damon nodded. "Blair's got a wash stall set up for her horses."

"Would I be able to wash the kennel there? I need to take it back to the shelter."

"I can do that for you, Char. You stay with the dog," Garrett said.

Charlotte squeezed Garrett's arm. "Thank you."

While Blair went to the house and Garrett washed and disinfected the plastic carrier, Damon filled the bowl with cool water and returned to the stall. He held the water close to the Border Collie's mouth, and she greedily lapped it up. Charlotte stroked her head.

"Poor thing," she whispered.

Charlotte put up a brave front, but she had a soft heart. Damon could see she was stressed.

"How are you doing, Charlotte?" he asked.

She blinked up at him, obviously not expecting his question. "I'm fine."

"Is that the truth?" Charlotte didn't like to admit to needing anything. But dammit, he was going to offer anyway. Someone had to look out for her. He stroked the dog while he waited for her answer.

"I'm fine," she repeated, then rolled her eyes at him. "Well, of course I'm worried. Most of the dogs at the shelter are unadoptable right now, and Best Friends doesn't have the money to cover all the expenses. It was already overcrowded and financially strapped before the hoarder dogs were apprehended."

Damon put his hand over hers. "This burden isn't one you have to bear on your own. Friends like Blair and Jamie and Cole will help you carry the load." He linked his fingers with hers. "And me. Whenever you need to talk, or to vent, I'm here."

She stared at him, her eyes wide. He read surprise in them, and wariness. Charlotte reminded him of one of Blair's rescue horses. Enormous patience was required to gain their trust. They needed proof they wouldn't be hurt again.

Who had hurt Charlotte?

She nodded and pulled her hand away from his. "Thank you, but I'll be all right."

Garrett returned to the stall with the kennel at the same time Blair arrived with a bowl containing a small amount of dog food. The dog sniffed at the food before gobbling it down in a few bites.

Blair stroked the dog's head with a gentle finger. "I'll bring her more in a couple of hours. It'll be easier on her stomach."

"Does she have a name?" Garrett asked.

"None that we know of." Charlotte shook her head. "I know this hoarder person had some kind of mental illness, but to treat animals this way is inexcusable."

Damon heard the barely repressed rage in her voice. "I know it's upsetting, Charlotte, but that person is sick. She probably thinks she's saving her animals. She can't see that they're suffering. She can't even identify her own suffering. She's likely physically ill herself from living in such squalid conditions."

He also knew that some animal hoarders had experienced a trauma in their childhood. The condition was complex and likely had many causes, but for this reason alone he felt a special empathy for them.

There but for the grace of God go I.

"I know what you're saying, and maybe someday I'll be able to understand, but right now I'm angry."

He wished he could touch her, comfort her, but she wouldn't welcome such a gesture from him in front of Blair and Garrett.

"The important thing is that we got the animals out of that squalor. At least now they have some hope." Blair turned to Charlotte with a smile. "Hope. That's what I'll call her. She needs hope, and so do we."

For the first time since she arrived, Charlotte smiled. "Hope is a perfect name for her."

"Do we know if she's had any vaccinations?"

"No idea. Jamie said we'll assume none were given and vaccinate her after she gives birth. Once her puppies are old enough, we'll vaccinate them, too."

"Is the shelter paying for vaccinations?" Garrett asked.

All traces of Charlotte's smile vanished. "The

shelter doesn't have the money. Some of the vet clinics in the area are donating vaccines, but we can't expect them to pay for it all. We're hoping to adopt out the puppies as soon as possible, with the stipulation that the new owners pay for their first shots before they take them home."

"I'll make sure Hope is vaccinated," Blair said with a determined nod. "And once her babies are weaned and she's in good shape again, we'll have her spayed. She's been through enough."

Charlotte stroked Hope again. "Yeah, she has. Thank you. I can't tell you how much this means to me."

Damon heard the sad note in her voice. Knowing that Charlotte was hurting was an unexpected blow to the gut. There was something about her that got to him.

Blair hugged Charlotte. "Don't worry, Char. We're going to figure this out. Okay?"

"Okay." Charlotte got to her feet. "I need to get back to the shelter. The staff is overwhelmed."

"Bye, Char. Let us know how things are going and if there's anything else we can do," Garrett said.

Charlotte hugged her brother. "Thanks, I appreciate that."

Damon rose as well. "I'll walk you out."

He picked up the plastic kennel. Charlotte walked silently beside him. He was sure she'd hoped for a quick getaway, but he wasn't letting her go quite so easily.

"Garrett's right. Keep in touch and let us know if there's anything else we can do. Don't try to take care of the world on your own."

She gave him an annoyed frown. "I'm not trying to

do that." She opened the tailgate of her Jeep and he slid the kennel inside.

"I meant what I said, Charlotte. Call me, and we'll talk about whatever's going on with you. Caregivers burn out if they don't look after themselves. And then they're no good to anyone."

Her shoulders slumped. "I suppose you're right. I'm thinking about asking for a leave of absence from the hospital so I can concentrate on the dogs for a while."

Damon couldn't stop himself from touching her. He laid his hand on her shoulder and was relieved when she didn't pull away. She stared up at him, her eyes wary.

"I think that's a good idea. You shouldn't stretch yourself too thin."

"I should go," she whispered. She didn't move.

"Yes." Damon took a step closer. The desire to kiss her, to pull her close and wrap her in his arms sang through his veins. But he knew that, like with the rescue horses, her trust didn't come easily. He'd need to take his time with her.

He'd been telling himself for weeks he should stay firmly in the friend zone with Charlotte. Had he decided he wanted her as more than a friend? Damon's heart thumped in triple time. He was afraid to answer that question.

"I have to go," Charlotte whispered.

Damon dropped his hand from her shoulder. He followed her as she walked around the SUV and opened the driver's side door. She turned to him with a grin before getting inside, her bravado firmly in place once more.

"I'll call. To make you feel better. I wouldn't want you to feel like your counseling skills aren't being put to good use."

Damon couldn't help but laugh. "Yeah. It'll make me feel a whole lot better."

With a wave, Charlotte drove out of the yard. Though he'd responded to her joke, she wasn't fooling him for a minute. She used humor to mask the pain she didn't want anyone to see.

It was a tactic he understood well. He'd used a mask to disguise his feelings for most of his life. Even from himself.

Chapter Five

The building inspector walked through the Fletcher Building, clipboard in hand, while Damon and Clayton followed silently behind her. Ms. Thompson took in the construction debris, the framed but unfinished walls, and the general disarray. She examined the framing near the ceiling.

"I don't see wiring for heat or smoke detectors. A multi-unit building like this requires alarms in each of the living quarters and in all the public spaces, including corridors." She made notes on her clipboard before pointing to the spot where the wall framing met the ceiling joists. "There's no fire blocking between the apartments."

"What's fire blocking?" Damon asked. He felt stupid for asking, but he had no knowledge of construction.

"It's when blocks of wood are fitted between the two by fours of the wall framing. Like this." She picked up a short piece of wood from the floor and held it horizontally between two wall studs. "If a fire starts in one room, or on one floor, it could spread through the walls very quickly if there's nothing to block its way. The blocking stops it long enough for people to escape and for firefighters to arrive. Saves lives and saves buildings."

She ripped off a sheet of paper from her clipboard

and handed it to Damon. "These fire safety components are in the building code, and because they're missing, I can't pass your inspection today. Call my office once you've met all the requirements, and we'll arrange for another inspection."

Damon stared at the paper, his heart sinking. The last thing they needed was a delay because of a failed inspection. But fire safety wasn't something they could compromise on. If he planned to house veterans in this building and to live here himself, it had to be safe.

He was perilously close to the end of his funds. The delays had to stop. Things had to be done right the first time.

Clayton gave the building inspector a smile. "Perhaps you can give me your card, and I can call you directly when the work is completed. Wouldn't it be best to deal with an inspector who is already familiar with our building?"

Ms. Thompson studied him calmly for a moment. She was an attractive woman in her thirties wearing a hardhat and a no-nonsense attitude. "The policy of my office is to send out the first available inspector. Like I said, when the deficiencies have been cleared up, call the office, and they'll send out an inspector as quickly as possible."

"We could save time and avoid a whole lot of red tape if you and I dealt directly with this matter." Clayton took a step closer to her, his gaze never leaving her face. Though his voice was calm, his stance appeared aggressive to Damon.

What the hell was going on?

"Clayton, Ms. Thompson has told you the policy of her office, and we are going to abide by it to the letter."

Clayton shot Damon a look of annoyance before dipping his head in acquiescence. "Of course. I was merely trying to speed up the process."

"You can speed up the process by completing the work in a timely matter," Ms. Thompson said. "The building department will be sure to do the same."

"My team will work very hard to make the changes happen." Clayton gave her a flirtatious smile as he touched her arm. "Don't worry. We'll get it done."

The flirting didn't work on Ms. Thompson. She stepped out of his reach and, unsmiling, turned to Damon.

"Goodbye, Mr. Greyson."

"Goodbye."

After a curt nod in Clayton's direction, she left the building. Clayton made a scoffing sound.

"Bitch."

The curse disgusted Damon. "Where the hell do you get off hitting on our building inspector?"

"In case you didn't notice, she didn't pass our inspection. I was merely trying to speed things along."

"Would you have flirted with the inspector if he'd been a man?"

Clayton curled his lip. "Of course not."

"Then why treat this woman any differently? She's doing her job. I suggest you do yours."

"What's that supposed to mean?"

"It means this building needs to be completed soon, and it needs to be done correctly."

Clayton narrowed his eyes. "Are you saying I'm not doing my job?"

Damon wasn't sure what he was saying, but he didn't like the vibe Clayton was giving off. "I'm saying finish the work and do it correctly. Plain and simple."

With that he left the Fletcher Building and got into his truck. He headed back to the farm and changed into his running gear. Maybe a long run would clear his head. Had his general contractor been trying to charm a passing grade from their inspector, or was something else going on? Either way, it gave him an uneasy feeling in his gut.

****

Chaos greeted Charlotte as she stepped into the shelter's reception area. Makeshift shelves had been brought into the front area and crates and kennels stacked on them. Even Michelle's reception desk had two crates perched on one end. The noise was deafening, and despite their best efforts, the smell was overpowering as well.

Shelter staff and volunteers had worked valiantly to care for the animals. A call had gone out for more volunteers to make sure the dogs were fed, walked, and kept clean. But the arrival of the hoarder dogs a week ago had tipped the scales. The shelter could barely keep its head above water. Charlotte was afraid the whole system was about to crash. If they ran out of food, or if another puppy mill or animal hoarder was found, the whole house of cards would crumble.

Like everyone else involved with the shelter, Charlotte called, cajoled, and begged friends, family, and co-workers to help in any way they could. Through their efforts, they'd managed to raise money for food and supplies. The local television and radio stations, along with the local newspaper, had covered the story, bringing attention to the shelter's plight. The news coverage brought in needed donations that bought food for the short term but didn't result in any permanent solutions.

So far, only three of the remaining twenty-nine hoarder dogs and five of the puppy mill dogs were deemed ready to go to foster homes. The hope was that after some time in a loving foster home, they'd be ready for adoption. But no one really knew how they'd react in a home situation.

That was, if they could find more fosters willing to take in the dogs. Three of the pugs from the puppy mill had been taken by a local pug rescue group that was willing to look after their many medical needs. Charlotte knew Gina had been in contact with several rescue groups, but so far this was the only one that had been in a position to help. Finding suitable homes for all the dogs would take time.

The three remaining pregnant dogs from the hoarder house, which she and the other volunteers had named Sally, Lucy, and Peppermint Patty, were special to Charlotte and consumed much of her time and attention. She snuck them treats and spent as much time with them as her busy schedule allowed. They were skinny and had itchy skin problems, but at least the one with diarrhea had recovered after receiving medication. She wished she could take them all to Blair's farm where they could rest in a quiet space, but that was impossible.

It would be some time before any of the dogs could be put up for adoption. In the meantime, resources were being stretched to the breaking point.

Charlotte went to work immediately, giving out fresh food and water and then taking three dogs at a time outside to walk according to the schedule Gina had established. She coached the new volunteers who'd stepped up to help during the crisis, showing them what to do and making them aware of sanitation protocols. Charlotte had asked for and was granted a leave of absence from the hospital. But despite her extra hours and the genuine efforts of the new volunteers, they couldn't keep up. The shelter simply had too many dogs.

When Charlotte returned after taking a group of dogs out for a walk, Gina was waiting for her.

"Can you come into my office for a minute, Char?"

"Sure. As soon as I get these guys settled in their kennels again."

When she was done with the dogs, she washed her hands and stepped into Gina's office.

"Close the door please, Char."

Charlotte pushed the door closed, her stomach making an apprehensive flip. Gina was pale and unsmiling, and she knew she was about to deliver bad news.

Very bad news.

"There's no easy way to say this, Char. The board of directors has decided the only way we're going to make it through this crisis is by euthanizing some of the dogs."

Charlotte's heart sank. She'd been afraid of this. "Isn't there some other way?"

Gina rubbed her forehead. "We have to prioritize the dogs that have a chance to be adopted. I know everyone's been working hard, but we've come to the end of our rope."

"Can't they give us more time? If we put out another appeal on social media, I'm sure we can raise more money. Maybe we can even get more foster families to step forward."

Gina shook her head. "The situation has become unmanageable, Char. We both know it." She paused and took a breath before facing Charlotte again. "The decision has been made to euthanize at least thirty of the sickest dogs, starting with the three pregnant females. We can't let them have their babies."

"No." For a second Charlotte couldn't move or even think. The idea of killing the pregnant dogs made her physically ill.

"No," she said again, shaking her head. "There has to be another way."

"I wish there was." Gina was on the verge of tears. "I've contacted shelters all over the country. We'll transport the eight dogs we identified as being ready to go into foster care, but that's all we've been able to place. No one is willing to take in pregnant or sick dogs. And even if they were, only healthy dogs can handle being driven across the country."

Knowing her friend, Charlotte was sure Gina had done everything she could. This wasn't her fault. It wasn't the board of the directors' fault. But she couldn't stand by and watch helplessly. She had to *do* something.

"When will the euthanasia begin?"

"Probably in a couple of days."

Charlotte closed her eyes. *So soon.* She pushed herself to her feet. "I should get back to work."

"I'm sorry, Charlotte. I didn't want this."

"I know."

Numbly, she made her way into the back, put leashes on three more dogs, and instructed a volunteer to disinfect the kennels while she was out.

Her mind whirled in a dozen different directions as she walked. What could she do? She'd already talked to everyone she knew to ask for support in one way or another. They'd given their money, their time, and in Blair's case, had fostered a pregnant Hope. How could she ask anyone to give more? She knew one of the volunteers had set up a campaign online on one of those funding pages where people raised money. But it was going to take time the dogs didn't have.

Especially the pregnant dogs.

Charlotte wanted to cry, to scream at the world. All she could think about were those unborn babies who would never have a chance at life. Guilt overwhelmed her.

She'd failed them. The only thing that gave her comfort was knowing that Hope was safe at Blair's farm.

She found a park bench near a playground and sat, too overcome with emotion to go any farther. The dogs sat at her feet, enjoying the sunshine after being cooped up inside their kennels for so long. Charlotte stroked the head of a large black Labrador named Molly. She was a sweet dog with a laid-back personality, but she was estimated to be over ten years old. People preferred to adopt a younger dog. Would Molly soon be on death row because of her age?

Out of the blue, she remembered her conversation with Damon. *"I meant what I said, Charlotte. Call me and we'll talk about whatever's going on with you. Caregivers burn out if they don't look after themselves. And then they're no good to anyone."*

She so wanted to talk to someone. Charlotte didn't

want to pile any more guilt on Gina. Her sister Lauren would listen and would probably understand, being an animal lover herself, but she and Cole had already done so much.

No, this was her problem. Maybe if she talked to someone, someone like Damon who was willing to listen, she could come up with a solution.

While the dogs lounged in the sunshine, Charlotte pulled out her phone and clicked on Damon's contact number before she could change her mind.

****

Damon's phone rang as he walked Hope around the farmyard. He tugged on her leash to bring her to a stop as he pulled his phone from his pocket. Was there another problem with his building? But when he saw Charlotte Saunders' name, he relaxed. A call from Charlotte was always welcome, and besides, he wanted to focus on something aside from Clayton Brown and the money pit that was the Fletcher Building.

"Charlotte, hi. I'm glad you're finally taking me up on my offer to talk."

"How do you know I'm not calling to hit you up for a donation to the shelter?"

Damon smiled at the irritation in her voice. "Just a hunch. How are you?"

"I'm fine."

"Really?"

There was a long pause. Damon waited, letting her take her time. Charlotte needed to tell her story in her own way.

"No. Not really. The shelter is in trouble, Damon, big trouble, and I don't know what to do. I'm hoping if I talk it out with you something brilliant will come to me."

Oh, Charlotte. He wished she wouldn't take the weight of the world on her shoulders. But at least she'd called. It was a start. "What's going on?"

"The shelter is overfull and on the brink of collapse. They're going to euthanize thirty dogs, starting with the three pregnant ones from the hoarder house."

Her voice was calm, almost matter of fact, but Damon sensed turbulent emotions beneath that composed exterior. He and Hope began to walk again. "I'm sorry. Is euthanasia really the only solution?"

"Gina says so. She's exhausted all possibilities to place dogs with other shelters. Best Friends Haven is overcrowded and financially strapped. If the mothers are allowed to have their puppies, it'll only get worse."

"And you want to find a way to save them."

"Yes."

"When are they going to be put down?"

She sighed. "In a couple of days."

"That's not much time to come up with a brilliant idea. Or even a not-so-brilliant idea."

"No, it's not."

Her voice quavered, and for the first time, Damon heard a crack in her composure. But she kept herself under control. He had a feeling Charlotte kept a lot of emotions locked behind a steely wall of control. He wanted to test the wall for cracks.

"How does that make you feel?"

"How do you think it makes me feel? It makes me angry. I'm angry with the puppy mill owner. I'm angry with a system that doesn't provide help to people with mental illnesses like the animal hoarder. And I'm angry at people in general for their apathy and disinterest and greed when it comes to animal welfare. If people cared, we wouldn't need shelters."

"That's a lot of anger."

She huffed out a breath. "You're not helping, Damon. I need a solution. I don't need you to analyze me."

"The way I see it, there's only one solution. To find someone, or several someones, willing to take in these dogs and look after them properly."

She sighed again, and this time he heard a note of sadness. "I know, but we've already been down that road, and it's a dead end."

"Sometimes there are no solutions. You have to be prepared to accept that."

"I will never accept that euthanasia is the only answer."

"I wish I could tell you miracles happen, but they don't. I'm sorry."

There was silence on the line. Then he heard Charlotte's brusque voice. "I have to go. Bye, Damon."

"Charlotte—"

The line went dead. *Dammit*. He hadn't handled that well. He'd wanted to prepare her for the inevitable, but she'd been looking for a miracle.

Damon wished he could conjure one up for her. For reasons he didn't fully understand, he wanted to be Charlotte's hero.

Chapter Six

After putting Hope back in her stall, Damon spent an hour tramping through the pasture, his brain working overtime to process his thoughts. It had been an all-around rotten day. First the weird situation with the building inspector and now Charlotte's disturbing news about euthanizing dogs at the shelter. He couldn't come up with any ideas to deal with either situation.

Eventually, he walked to the farmhouse, his steps heavy. He found Blair and Garrett in the kitchen preparing dinner. Damon washed his hands at the sink and turned to his sister. "What can I do?"

"You can wash lettuce for salad." She handed him a head of romaine.

Damon ran the leaves under the faucet. He wondered what Charlotte was doing right now. She had to be hurting and was probably still searching for a solution.

But there was nothing Charlotte could do in this case. It had to be killing her.

"You're awfully quiet, Damon," Blair said. "What's going on?"

He sighed. His sister would likely be as upset by the news as Charlotte.

"Charlotte called with some news regarding the shelter." He relayed the situation to Blair and Garrett. "There doesn't seem to be any way to stop the thirty sickest dogs from being put down."

"We have to help," Blair said. "We have to take in those dogs, especially the three pregnant ones."

Garrett shook his head. "Blair honey, I don't like this situation any more than you do, but there's no way the three of us can look after so many dogs. And aside from that, feeding that many dogs would cost a fortune."

Blair shook her head. "I know you're right, Garrett. In my head, at least. But in my heart…it hurts, you know."

Garrett put his arms around her and kissed her forehead. "Yeah, I know."

Damon went back to washing lettuce. Why was there so much hurt in the world? The toll on good people like Blair and Garrett, and Charlotte, was staggering. It was a question he'd asked himself since childhood, and he still didn't have an answer.

His phone rang, and Damon welcomed the distraction from his dark thoughts. He dried his hands on a towel and pulled his phone from his back pocket. The screen showed the caller was from the Veterans Administration.

"Damon Greyson speaking."

"Mr. Greyson, this is Tony Cunningham. I'm calling from the VA in Minneapolis. Do you have a few moments to speak?"

"Yes, of course. What can I do for you?"

"I'm hoping you can help me with a situation. We have five men we need placement for immediately. They've come forward asking for help with their PTSD. We've done what we can for them at the hospital, and we feel they'd benefit from a country setting like yours.

I understand the counseling program you've proposed has been vetted and approved. Is that correct?"

Damon's heart fell, knowing he wasn't going to be able to help. "Yes, it has, but unfortunately we've had several construction delays on my property. I can't house these men. It could be weeks until my building is ready."

"Oh." Damon could almost hear the man deflating. "That's too bad. I was told it was a long shot, but I'd hoped... All of the facilities in the area are at capacity. When someone reaches out for help, you want to be able to answer that call right away, you know?"

"Yeah, I know exactly what you mean." Frustration made Damon want to hit something. "I'm sorry I can't help. I hope you'll be able to find help for these men."

"Yes, so do I. Please let me know when you're up and running."

"I will."

Damon had no idea when that day would arrive. In the meantime, veterans were suffering, and there wasn't a damn thing he could do about it.

****

After talking to Damon, Charlotte felt restless. And vaguely depressed. He was right. Sometimes there were no miracles to be found, no matter how hard you searched for them.

She took the dogs back to the shelter, leashed three more and walked them around the neighborhood. She spent the rest of the afternoon cleaning and disinfecting the kennels, administering treatments to dogs with skin issues, and making sure each one had fresh water. By six p.m. she was emotionally and physically exhausted, and needed to go home. After saying goodnight to Gina and Michelle and the other volunteers, Charlotte dragged herself to her Jeep and drove away.

Though she wanted nothing more than to head straight home and put on her pajamas, she remembered she was nearly out of dog food. With a sigh, she pulled into the parking lot of a supermarket on the outskirts of Bismarck.

Charlotte pushed her cart through the aisles. She picked up a month's supply of dog food for River and Daisy, and decided that while she was here, she might as well get something for her own dinner. At the deli counter, she examined the ready-made salads and tried to decide what she felt like eating.

"Look who it is. I never imagined I'd see you here, Charlotte."

Charlotte's whole body went cold at the sound of the remembered deep, male voice. Slowly, she turned her head to see Clayton Brown standing next to her wearing the arrogant grin she'd once found so attractive. It was the same grin that had haunted her dreams for the last ten years.

She lifted her chin and narrowed her eyes. She refused to let him see that her insides were quaking. "What are you doing here?"

"My company's got a construction job in the area." Clayton stepped closer. "I was feeling lonely away from home, but now that I've found you, things are going to get much more friendly. And interesting. How about having a drink with me?"

Charlotte's fear and shock morphed into anger. How dare he talk to her like they were friends, as if he hadn't destroyed her ten years ago?

"I'd rather gouge out my eyes with a spoon."

She turned her cart. Clayton stopped her with a hand clamped to her arm, his fingers pressing into her flesh. His face lost its faux-friendly expression as he lowered his head to whisper in her ear.

"Don't make a scene, Charlotte. There's no need to be rude to an old friend."

Charlotte raised her voice. "Get your hand off me or I will scream this store down."

The female deli clerk's gaze darted from her to Clayton and back. "Is there a problem, ma'am? Do you need help?"

Clayton immediately dropped his hand, raising it in surrender before walking away. But not before giving her a look of pure venom that chilled her to the bone.

"Are you okay?" the clerk asked.

"Thank you for your concern, but I'm fine."

Charlotte hurried away from the deli counter without buying anything, her appetite gone. She pushed her cart toward the exit. Her first instinct was to ditch the cart and race to the Jeep. But Clayton might be waiting out there for her. He could follow her to the Jeep, or worse, track her back to Masonville, to her house.

The thought caused gooseflesh to rise on her arms.

She stayed close to other shoppers and kept a careful eye peeled as she pushed her cart around the store. Maybe if she delayed long enough, Clayton would get bored and take off.

At the checkout, she asked for someone to help take her purchases to her vehicle. A teenage boy pushed her cart loaded with the bags of dog food to her Jeep. While he stacked the bags in the back, she scanned the parking lot and held her keys threaded between her fingers to use as a weapon if the need arose.

The teenager closed the tailgate. "There you go, ma'am."

"Thank you." She handed him a couple of dollar bills, and he headed back to the store. As Charlotte opened the driver's side door, a truck drove by slowly, its horn honking. From inside, Clayton grinned at her and waved. His message was clear.

I see you.

Charlotte watched as his truck exited the parking lot and merged onto the main street. And then she turned and vomited beside her vehicle.

The man who had raped her was back in her life.

****

After exchanging email addresses with Tony Cunningham, Damon ended the call. He turned to face his sister and brother-in-law.

"That was someone from the VA. They wanted me to take in some men."

"How many?" Garrett asked.

"Five." Damon groaned in frustration. "It might as well be five hundred. I can't help anyone until the building is ready. There's no place for them to stay."

"Wait." Garrett gripped Blair's hand. "Sweetheart, what if we had the men stay here in the house with us? Now that Chris and Alison and the kids have their own place, we have those two empty bedrooms on the second floor."

"You want to bring five men we don't know into our house?" Blair frowned. "It's one thing to have them spend time on the farm working with the horses, but to have them live with us? I don't know."

"You didn't know Chris in the beginning either,

and you let him stay."

"That was different. He was your friend, and I trusted you."

"I understand your concerns, but I'm asking you to trust me again. These men are fellow veterans, and they need our help. If you're dead set against them living in our house, the conversation ends right here. What do you say, Blair?"

"How long would they be with us?" she asked.

"The program is twelve weeks," Damon said.

He held his breath as Blair looked up into Garrett's face, her hand in his. Finally, she nodded.

"If we fixed up the attic, we could probably put a couple of beds up there. We'd need an air conditioner, though."

"Yes, we would." Garrett leaned down to kiss her. "Thank you, sweetheart. That gives us accommodation for four men."

"My room gives us five." Damon began to feel their excitement. "Hell, if the VA approves this arrangement, I don't care if I sleep in the barn."

"Don't joke. You may have to," Garrett said with a grin. "With only five men, you could hold group counseling sessions here in the kitchen or outside on the porch in good weather."

"I know Chris is anxious to get back to work and start cooking for a crowd again," Blair said. "Alison says the delays in getting the retreat running have been hard on him. He needs the programming as much as these five men do."

Damon nodded. Chris Redwick and Garrett had served in Afghanistan together. Chris was in an armored vehicle with Garrett when a roadside bomb and the subsequent explosion resulted in Garrett's amputation. Though Chris had left Afghanistan physically unscathed, his psychological wounds meant he'd almost succeeded in taking his own life on his return home. Garrett had brought Chris to the farm to heal, and his wife Alison and their two daughters eventually joined him. They'd lived at the farm for several months until recently finding their own place.

Damon pulled out his phone. "I'll call Tony Cunningham at the VA and see if this arrangement will work for them."

"Damon, wait." Blair bit her lip. "What if we could solve both problems?"

"What do you mean?"

"What if the veterans could help themselves by helping the dogs? You were going to have them work with the horses for their therapy, right? What if you included the dogs the shelter is about to put down? If the veterans could devote themselves to caring for the physical needs of the dogs, we'd be able to give the animals the attention they need and at the same time the veterans will receive the love and devotion of an animal."

Damon recognized that for some veterans, caring for a dog could be therapeutic. But could they manage so many? "That's a lot of dogs, Blair, as many as thirty. And counting. Hope will have her pups any day now."

"With any luck, the shelter will be able to find people willing to adopt once the dogs are in better shape."

"Yeah, but thirty dogs…Blair, I don't know."

"It's only until the shelter can find forever homes. We'll simply be giving them time to regroup." Her eyes implored him. "We have the opportunity to stop a tragedy, Damon. Don't you want to do that?"

He sighed. "Blair, I don't want those dogs to be euthanized any more than you do. But the numbers are crazy." He turned to his brother-in-law. "Garrett, how do you feel about bringing all these dogs here?"

"I agree with you. The numbers are crazy." Garrett reached for his wife's hand. "After my amputation, I didn't know what I was supposed to do with my life. I didn't even know who I was any more. It wasn't until I started working here on the farm that I was able to build some self-worth again. I had purpose and I was needed here. Just like these five men and Chris will be needed here. I say we go for it."

Damon watched as Garrett put his arm around Blair. She looked up at him with love in her eyes. Like he was her hero. Damon had to look away.

Psychologically speaking, Garrett's case was probably different from that of the five men the VA proposed to send to the farm. But one thing remained the same. These vets required help to overcome the experiences of the past. They needed empathy from others, and from themselves.

Damon nodded slowly. "If the VA is okay with having the vets look after thirty dogs, then so am I."

Blair threw her arms around him. "Thank you."

Damon held her close. "Don't thank me yet. The VA still has to approve."

She looked up at him with a smile. "They will. I can feel it. Charlotte's going to be thrilled. And so relieved."

He was shocked by how badly he wanted to give Charlotte everything she wanted. But he couldn't let his desire to be Charlotte's hero influence what was best for the veterans' retreat and for the veterans themselves.

Damn, he wanted this to work.

"Call the man from the VA right now and find out for yourself," Blair said. "They're going to go for this. You'll see."

"Okay."

Damon pulled out his phone and hit Tony Cunningham's number. When he answered, Damon began his pitch. "Mr. Cunningham, we have a proposition for you."

****

Charlotte pounded the heavy bag over and over, until her hands began to hurt even though they were protected by her boxing gloves. For good measure she kicked the bag with her left foot, then whirled and hit it again with her right foot.

After working herself to exhaustion, she rested her hands on her knees and caught her breath. Thumping the bag helped, but it hadn't completely pushed thoughts of Clayton Brown from her head. He was still there, sneering at her. Now that she knew he was close by, she had to be on alert every second.

The thought drained her.

And she couldn't stop thinking about what was going to happen to Sally, Lucy, and Patty either. She imagined their unborn pups, in a variety of colors from pure white to pure black. She could see them at six months of age as they fought and played and tested their baby teeth on each other.

She shook her head. She had to give up this game of make-believe before she lost her mind.

She peeled off her gloves and the cotton wrapping

beneath them. River and Daisy watched her patiently from the sofa. It was getting late, and they needed a quick walk before they all turned in for the night. Despite everything going on with the shelter, she couldn't forget that her first responsibility was to the dogs she'd already adopted.

She gave a whistle. "Come on, guys. Let's go."

They didn't have to be told twice. They jumped off the sofa and raced up the basement stairs, anxious for their walk. Charlotte followed them, her steps slow. The lateness of the hour gave her pause. She'd never been afraid to walk after dark in her hometown before, but after seeing Clayton again...

As she got to the top of the stairs, the doorbell rang. The dogs barked madly, and her heart jumped into her throat. Had Clayton followed her? She'd been so careful on the way home, taking roads that were out of her way and doubling back a couple of times. Charlotte glanced at the clock on the kitchen wall and noted it was nearly ten o'clock. In trepidation, she peered through the peephole in the door and nearly fell over in relief at seeing Damon Greyson on the stoop at her side door. She grabbed a fleece jacket from the nearby closet and slipped it on over her sports bra and shorts.

With shaking hands, she opened the door a crack and peered out at him. "It's a little late for a social call, isn't it?"

"I'm sorry. I know it's late, but something's come up, and I needed to tell you in person. It's important. Can I come in for a minute?"

"All right." She opened the door wider, and he came inside. What could be so important that he had to speak to her in person?

Damon turned to her, about to say something, then closed his mouth and cleared his throat before trying again. "Ah, were you working out or something?"

Charlotte's breath caught. She zipped up the fleece jacket, embarrassed that Damon had caught a glimpse of her in her fighting gear. Especially when she saw a look in his eyes she'd never seen before.

"What do you want, Damon?"

He schooled his features into a neutral expression. "I want to tell you something."

"So you said." She wished he would just spit it out and get out of her house. "What?"

"I have some news about the hoarder dogs at the shelter."

"Oh, no." Tears sprang to her eyes. "They've put them down already? Why didn't Gina call me?"

Damon stepped forward and grasped her hands. "No, no. Charlotte, I'm sorry. Just the opposite has happened. We've found a way to save them."

"What? How? What do you mean?"

"I've made a deal with the VA. Five veterans are coming to the farm, and part of their therapy will be to care for the dogs." He explained the details of what was about to happen.

She stared at him. "So, Sally and Lucy and Peppermint Patty aren't going to die?"

He gave her a quizzical grin. "The kids from the Peanuts cartoon?"

Fresh tears poured down her face that she was helpless to stop. "The three pregnant hoarder dogs. They were going to be the first to be euthanized."

Damon tenderly brushed a tendril of hair from her face. "No, sweetheart. They're going to be okay. You don't have to worry about them anymore."

Charlotte lost it. Sobs burst out of her, her profound relief nearly bringing her to her knees. Damon gathered her into his arms and held her tight. She clung to him, and for the first time in a very long time she felt safe.

It was Heaven to be in his arms. But she couldn't let herself enjoy it too much.

Gradually, she forced back her tears and pulled away. "Sorry about that."

"Don't apologize. I know the dogs are a very emotional issue for you."

"Yeah. Thank you, Damon. If it weren't for you…" She shook her head, unable to finish.

"You should thank Garrett and Blair. They're the ones who had the crazy idea to put the vets and dogs together. And they're the ones who will be keeping five men they've never met in their home."

"I'll thank them profusely next time I see them." Charlotte wiped at her tear-streaked face with her hand. "I hope these guys like dogs."

"They do. The VA checked with each of the men to make sure they were comfortable with the situation. From what our contact told me, they were all happy they'd have something to do aside from sitting around and talking about their feelings."

Charlotte couldn't help but laugh. "I know where they're coming from. I can't imagine anything worse."

Damon grasped her hand once more, intertwining his fingers with hers. "Why don't you like to talk about your feelings?"

She tugged on her hand, but he wouldn't release her. "Don't go all Sigmund Freud on me again,

Greyson. I'm not your patient."

"No, but you're my friend. The offer's always open. Any time you want to talk, I'm here."

Charlotte stared into his sincere gray eyes. Emotion overcame her, and tears filled her eyes once more. She attempted to cover it with a shaky laugh. "I can't seem to stop crying tonight. It's all your fault."

"Don't cry, Charlotte. It'll be okay."

He slowly lowered his head, his breath mingling with hers. But he held back, as if waiting for her permission.

Charlotte stood toe to toe with him, her lips mere inches from his, their only connection his hand holding hers. Her senses filled with him, with his scent, with the look in his eyes, and the sound of his ragged breathing. She trembled, but she wasn't sure if it was with excitement or fear. Perhaps it was both.

All she knew was that right now she wanted to kiss Damon Greyson more than she'd wanted her next breath. She stretched up on her tiptoes and touched her lips to his.

Damon's arms came around her and crushed her against his broad chest. Somehow her arms wound themselves around his neck and hung on tight. Every part of his body seemed to fit perfectly with hers, as if they were puzzle pieces made only for each other.

And his mouth. Oh, his clever, wonderful mouth. His kiss was demanding, and yet so utterly tender it made her want to weep. It had been a long time since she'd been kissed like this.

No, she corrected. *I've never been kissed like this.*

The thought terrified her. She broke the kiss and backed away, though she couldn't quite make herself let go of him. She clung to his hand and said the first thing that came to her mind.

"I need to walk the dogs."

He nodded, his breathing still heavy. "Okay. I'll come with you. It's late."

"You don't have—"

"Don't argue. I'm coming with you." A grin curled Damon's lips as he stared at her bare legs. "You may want to put on pants."

She dropped her hand and took another step away. "Umm, yeah. I'll be right back."

Charlotte hurried to her room and rifled through her closet, her nerve endings on fire. What the hell just happened? Damon's kiss, coming so soon after seeing Clayton again, blew all the circuits in her brain.

She pulled on a pair of sweatpants and rushed back to the kitchen. Damon had found the dogs' leashes in the closet and clipped them to their collars. Charlotte slid her bare feet into flip-flops, grabbed a set of house keys, and opened the door.

"Let's go."

For the first few minutes of their walk, neither of them said anything. Charlotte wondered if Damon felt as confused and thrilled about their kiss as she did. What did it mean? Maybe to him it was simply a kiss. It didn't have to mean anything.

It sure felt like it meant something.

She didn't want to examine it too closely. Best to concentrate on something else.

"When will the dogs be brought to the farm?"

"In the next few days. Blair arranged things with your friend Gina. She and Garrett plan to buy wire kennels that we'll set up in the barn. We can't have that many dogs running around loose."

"Yes, of course. I'll buy the kennels."

"You don't have to do that."

"Paying for the kennels is the least I can do."

Damon held up his hands. "Fine. But talk to Blair, because I think she was going to order them online very soon."

"I will. When are the veterans arriving?"

"In a few days. We have to get rooms ready for them first. Garrett plans to insulate, drywall, and install air conditioning in the attic. I'm buying a couple of new beds tomorrow. We have to move fast."

"I'll be there first thing in the morning. Just give me a job."

"Good. We'll need all the help we can get."

They were silent again for a few more blocks. When Daisy squatted next to the sidewalk to pee, Charlotte managed to find her voice again.

"I want to thank you again for everything you've done. For the dogs and for the vets. No matter what you've said about Blair and Garrett, if it weren't for you, none of this would be possible. You should be proud."

Damon shook his head. "You're giving me too much credit."

"No, I'm not. Take the compliment, Damon. And be proud of your accomplishments."

He turned to her with a grin. "Okay. If you say so."

She smiled back. "I do."

They turned for home, Daisy and River in the lead. When they reached Charlotte's front door, Damon handed her River's leash. "I should go. I'll see you tomorrow, then?"

"Yeah, for sure. Thanks for giving me the news in person. I really appreciate it. Even if I did blubber all over you."

He grinned. "You can blubber on me any time you want. Goodnight, Charlotte."

"Goodnight."

He headed to his old Chevy truck parked in front of her house and waved to her before getting inside and driving away.

Something had happened between them tonight. Something both wonderful and scary.

Charlotte wished she could run toward that something wonderful and hang on to it for all she was worth. The irony of experiencing Damon's kiss on the same day she'd seen Clayton Brown again after ten years wasn't lost on her.

Maybe wonderful wasn't possible for her. And maybe someone like her didn't deserve wonderful.

Chapter Seven

Damon helped Chris and Ben clear out the contents of the attic. A lot of what they found was junk, like the stacks of old magazines that went straight to recycling. But some things still had value, even if it was of the sentimental variety, like the Christmas decorations and old photographs they found. There was wooden furniture, and boxes of china that had probably been handed down to Grandma Anna from her mother and grandmother.

He carried a box of dishes into the kitchen. "Where can we store these, Blair?"

"The only place I can think of is the potting shed." Blair took a teacup out of his box and examined it. "Someday, when life isn't quite so crazy, I'd like to go through all the boxes with you and Ben."

"Yeah, I'd like that." It would be fun to reminisce with his brother and sister about his grandparents. They were the stabilizing force in his life growing up. Because of them, he always knew he was loved. And was worthy of love. Sometimes it had been hard to remember.

Thinking of the past reminded him of his father's phone call a few weeks ago. He hadn't heard anything from him since, which made Damon wonder if Peter had been drunk when he made the call. It would explain the secrecy and paranoia Peter had exhibited.

But he'd also been clear in his thinking and hadn't sounded drunk. And it certainly wasn't out of the realm of possibility for his mother to be scheming about something. If Peter was to be believed, Victoria had used Damon's name when speaking to a mysterious third party. That gave him pause. He preferred when Victoria totally ignored him.

He hadn't mentioned Peter's call to either of his siblings. It could be nothing but the ramblings of a drunk, so why alarm them over nothing?

Charlotte walked down the stairs carrying a paint roller. "Blair, do you have more paint? I'm almost done with the first bedroom."

"Yes, it's on the porch. I'll stir it up and bring it to you."

Blair stepped outside, leaving Charlotte and Damon alone in the kitchen. Charlotte looked everywhere but at him, appearing ill at ease. He was sure their kiss last night was the cause of her discomfort.

"How are you this morning, Charlotte?"

She shrugged. "I could use more coffee, but other than that, I'm good."

"We'll take a coffee break later." He set his box on the table and moved closer to her, keeping his voice low. "I don't regret our kiss last night for a minute, but I don't want you to be uncomfortable around me, okay? I won't say anything. It's no one's business but ours."

She gave a slight nod. "Okay."

"I would never hurt you, Charlotte." His fingers itched to touch her, but he sensed it would be exactly the wrong thing to do right now.

For the first time, Charlotte lifted her eyes to his

and met his gaze directly. Again, the image of the skittish colt came to mind. Last night, in a moment of high emotion, she'd let down her guard, and he'd experienced the passion that lay just under the surface of her control. He wanted that again, he realized. Again and again.

"How do you know *I* won't hurt *you*?" she whispered.

Before Damon could even consider an answer, Blair came back into the kitchen with a gallon of paint. "Here you go, Char. I'll start cutting in with my brush if you keep rolling."

"I can do that. Are we painting the second-floor bathroom?"

"I don't know yet," Blair said. "It depends whether we have enough paint and enough time. I want to make sure we get two coats on the three bedrooms first."

"Okay."

Damon wished he could take Charlotte aside and ask her what she meant by her enigmatic statement, but the moment was gone. She avoided his gaze as Ben and Chris carried an old wooden dresser down the stairs.

"That's really a nice piece of furniture," Charlotte said.

Blair frowned. "You think so? It looks kind of beat up to me. The finish on the top is ruined. It looks like something spilled on it."

"I'm pretty sure it's solid wood. I think that blemish could be sanded out and the piece re-stained. Or maybe painted. You'll need some furniture in the attic, won't you?"

"Yeah, we will," Blair said with a shrug. "Damon bought two new beds, but we have nothing for the men to store their things in. I want them to feel at home, not like they have to live out of a suitcase."

Chris and Ben set the dresser on the kitchen floor and Charlotte examined it. She opened the drawers and ran her hands over the wooden top. "I've refinished some old furniture for my house. I'd love to try my hand with this dresser."

"Knock yourself out," Blair said. "Ben, could you and Chris take the dresser to the barn? Charlotte can work on it out there."

"Sure. There's a couple of other pieces of furniture in the attic," Ben said. "A small wooden table and another dresser with two drawers that looks like it could be used as a nightstand. We'll take them out to the barn and you can figure out if they can be saved."

Damon and Ben and Chris finished clearing the attic. Just as they carried out the last load, Garrett pulled into the yard, the back of his truck piled high with bats of insulation. He stepped out of the truck and opened the tailgate. "Can you help me carry the insulation to the attic?"

"Sure." Damon hoisted himself up onto the tailgate and threw down a bat. "Are we hanging the drywall in the attic, too?"

"No," Garrett said. "I was able to find a crew who'll hang the drywall and get it ready for paint. All we have to do is carry the sheets of drywall up two flights of stairs to the attic."

"Oh, man," Ben said with a groan. "Is that even possible? Those attic stairs are pretty narrow."

Garrett grinned. "I guess we'll find out this afternoon when our delivery arrives."

They worked for the rest of the morning, dragging

insulation up to the attic and stuffing it between the two-by-four ceiling rafters and wall studs. The sloped ceilings made for interesting lines, but they were going to be a challenge to finish.

There'd been no opportunity to speak to Charlotte privately again. There were too many people around, and even when there was a quiet moment, she'd avoided him. Damon was left to wonder why she thought she could hurt him.

Just after noon, Chris's wife Alison arrived with lunch, and they all gratefully stopped for a break. They ate outside at the picnic table beneath the cottonwood trees. Damon chugged back a cold can of cola.

Alison handed him a plate of potato salad and a ham sandwich. "I think what you're doing is wonderful, Damon. Those men will benefit from living here as much as Chris and I did."

"That's what I'm hoping," Damon replied. "I think our grandparents would be pleased that their farm is being used to help people."

"And dogs," Charlotte said with a smile.

Damon returned her smile. "And dogs. I'm pretty sure they'd be pleased about that, too."

"The only person who's not going to have a place to stay is Damon," Chris said. "Alison and I were talking, and we figure our girls can bunk together till your place is ready. You could have Hannah's bedroom in our basement."

"That's really generous, Chris, but I don't want to throw your daughter out of her room."

Ben set down his drink. "We've got an extra bedroom in the basement. Why don't you stay with us?"

Damon hesitated. Ben and Jamie had two children and were about to have a third. They already had a full house. More importantly, they were essentially newlyweds. They needed time to be a couple and a family. Damon didn't want to interfere with that. But where the hell *was* he going to stay? He really might have to sleep in the barn.

"Damon's staying at my house," Charlotte said. "I've got an extra bedroom, too. Isn't that right, Damon?"

Everyone stared at her, including Damon. He cleared his throat and tried not to look too shocked.

"Ah, yeah, right. I'm staying at Charlotte's house."

"I thought it was the least I could do since he's helping to save so many dogs," she said.

Wasn't this an interesting development? Damon saluted her with his soda can and grinned. "Yeah, it really is the least you could do. Me being a hero and all."

Charlotte frowned. "I'm starting to regret my offer."

Everyone at the table laughed. Charlotte laughed with them, but when she looked at him, Damon saw apprehension in her eyes. Was she afraid of him? If she was, why would she offer to let him stay?

Her previous words played in his head. *How do you know I won't hurt you?* Maybe she was afraid of herself.

****

At Damon's knock, Charlotte opened her front door. She stood aside while he hauled in one large suitcase and a small carry-on. He shut the door behind him.

"Is that everything you have?" she asked.

"Pretty much. I left a couple of boxes of memorabilia I didn't want to part with at Blair's house, but other than that, this is it. I travel light."

Blair had told her that Damon had moved several times in the last few years. He must have become used to traveling light. She wondered how long he planned to hang around Masonville.

"You certainly do. I'd need one suitcase just for my shoes." Charlotte swept out her hand. "Come on. I'll show you to your room."

She led the way through her living room to the two bedrooms at the back of the house.

"Here's the bathroom," she said indicating the door between the two bedrooms. "And your room is here on the right."

He followed her inside, and, looking around, set his suitcases on the floor. Damon filled the space with his presence, making the small room feel even smaller. Charlotte fought the urge to flee.

"So, here it is. I know it's not very big, but there's a decent-size closet, and the bed is fairly new. I just put clean sheets and blankets on it, so everything's fresh."

"It's perfect, Charlotte. Thank you."

She nodded and clutched her hands together. Her nerves jangled. Why was she so nervous? "The laundry room is downstairs on the other side of the rec room. Anytime you need to wash clothes, help yourself to detergent. Unfortunately, I only have this one bathroom, so we'll have to share."

"I'm fine with that. I'll try to stay out of your way as much as possible."

"I don't expect you to isolate in this bedroom while

you're here. I want you to feel at home."

Damon glanced around the room. "I appreciate the sentiment, but I'm not sure I've ever felt at home anywhere."

A wave of empathy for Damon made Charlotte want to reach out to give him comfort, but she held herself still. It occurred to her that the trauma in their pasts meant they had much in common. In so many ways, he'd overcome the harm done to him as a child. But he hadn't yet found a home the way she had. This house represented sanctuary and refuge for her. It was the place she could truly be herself, and she was thankful for the safety it provided.

"Come on. I'll show you the basement."

She led the way down the stairs. Damon stopped on the last step.

"You have a heavy bag hanging from the ceiling. What do you do with it?"

"I punch it. What else do you do with a heavy bag?"

"Do you box?"

"Some. Mostly I practice Krav Maga and some Muay Thai, or Thai boxing."

"Krav Maga is a form of self-defense, isn't it?"

"Yeah. It was originally developed by the Israeli army."

"Do you go to a gym for lessons or just work out at home?"

"Both. I take Muay Thai classes at a gym."

"How long have you been practicing?"

She squirmed, uncomfortable with his questions. "A few years. I find both disciplines challenging, and they keep me in shape."

"Do you mind if I use your bag? I had one in the barn, but with all the dogs coming, I had to take it down."

"Of course. You can use it any time you want. Why don't I show you the laundry room?"

Charlotte was grateful when Damon nodded and kept any further questions to himself. After showing him around, they headed back up the stairs.

"Help yourself to anything in the kitchen." She opened the refrigerator and stared at the nearly empty shelves. "Although the cupboard is pretty bare right now."

He grinned. "I don't imagine we'll be spending much time here anyway. We'll be at the farm most of the time."

"Which reminds me, the wire kennels I ordered for the barn will be ready for pickup on Saturday. Can you help me with those?"

Damon dipped his head in a nod. "Sure. We can take my truck."

"Once they're set up, Gina said, the volunteers will bring the dogs to the farm."

"The veterans will all arrive by the end of next week. We've got a lot of work to do on the house before they get here."

"Speaking of which, we need to get up early tomorrow, so I'll say goodnight. Sleep well, Damon."

"Wait."

He stepped forward and set his hand on her arm. "Why did you tell everyone I was staying here?"

She looked into his warm gray eyes, mesmerized by flecks of green surrounding the iris. She swallowed. "You seemed uncomfortable with the idea of staying with Ben and Jamie. So I offered."

Charlotte wasn't sure what had come over her in that moment. She'd felt Damon's reluctance to stay with his brother and his family, even temporarily. She understood well the feeling of being in the way, of being the odd man out. And the words were out of her mouth before she had time to reconsider.

"Thank you. Jamie and Ben are finally in a great place in their marriage, and I didn't want to interfere with that. And besides, they've already got a houseful."

"Yes." Charlotte stared at Damon. Part of her screamed to race to the safety of her room and keep her distance. Still, she didn't move.

"I want you to know you're safe with me. I'd never hurt you or take advantage of you." Damon's voice was barely a whisper. "I'd never force you to do something you don't want to. I hope you can believe me."

It was good to hear him say the words, but she realized that, on some deeper level, she already understood she could trust him. Otherwise, she never would have offered him a room in her home.

Or perhaps, with Clayton in the area, she didn't want to be alone. Damon's presence in her house would give her some peace of mind.

"Yes, of course I believe you."

Damon's eyes never left her face. "If someone forced himself on you in the past, you know you can talk to me about it. I'll always listen."

Charlotte's heart pounded against her ribs. She tried to appear calm and in control, even as her hands began to shake. She averted her eyes, no longer able to look at him directly.

"Nothing like that has ever happened to me." She

tugged at her arm, and he let her go. "Goodnight, Damon."

"Goodnight."

The dogs followed closely on her heels as she hurried out of the kitchen and sought the refuge of her bedroom. Once inside, she locked the door, sat on her bed, and stared at her feet. She stayed that way until her heart rate slowed.

Damon was incredibly perceptive. Whether his ability to read people stemmed from being a counselor or because he'd been abused himself, she didn't know. All she knew was that having him live in her house was going to be far more difficult than she'd ever imagined.

Chapter Eight

Charlotte pulled up to her sister's house and shut off the engine of the Jeep. It was Friday, and Lauren and Cole had likely just returned home from work. They probably wanted to relax and spend time with each other and their daughter Piper.

She hadn't called ahead, but she needed to speak to Lauren, though she wasn't exactly sure what she wanted to say to her. She'd been unsettled since last night when Damon indirectly asked if she'd been raped. No one had ever asked her such a question before. As far as she knew, no one even suspected what had happened, and she wanted to keep it that way. She'd fooled a lot of people, but apparently, she couldn't fool him.

She'd avoided Damon most of the day by staying in the barn to sand the old furniture from the attic. She'd even dodged driving out to the farm with him that morning by saying she needed to run to Bismarck to get supplies for her refinishing projects and needed her own vehicle.

But she couldn't evade him forever, and she couldn't escape his questions, either. So here she was, wanting to confide in her sister but unable to.

Charlotte slumped in her seat, her head bowed. Keeping her secret was exhausting, but she had no choice. The shame of her rape weighed her down, threatening to drown her. She couldn't let anyone know.

Finally, she blew out a breath and opened the door of the Jeep. She'd say hello, play with her baby niece for a few minutes, and then leave. No big deal.

Cole answered when she knocked on the door. "Hey, Charlotte. How are you?"

"I'm good, but tired. We've been busy." She told him about the work they'd been doing at the farm, and about the imminent arrival of the dogs and veterans that had necessitated the work.

"I've got to give all of you credit. You've found a way to solve two difficult problems."

"We haven't solved anything yet. We could still fall flat on our faces."

Cole grinned. "Have faith, Charlotte. If there's anything I can do, let me know."

"Jamie's got our veterinary needs covered for now, but with the baby coming, she's going to need assistance soon. Eventually we'll want to spay and neuter all the dogs coming to Branson Farm."

"Don't worry. I'll help you out."

"Thanks, Cole."

Charlotte adored her brother-in-law. No one was kinder than Cole. Lauren was a very lucky woman. How wonderful it must be for her to simply love her husband without having to worry about the past.

That wasn't fair. Until not long ago, Lauren had worried about the past a great deal. She'd once been married to Cole's philandering brother. Billy died in a car crash, and on the day of his funeral she and Cole had turned to each other for solace. The result was Piper, but everyone in Masonville had assumed she was

Billy's child. It had taken courage for them to stand up and tell everyone that Piper belonged to Cole.

Lauren walked into the living room carrying Piper. Charlotte extended her hands, and her niece reached for her.

"An-tee, an-tee!"

Charlotte held her close and breathed in her sweet baby scent. "How's my favorite niece?"

Lauren chuckled. "Your only niece."

"Still my favorite."

"Did we have something planned for tonight?" Lauren asked. "I didn't forget, did I? Things get so busy at work I blank out sometimes."

"No, we didn't have anything planned. I just wanted to see you guys."

She rested her forehead against Piper's, and the toddler put her tiny hands on her cheeks. Since Piper's arrival, Charlotte had thought a lot about babies. If things had been different…

But they weren't. She'd content herself with being the world's coolest aunt and hope her siblings had lots of children.

Because she'd never have any children of her own.

Charlotte closed her eyes and let the grief of that loss wash over her.

Lauren turned to Cole. "Honey, your mom said the other day she doesn't spend enough time with you and Piper. Why don't you take Piper over to Ella's for a short visit?"

Cole blinked at her. "Now?"

"Just for a half hour or so. Okay?"

Cole glanced at Charlotte, then nodded at Lauren. "Sure, no problem. We'll make Mom's day. Come on, sweetie."

He took Piper from Charlotte, grabbed a diaper bag, and headed out the door. Charlotte rolled her eyes at Lauren.

"You didn't have to make Cole leave."

"I had the feeling you wanted to talk." She looped her arm through Charlotte's. "Come into the kitchen, and I'll make tea."

Lauren put a kettle on to boil. Charlotte sat silently at the table while Lauren set out cups and a small pitcher of milk. By the time the tea was made, she still hadn't figured out what she wanted to say. What she *could* say.

Lauren sat across from her and sipped her tea, waiting. Charlotte tapped her fingers against the table.

"I invited Damon Greyson to stay with me while his place is getting ready."

"Oh. Okay." It was obvious from the look on her face that Lauren was surprised by this news but was trying hard not to show it. "I don't know Damon well, but he seems nice. So why did you invite him to stay at your house?"

"Because he needed somewhere to stay, and he felt he'd be in the way at Ben and Jamie's house."

"I see." Lauren sipped her tea. "Aside from me, you've never had a roommate in your house before. And you've certainly never had a male roommate. What's different this time?"

Charlotte wasn't sure how to answer her sister. She certainly couldn't tell her she was nervous about Clayton Brown being in the area. She went with a half-truth.

"I trust Damon."

It went so much further than that, she realized. She cared about Damon, cared about his feelings, for one thing. And also, she liked him for the funny, self-deprecating, compassionate person he was.

And he was an incredible kisser. She smiled at that thought.

Lauren nodded. "I'm glad you trust him. There's not many people you can say that about."

"What do you mean? I trust people. I trust you and Cole, Mom and Dad, Garrett and Blair. I trust lots of people."

Lauren tilted her head as if contemplating a particularly vexing problem. "Let me rephrase that. There's not many people you trust outside of family, especially men."

Charlotte opened her mouth to disagree and then closed it, unable to refute the point. She trusted people at work, her friends at the shelter, some old friends from college, but nearly all of them were women. It surprised her to realize that outside of male family members, she had cut herself off from most men.

"I think if you trust Damon, it's a good thing, and I'm happy for you. He must be a very special person."

Charlotte lifted her teacup to her lips. "Nothing's going on between us. Don't go getting any crazy ideas."

Lauren blinked in indignation. "What ideas? I have no clue what you're talking about."

Unfortunately, Lauren ruined the indignation act with a satisfied grin.

****

On Saturday morning, Charlotte jumped into Damon's truck for the drive to Bismarck to pick up the new dog crates. She handed him a to-go cup with the coffee she'd brewed. Damon took the cup from her with a grateful smile.

"Thanks." He sipped the coffee, his eyes on the road. "So what do we have to pick up today?"

Charlotte referred to the receipt the big box store had emailed to her and she'd printed. "Twenty-six large wire dog crates, two large cooling fans, sixty stainless steel feeding bowls, and thirty holders."

"What are the holders for?"

"A holder can clip onto the side of the wire crate and hold one of the stainless-steel bowls. That way we can keep water for the dogs inside the crate all the time. If it's on the ground, they tend to knock it over."

"Sounds like you've thought of everything."

"I hope so. I wonder if two fans are enough. It could get very hot in the barn in the summer."

"We can always add another fan later if we need to," Damon said. "It's very generous of you to buy all this equipment."

"Not generous. Just practical." Charlotte turned to examine his profile as he drove. He had a long, straight nose, a strong chin, and a beautifully shaped mouth. She shivered in remembrance of his mouth on hers, then forcibly pushed the memory aside. "If it weren't for me, Garrett and Blair wouldn't have become involved in trying to save these dogs. I don't want them to have to bear the financial costs of housing them."

Damon sighed, his mouth turning down in a frown. "I know what you mean. If it weren't for me, they wouldn't be spending all this money on fixing up the house. It can't be cheap. Insulation, framing, drywall, paint. Yesterday a crew hung the drywall in the attic and then taped and mudded. Another crew installed a heating-and-cooling unit up there, while a window company put in two new, larger windows. The costs have got to be adding up."

"This isn't only because of you. Working with fellow veterans means as much to Garrett as it does to you, maybe more. And besides, they just gained a bunch of square footage for their house. With any luck, they'll fill the place up with kids one day."

Damon chuckled, and Charlotte enjoyed the way his mouth curved into a smile.

"I hope so, too. I think it would mean a lot to Blair," he said. "But still, I hope they haven't overextended themselves financially. I wish I could help more, but all my money is tied up in the Fletcher Building."

"It'll be worth it, Damon. Once the Fletcher Building is up to snuff and you're able to help veterans, all the stress of these renovations will be a distant memory," Charlotte said.

"I hope so. Because it's killing me right now."

"When did you say the first two veterans are arriving at the farm?" she asked.

"Monday. Just two days from now. The drywall crew should finish sanding today, and Chris and Garrett are going to start painting."

Charlotte knew Blair had chosen white paint to keep the third floor light and bright. A wall had been erected down the middle of the attic to create two small, private rooms. Hopefully, the light color would give the illusion of space.

They soon reached the outskirts of Bismarck and entered the parking lot of the big box store. "Do you think we can go inside before we pick up the crates at the loading dock? I want to buy some dog food so Blair doesn't think she has to supply it all," Charlotte said.

"Sure. No problem."

They parked the truck and headed inside. Charlotte grabbed a shopping cart in the vestibule and pushed it through the inside doors of the store. Even at this early hour, the place was packed. Beside her, she sensed Damon's tension. He watched fellow shoppers, seeming to examine each of them closely. When he stopped to watch a man talking to a boy who looked to be about ten, Charlotte brought her empty cart to a stop.

"Damon? What's wrong?"

He blinked at her as if he'd forgotten she was there. "Nothing. Let's go."

They headed to the pet food aisle and loaded four large bags of dry dog food into the cart. As they were making their way to the check out, the cries of a screaming toddler pierced the air. Charlotte saw the boy, who was maybe four, drop to the floor and throw a full-blown tantrum, his legs and arms kicking as he continued to scream. The exasperated father picked up the child and started carrying him toward the exit, even as the boy continued to scream and kick.

To Charlotte's shock, Damon went after them. He grabbed the man's arm and forced him to turn around.

"Who are you?" he demanded. "What's your relationship to this child?"

"It's none of your damn business."

The man took a few more steps toward the exit, but Damon blocked his escape. "You're not leaving this store until I'm sure this child belongs to you."

"You're crazy," the man said. A group of onlookers now surrounded them. "I'm calling security."

"By all means, please do."

Damon stepped closer to the man, the look on his face one Charlotte had never seen before, and it scared her. It told her he was prepared to take this man apart limb by limb if he meant the child harm. There was no way he was letting him leave with the toddler until he knew the truth.

The boy stopped crying, his attention caught by Damon's actions. He stuck his thumb in his mouth and watched him, one arm slung around the man's shoulders.

Damon addressed the child with a soft voice and a smile. "Hi there. What's your name?"

The boy popped his thumb out of mouth to answer. "Joey."

"How old are you, Joey?"

He held up his hand, his thumb tucked into his palm. "I'm four."

"Why were you crying?" Damon asked gently.

"I wanted the candy." Joey laid his head against the man's shoulder.

"And who is this?" Damon pointed at the man.

"Daddy," Joey whispered, his mouth turning down in a frown as if he were getting ready to cry again. "Daddy won't let me have candy."

Damon looked straight into the man's eyes. "Listen to your daddy, Joey. He knows what's good for you."

Damon stepped away. With his child in his arms, the father hurried to the exit and soon disappeared.

Charlotte continued to the checkout and paid for the dog food, her heart racing. What was that all about? She'd seen a toddler having a meltdown. She hadn't given it a second thought, and neither had most of the other shoppers. But Damon had interpreted it as something far more sinister.

Neither of them said a word as Damon pushed the cart back to his truck and stowed the bags in the back seat. They then headed to the loading dock to get the crates. Once the crates and the other supplies were loaded into the back of the truck and they were on their way back to the farm, Charlotte turned to Damon.

"What happened back there? What made you decide to intervene?"

Damon's jaw clenched. "I can't seem to help it. Every time I go into a public place, I wonder if any of the adults shouldn't be around kids."

"You mean, you wonder if they're going to hurt them?"

"Yeah. I keep asking myself, 'Did that touch on the shoulder look normal? Is that man the kid's father, or someone he doesn't know? Is that person standing too close to that little girl?' It's exhausting."

"I imagine it is."

Charlotte's heart cried for him. They hadn't talked about the abuse that had been perpetrated on him as a child since he'd mentioned it on the night of Blair and Garrett's wedding. This hypervigilance must be a residual effect of that abuse.

"If I knew—or even suspected—that a child was being abused, I couldn't live with myself if I stood by and did nothing," he said. "No one stepped in to help me. I'm not going to let that happen to another child."

Charlotte was too choked up to reply. Most of the time, Damon appeared so totally in control, so together, that she forgot what had been done to him. He must have worked very hard for the peace of mind he normally showed the world. The strength it must have taken to overcome that abuse awed her.

And it filled her with anger. Why hadn't his parents protected him?

She was angry with herself, too. When he'd confronted the father, her first reaction had been embarrassment.

She wouldn't make that mistake again.

****

After asking about the incident in the store, Charlotte had been silent the rest of the drive. Damon's heart fell. He'd made an utter ass of himself. Who confronts a father with a kid throwing a tantrum? He was sure she'd never known anyone as paranoid as him.

When they arrived at the farm, Damon backed his truck to the double doors of the barn. He searched for something to say to her, something normal. As he and Charlotte began unloading the flat cardboard boxes containing the wire crates, Damon noticed the old wooden furniture they'd found in the attic had been sanded down to the bare wood.

"Hey, you've been busy," he said.

"I have. I know they don't look like much now, but once I apply the stain, they'll be beautiful. The wood on the dresser is especially nice. It must have been an expensive piece at one time."

"It was."

Damon remembered asking his grandmother about it one summer when he'd been exploring in the attic. In his ten-year-old mind the small three-drawer dresser with the oval mirror and curved drawer fronts was elegant looking. Grandma Anna had explained that as a teenager, his mother Victoria had insisted on having the antique dresser, but after spilling nail polish remover on the top and ruining the finish, she'd demanded new furniture. Granddad had given in, but he'd refused to throw out the old dresser. Grandma said he'd always meant to refinish it but had never found the heart to do it.

"I think Granddad would be pleased you're fixing it up."

Charlotte smiled. "I'm glad. Everett was one of my favorite people."

Once they unloaded all the crates, they opened the cardboard boxes one by one and assembled each crate. By the time they were finished, twenty large crates lined the main hallway of the barn on both sides and six more were placed in a stall for the dogs with the worst skin problems. A mountain of cardboard sat near the open door.

"We want to keep the males and females separated as much as possible," Charlotte said. "We'll put as much space as we can between each crate to prevent the dogs from fighting, and diseases from spreading."

Damon and Charlotte moved the crates around until she was satisfied. When they were done, Charlotte stood back to admire their work.

"I can hardly wait to see the dogs in their new homes. I texted Gina to tell her we've got the crates now, so volunteers will start bringing the dogs tomorrow."

"You did good, Charlotte."

She smiled. "So did you."

"Charlotte…" Damon cleared his throat and tried again. "I'm sorry about what happened earlier. I embarrassed you."

She shook her head. "No, I'm the one who should be apologizing to you. You had the guts to question the situation when no one else did, including me."

They stared at each other. Aside from his counselors, he'd never revealed so much about his abuse and its lasting effects as he had with Charlotte. In the past, when he was involved with a woman, he'd avoided visiting public spaces with her, especially places where children might be present. He preferred not to have to explain his strange hypervigilance, or any confrontations. It was too embarrassing to go into his whole sad history. Too draining.

But it was different with Charlotte. For one thing, she already knew. And on some level, she understood. Maybe that was because she understood abuse on an intimate, personal level.

Damon wished he could touch her, wished he could kiss her the way he had a few nights ago. He couldn't stop thinking about it. He'd never experienced a kiss like that before, one that nearly brought him to his knees.

But then, he'd never kissed Charlotte Saunders before.

He hadn't believed her when she'd said no one had ever forced her. Something had happened to her, he could feel it. He only hoped that when she revealed the truth to him, he'd be strong enough to support her. Because the idea of someone hurting her undid him.

A keening whine drew his attention. Charlotte turned toward the stall where Hope was kept.

"It's Hope. Maybe she's in labor."

They hurried to the stall and found Hope panting and pacing between the straw on the floor of the stall and the cardboard whelping box. She pawed at the blankets lining the bottom of the box, rearranging them to her satisfaction. Soon she started restlessly pacing the straw again.

"Do we need to call Jamie? Does she need veterinary care?" Damon asked.

"I don't think so, at least not yet." Charlotte kept her voice low as she knelt on the straw and scratched Hope's ear. "I think she's in the first stage of labor. For now, I'll stay close by and monitor how she's doing."

"I'll stay with you."

"There's no need for you to stick around, too. It could take hours."

Damon knelt beside her and laid his hand on her shoulder. "You don't have to do this alone. You have people here who care about you and want to help you."

Charlotte's eyes softened as her gaze met his. "I appreciate that, Damon. I really do. But I've got this. Why don't you come check on us once you get rid of all that cardboard out there?"

She was the most stubborn woman. Her inability to accept help was frustrating when he only wanted to make things easier for her. But at least she wasn't closing the door completely on the idea of him waiting out the birth with her.

Damon sighed and got to his feet. "All right. I'll clean up here so we're ready for the other dogs tomorrow. But I'll be back. You don't get to have all the fun."

Charlotte grinned as she rose. "Don't worry. I'm sure there will be plenty of fun to go around. Remember, we have three more pregnant dogs. You can play midwife another time."

"Right." *What the hell were they going to do with all those pups?* He tucked that worry away for another day. One problem at a time.

Damon loaded the cardboard boxes into the truck bed and tied them down with bungee cords to keep them from flying out of the truck during the drive to the nearby recycling center. By the time he'd finished loading, Charlotte was brushing stain on the dresser.

"Looks good," he said.

"Thanks. I've still got some work to do if they're going to be ready in time for the vets."

"Do you need anything while I'm out?"

"I've got all my refinishing supplies here. But a cold drink would be nice."

"Coming right up." Damon headed to the cab of his truck.

"Damon, maybe let Blair know that Hope's gone into labor." For the first time, she looked worried. "In case we need her or Jamie to come in a hurry."

"Okay, I will. I'll be back soon."

She waved as he drove out of the yard. Before he hit the main road, he was on the phone with the veterinary clinic.

"Masonville Veterinary Clinic."

"Hi, Lauren? It's Damon Greyson here. Is Blair available?"

"Hi, Damon. Sorry, she's out on a farm call with Cole. Can I take a message?"

"Yeah. Can you let Blair and Jamie know that the pregnant dog we brought here to Branson Farm has gone into labor? Charlotte says she's in the first stage, and she thinks everything is fine, but she wanted to let them know, just in case."

"Is that the one they named Hope? The Border Collie cross?"

"Yeah, that's her."

"I'll let them know." He heard Lauren sigh. "Is Charlotte okay? She gives so much of herself to the shelter that it worries me sometimes."

He understood what she meant. "She's okay. But she's trying to carry the responsibilities of the world on her shoulders."

"Yeah. She does that." She hesitated, and Damon heard her sigh again. "She wasn't always so serious. She used to like to have fun. Her partying and her constant string of boyfriends used to drive my mother crazy with worry. But once she finished college and started working as a nurse, she did a total one-eighty. I can't remember the last time she had a boyfriend. In fact, you're the only man she's shown any interest in, in a very long time."

He didn't want Lauren to think he was taking advantage of Charlotte's vulnerability. "If you're asking if something's going on between us, the answer is no."

"I know my sister, and I know she trusts you. That's a big deal for her."

Lauren was right. Charlotte's trust didn't come easily. He needed to do everything he could to show her he was worthy of that trust.

"Just…be careful with her. Okay?"

"I'll be careful. I promise."

"I appreciate that. I'll let Jamie and Blair know about Hope."

Damon ended the call. Lauren's comment about Charlotte once having lots of boyfriends and being the life of the party stuck with him. People changed, of course. They grew up, matured, developed new tastes.

But to turn away from relationships seemed drastic. Though Charlotte had denied it, he was afraid he knew what had happened to her.

He wished she'd let him support her. But until she asked for his assistance, all he could do was be her friend.

Chapter Nine

Charlotte watched helplessly as Hope pushed and strained. The Border Collie was obviously in deep discomfort. She'd paced and panted for over five hours.

She tried to call on her medical training to stay calm so she could assess the situation. But with every passing minute she grew more worried that Hope and her babies weren't going to make it. And with every passing minute she grew more paralyzed, unable to think through the fog of fear.

She was going to lose them.

Damon slipped through the door of the stall and sat next to her on the straw. The only thing that had kept her from falling to pieces all afternoon was Damon's frequent appearances. She had the feeling he was checking on her as much as he was checking on the dog.

He handed her a sandwich and a bottle of orange juice. She handed it back, her stomach rebelling at the idea of food.

"I can't, Damon."

"You need to eat something. And you haven't had anything to drink since I brought you that cola hours ago. You're not going to do Hope any good by making yourself ill."

He had a point. She reached for the orange juice. "All right, fine. I'll try some of this."

"Good." He turned to Hope, who sat in her whelping box, panting and staring at them as if asking why they didn't do something. "So there's no change?"

"No." Charlotte checked her watch. "It's been nearly six hours."

"I talked to Blair, and she said it's not unusual for labor to last this long. She'll be home soon. And Jamie's going to drop by as soon as she finishes with her last patient of the day."

Tears of relief filled Charlotte's eyes. "Thank goodness the cavalry's coming. I can't bear the thought of losing those babies."

Damon tucked a strand of hair behind her ear. "Help is coming, and everything's going to be okay. Now, eat."

He placed the sandwich in her hands. Normally, chicken salad was one of her favorites, but she had no appetite for it today. Charlotte stared at it. "I should have been able to help Hope, but I couldn't."

"You don't have any power over the length of Hope's labor."

"Yes, but I should have—"

"Stop right there. Don't blame yourself for something that's beyond your control. If one of your patients came to you with a broken arm, would you blame yourself for their injury?"

"No, of course not. But—"

"No buts. This is exactly the same." He cupped her face with his hand. "You don't need to feel guilty in any way about Hope, or about reaching out for assistance. We all need help sometimes. If we didn't, I'd be out of business."

She smiled at that. "You're lucky so many of us are

needy puddles of emotion."

"I am. Business is booming."

"Thank you, Damon."

"For what?"

"For being here. For understanding. This may come as a surprise to you, but it's not easy for me to admit when I can't manage on my own."

He grinned. "Shocking. I hadn't noticed."

She lightly punched his arm. "Jerk."

He lowered his head towards hers, and her breath caught as she anticipated his kiss. Instead, he whispered in her ear.

"Eat your sandwich, Charlotte."

Hands trembling, she removed the sandwich's plastic wrapping and took a bite. To her surprise, the chicken salad was delicious, and she polished it off in a few bites. She hadn't realized how hungry she was.

She washed down the sandwich with orange juice. "Are you happy now?"

"Ecstatic." He stretched his long legs out in front of him. "The old furniture looks good."

"Yeah, it does." She'd worked on the furniture over the afternoon while running back and forth to check on Hope. "I'll give it another coat of polyurethane tomorrow morning, and once it dries, it'll be ready to go back into the house."

"Not a moment too soon. The first two vets get here on Monday."

"Are you worried about treating them?"

"No. I'm confident I've developed a solid program that can help people with PTSD. A combination of cognitive behavioral therapy and exposure therapy has benefited a lot of people."

Charlotte was happy to talk about something other than herself. "I've heard about those therapies, but I don't really know what they entail."

"In cognitive behavioral therapy, or CBT, we talk about the traumatic event and how it affected the vet's life. Sometimes they write about the event, which gives them a chance to examine how they feel about their trauma. I try to give them new ways to deal with it, so they don't blame themselves for what they did or didn't do. If someone avoids thinking or talking about their trauma, exposure therapy aids them in facing it. We continue to look at the trauma until it loses its power. It's like washing the wound over and over again until it's clean."

Charlotte nodded. She had no doubt in Damon's abilities. "Any idea when your building will be ready?"

He shrugged. "No clue. I'm starting to worry it'll never be ready. What if the costs to fix it are beyond my means? What if it's unfixable? Housing the men here is a temporary measure, and even if Garrett and Blair were willing to open their home permanently to veterans in need, we couldn't help more than five at a time. The need is much greater than that."

Charlotte examined his tense face. Damon's jaw was clenched in frustration. He was so sincere about wanting to be of service to others. She wondered if it stemmed from his experience of being abused as a child.

"Maybe all the bad stuff has been found, and it'll be clear sailing from now on."

"Maybe." His frown told her he didn't believe the trouble was over.

Hope whined and began to strain once more.

Charlotte moved closer to the box. Something that looked like a water-filled bubble began to emerge from Hope's vulva. From her experience at the shelter witnessing other canine births, she knew this was the water bag that should precede the birth.

"It's finally happening!"

Damon crouched beside her. The world narrowed to the two of them alone together in this stall with a dog giving birth. Somehow it was all she needed.

"Hello? Charlotte, are you here?"

Her cozy bubble was burst by the sound of a familiar voice coming from the entrance of the barn. As glad as she was for Jamie's arrival, Charlotte found herself wishing for a few more minutes alone with Damon.

Thoughts like that were dangerous.

She moved away from Damon and opened the stall door. "Over here, Jamie."

Jamie stepped into the stall and gave Charlotte a hug. "How long has Hope been in labor?"

"Too long for my liking, but it looks like something is finally happening now."

She gave Jamie the rundown on Hope's condition and the length of time she'd been straining. Damon supported Jamie as she got down on her knees to examine Hope in her box.

"I know it seems like a long time, but it's perfectly normal, especially if this is Hope's first litter." Jamie took a pair of latex gloves from her bag and pulled them on. "The x-ray we took at the clinic showed six puppies. With any luck, they'll come quickly."

Jamie's words were prophetic. The first three puppies came out one after another in quick succession.

Hope licked them thoroughly, breaking open the water sac surrounding each one and chewing off the umbilical cord that attached the pup to her body.

"Is she supposed to do that?" Damon asked as Hope ate the placenta that followed the birth of one of the pups.

"It's perfectly normal," Jamie replied. "It's an instinct dogs have retained to remove any evidence of the birth from prey. But we won't let her eat all six because it could make her vomit or give her diarrhea. The important thing is to see the placenta come out after each birth."

By the time the fourth puppy was born, it was obvious Hope was fatigued. While the first three puppies nursed, Hope rested on her side, too tired to give much attention to number four. Jamie grabbed the towel Charlotte had brought from home and began rubbing the fourth pup until the membrane around its nose and mouth broke and it began to breathe. Its tiny cries were a welcome sound.

After drying it as much as she could, Jamie put the puppy close to Hope's head. The dog immediately began licking it.

"Damon, could you get more clean towels from the house? We're going to need to assist Hope with the next two. She's exhausted, poor thing." Jamie chuckled. "Glad I'm not giving birth to six babies at once."

"Amen to that. Ben would have a heart attack." Damon jumped to his feet. "I'll be right back."

After he left the barn, Jamie turned to Charlotte. "How are you doing, Char?"

"I'm fine. A little stressed after watching over Hope all day, but I'm good."

"How have you and Damon been getting along since he's been staying with you?"

"We're good. We're here most of the time."

"Both of you have worked so hard." After Hope finished licking the fourth pup and then chewed off its umbilical cord, Jamie placed it near a teat so it could nurse. She moved the placenta out of the mother dog's reach. "Damon's a good man. Ben says he couldn't have made it through the rough times we went through without him. He helped Ben see what was really important. If he hadn't, Ben and I may not have found our way back to each other."

Charlotte hadn't realized their problems had been so serious. "I'm glad you were able to work things out. You and Ben are good together."

"We are. And now with the baby coming, I couldn't be happier." Her attention was diverted by Hope's whine. "Looks like something's happening."

A pup began to emerge. Hope lay on her side panting. Charlotte stroked her head.

"Just two more, Hope. You can do it."

Pup number five spilled out onto the blanket, followed by the placenta. Hope lifted her head briefly to look at it and then lay back down.

"We'll need to help her," Jamie said.

Damon rushed back into the stall with several towels. He handed one to Jamie, and she immediately began rubbing the new pup. Once she removed the membrane from the pup's mouth and nose, she handed it to Charlotte.

"Keep drying it. I'm going to cut the cord myself."

Jamie tied the cord with a fine string in two places between the pup and the mother dog, and then cut the cord between the two tied-off points. She took the pup from Charlotte and again placed it near Hope's head. As tired as the dog was, instinct took over, and she began licking it clean.

"One more to go," Jamie said.

Charlotte blew out a breath. "I can't wait for this to be over."

Damon grinned at her. "You look almost as tired as Hope."

She grinned back. "Don't be silly. I plan to run a marathon after this."

Their eyes met and held in an unspoken moment of silent communication. Damon was the first man she'd met in ten years who'd made her think that maybe she could have a normal life.

Whatever normal was.

"Here comes number six," Jamie said.

The final birth came swiftly. Again, Jamie wiped the pup's nose and mouth to allow it to breathe, then handed it to Charlotte to dry while she tied off the cord. Once Hope gave the last pup a thorough licking, Jamie moved it close to Hope's belly. In seconds, it latched on to a teat and began nursing.

"There we go," Jamie said with a satisfied smile. "Family complete."

Jamie's simple words brought a lump to Charlotte's throat. She swallowed and blinked, struggling to get herself under control, and not even sure why she was so emotional.

"Hey." Damon put his arm around her shoulders. "It's okay. They're all fine now."

"Yeah." Charlotte swiped at a tear running down her cheek.

"I promise they'll be fine, Char. I've got a heat lamp in my car that we can set up over the whelping box to keep the puppies warm. I'll come check on them for the next few days." Jamie extended her arm. "Now, if you don't mind, Damon, can you help me up?"

Damon laughed and gently pulled her to her feet. Just then Blair opened the stall door and stepped inside.

"Sorry I'm late. Cole and I got tied up on the farm call with a stubborn bunch of calves. How's Hope?"

"See for yourself," Jamie said. "She did great."

"With some assistance from you and Charlotte," Damon added.

Blair knelt on the straw. "Oh, aren't they cute!"

Now that the puppies were dry, their coloring was discernible. Charlotte noted that five pups were black and white like Hope, but the smallest one, Number Six, who'd been late to the party, was mostly brown.

"What are you going to name them?" Blair asked.

Charlotte didn't have the brainpower to come up with names right now. "I don't know yet. Give me a couple of days."

Relief at seeing Hope nurse six healthy babies made Charlotte want to cheer and shout. But it also made her want to weep. Life could be so precarious for animals.

And for humans.

Perhaps it was seeing Clayton Brown so unexpectedly that caused her to feel so emotional and unsettled. He represented a dark period in her life, one she'd been trying to put behind her for ten years. Every time she thought she was over the rape something would happen to make the memories come rushing back.

Maybe she'd never be over it.

Charlotte glanced up and saw that Damon was watching her. She quickly looked away. He'd said everyone needed assistance at some point in their lives, but she'd never been able to ask for support. She'd never told anyone about the rape, not even Lauren. The idea of telling her family, especially her parents, filled her with such overwhelming shame that she'd kept it hidden deep inside. They'd be so disappointed in her. So ashamed of her.

Because the rape had been her own fault.

Chapter Ten

It was close to ten p.m. when Charlotte arrived home. As Damon pulled his truck into the driveway, she parked her Jeep behind him and turned off the ignition. Despite knowing she had another busy day tomorrow and she needed sleep, Charlotte was too keyed up to relax. The birth of the puppies, though exciting, made her feel strangely restless. She needed to move, to do something.

She considered taking the dogs for a walk, but it was dark, and with Clayton Brown somewhere close by, she no longer felt safe walking alone. She hated that once again he'd taken away her sense of security.

She let the dogs out of the back seat of the Jeep and they chased each other around the front yard before heading to the door with her. She unlocked the front door, her gaze not quite meeting Damon's.

"I think I'm going to work out downstairs for a while," she said.

"Mind if I join you?"

His question surprised her. "You want to watch me hit the heavy bag?"

"I'd like to see some of your self-defense moves. Maybe you can give me some pointers."

Charlotte stared at him, trying to figure out what he wanted. Did he think he could cop a feel by getting her in a clinch? Damon was bigger and stronger than she was, of course, but she knew ways to take him down. If he wanted to see her moves, she'd show him.

"Fine. I'll meet you downstairs as soon as I change."

Ten minutes later she headed to the basement. From the stairs, she watched, unobserved, as Damon pounded the heavy bag, the muscles in his arms and across his bare back bunching and straining. Her breath caught. Damon was seriously built.

"Are you going to stand around and watch, or are you going to work out?"

Damon's question caught her off guard since she'd thought he hadn't seen her ogling him. It reminded her to never underestimate an opponent, something she'd been taught in her training.

Charlotte stepped forward. Rather than her usual training gear of sports bra and short shorts, she'd opted for yoga pants and a T-shirt. "Just staying out of the line of fire, Greyson. How do you want to do this?"

"Show me how you'd stop someone who tries to grab you."

"All right. Help me move the crash mats first."

She'd purchased a couple of mats like the kind used at the gym. She usually practiced hitting the heavy bag in her bare feet, so the mats cushioned her from the concrete floor. She could also practice falls and rolls on the mats without injuring herself. But tonight she'd decided to wear running shoes. Damon helped her move the mats to the center of the room, then faced her on the mat.

"I'll come at you from the front. Okay?" Damon said.

"Attackers don't usually announce the direction

they plan to hit you from."

"I don't want to hurt you."

"Worry about yourself, Greyson. I'll look after me."

"All right, if that's the way you want to play this."

Without warning, he grabbed her upper arms and pulled her close. Her nostrils flared as his scent reached her, a combination of spicy aftershave and sweat.

"Now what are you going to do?" he asked.

She grinned. "Brace yourself."

With one quick, hard move, she jerked her arms down, breaking Damon's hold. Then she slammed her shoe into the top of his foot. As he cried out in surprise, she pushed the heel of her palm into his nose, just above his mouth.

"Now if you were a real attacker, I'd slam my hand hard enough into your nose to break it, or at least cause a nosebleed and a lot of pain. But I prefer not to get blood on my mats."

"How did you do that? How did you manage to free your arms so easily?" he asked.

"By applying pressure to the weakest point of your hold. Here, I'll show you." Charlotte wrapped her hands around his wrists. "See how my thumb and pointer finger don't quite meet? That's the weakest point. Even if I hold onto to you as tightly as I can, if you thrust your arms hard in the direction of that weak spot, you'll be able to break the hold. Try it."

"Okay, I'll try."

Damon stared into her eyes, and Charlotte forgot the point of what they were doing. He had the most amazing eyes, with the uncanny ability to change color. Perhaps it was because of the way the light hit them, but she imagined they reflected his mood as well. Right now, they appeared a stormy gray. Was that because he was concentrating on his lesson, or were more sensuous thoughts at play?

Without warning, he thrust his arms down hard and fast, breaking her hold on him. He grinned at her.

"Hey, it works!"

"Told ya."

The grin left his face. "Okay, I see it's possible to break a hold, but what if things go sideways after that? What if you don't hit me hard enough in the nose? What if I grab you again?"

"There's always a counterattack." She lifted her knee and pressed it against his groin. "You've let me get close enough to injure you. One hard knee in the balls and you'll drop like a sack of potatoes."

They were so close, Charlotte could see the green flecks embedded in his storm gray irises. Suddenly aware of intimacy of the position, she lowered her knee and stepped back.

"Let's…" Damon cleared his throat. "Let's try it again."

This time Damon grabbed her forearms and held tight, using his superior strength to immobilize her. Again, she was able to break his hold with a hard downward thrust. Then she grabbed him, wrapped her arm around his, and tucked it under her armpit.

"If you try to escape this hold, I can dislocate your elbow. Or I can incapacitate you again with a few knee jabs to the groin." Charlotte opted not to lift her knee in demonstration and quickly let him go.

"What if I came at you from behind?" Damon demonstrated with an arm crooked around her neck.

"What if I held a knife to your throat?"

Charlotte stomped on his foot again and head butted him under the chin, being careful not to hit him too hard. "Does that answer your question?"

"Yeah, it does." Damon grinned and rubbed his chin. "Have you ever had to use any of these tactics to protect yourself in a real-life situation?"

"No, fortunately not."

"Do you think you could?"

"I hope so." Charlotte wished she'd known how to protect herself from Clayton. Now that she had the tools to fend off an attacker, the only thing she was afraid of was freezing with fear and being unable to react quickly enough.

If the need arose, she prayed she'd be strong enough to defend herself. She'd rather die than be raped again.

****

Damon woke early, with sunshine streaming in through the window. He'd slept so soundly he was momentarily disoriented and couldn't remember where he was. As he glanced around the small bedroom, he remembered he was in Charlotte's house. And Charlotte was down the hall. In her bed.

Damon rolled over and groaned into his pillow. He'd underestimated how tortuous living with Charlotte would be. In each of the four nights he'd lain in this bed, he imagined Charlotte in hers. Did she sleep in T-shirts and cotton boxer shorts, or in silk nighties? He wanted the silk. He imagined running his hands over the soft material, and then her bare skin, unable to tell where the fabric ended and the silk of her skin began. His body burned with wanting her, burned with wanting to sink inside her, to love her.

But it wasn't what Charlotte wanted. Or needed. Damon groaned into his pillow one last time before pushing himself to a seated position. Time for another cold shower.

He threw on a pair of sweatpants, grabbed his bag of toiletries, and opened his door. Charlotte emerged from the bathroom at the same moment, a fluffy white towel covering her from just above her breasts to her upper thighs. Her wet hair clung to her bare shoulders, and little rivulets of water disappeared beneath the towel. She was like an exotic mermaid rising from the sea. Damon stared transfixed at the streams of water flowing over her skin before lifting his gaze to her face. Her eyes were wide, her mouth partially open in an expression of surprise. She clutched the top of the towel with one hand, hiking it higher up her thighs.

She was so damn beautiful she rendered him speechless. Hell, he could barely breathe.

"Sorry." Charlotte's cheeks flushed pink. "I forgot my robe. I'm used to being on my own."

Damon cleared his throat and tested his voice. "I...I'm the one who should apologize. I just woke up. I didn't hear the shower."

She nodded and bit her bottom lip. Damon watched her mouth, his body on fire despite the awkwardness of the moment.

"I should go," she whispered.

"Yeah, me too. I need to shower."

For a second, neither of them moved. Then Daisy approached and barked once, then twice more. Charlotte blinked as if waking from a deep sleep. She tightened her hold on the towel.

"I have to go."

With that, she hurried to her room and closed the door. Damon stood immobile, staring after her. It took all his self-control not to go after her. The only thing stopping him was the knowledge that she didn't want him.

Someone had forced himself on her in the past, he was sure of it. If he and Charlotte ever made love, it would be because she initiated it.

Damon entered the bathroom. He stepped under the shower and turned the water as cold as he could stand.

****

By noon on Sunday, volunteers began arriving with the rescue dogs. Charlotte and Blair helped the dogs out of the travelling carriers and led them to their new crates. Some of the animals were obviously afraid, and extra time had to be spent getting them used to their new surroundings. It was no wonder they were afraid. In the space of a couple of weeks, they'd gone from the squalid conditions in a hoarder's house to an overcrowded shelter, and now to another strange new location.

She hated that the dogs had to be keep in crates and could only go out a few times a day. She would have loved to see them run free, but there were simply too many of them. For their own safety and for the safety of the horses, they'd have to be kenneled, at least for now. Local animal protection officers had come out to the farm to inspect their facilities. They were satisfied with the arrangement as long as the dogs were let out of the kennels regularly. Maybe in the near future some sort of dog run could be built that would allow the dogs to have more freedom. Where they'd find the money to build such a thing, Charlotte had no idea.

She'd worry about a dog run later. For now, it was enough to know the dogs had been saved and each had a chance for a happy life.

Charlotte wondered if she could say the same for herself. She kept seeing the look of hunger on Damon's face when she'd stepped out of the bathroom that morning. He'd wanted her.

And she'd been tempted in a way she'd never been before. After her rape, she had shut down that part of her life, too afraid to be intimate with anyone. Somehow Damon had worked his way past her defenses and made her consider taking a chance. She trusted him more than she'd trusted any man in the last ten years.

But was she ready to take a big step like having sex with him? Her stomach fluttered at the thought, though Charlotte wasn't sure whether it was fear or arousal that caused the reaction.

Keep it together, Char. You've got work to do.

As if her thoughts had summoned him, Damon appeared in the barn. He'd spent most of the morning working in the house with Garrett and Chris, putting the finishing touches on the rooms for the vets. Or perhaps he'd been avoiding her as much as she'd been avoiding him.

"What can I do, Charlotte?"

"Can you make sure each of the dogs has a bowl of water in their crate? It's pretty hot today."

"Sure. Where are the bowls?"

"In the wash stall. They're cleaned and ready to go. You just need to put them in their holders and attach the hooks to the inside of the crate."

"I'm on it."

She watched him head to the wash stall, her heart heavy with longing. Charlotte almost hated him. Until he came into her life again, she'd been fine on her own. She had a full life with her family, her career, and her volunteer activities. And then Damon arrived and made her want more. He showed her what she was missing, what could be if she was brave enough to make a leap of faith.

Charlotte blew out a breath. That was a hell of a scary leap.

A van driven by a volunteer entered the yard. Inside the van were the six dogs with the worst skin problems. Charlotte and the volunteer moved them to the largest stall, where they would be kept a safe distance away from the rest of the dogs. Jamie had warned that strict protocols needed to be in place to ensure the skin diseases didn't pass to the other dogs. The veterans and anyone else who worked with them would have to wear latex gloves and protective clothing when taking them out for walks or administering ointments. These six dogs had to be walked one at a time, a safe distance from the other dogs. Everyone had to be meticulous about handwashing. Charlotte hoped the protocols and the distance were enough to prevent any diseases from spreading.

Another volunteer soon arrived with the three pregnant dogs, Sally, Lucy, and Peppermint Patty. Charlotte helped the volunteer unload.

"I've got just the place for our girls," she told her.

They carried Sally's kennel to the stall next to Hope's. Charlotte could hear the soft mewling of the pups next door. She gently pushed aside her two dogs and Frisco before opening the stall door.

"Go find somewhere else to play, guys."

When they wandered off to find more adventures, Charlotte entered the stall and set the plastic kennel on the floor. She and Garrett had spread straw in the stalls meant for the pregnant dogs and prepared whelping boxes lined with old towels and blankets their mother had donated. All the stall doors were full-length and made of solid wood. They closed securely, so Charlotte didn't have to worry about other dogs or wildlife wandering inside and hurting either the mothers or the pups.

She opened the door of the kennel. The volunteer, Jean, knelt in front of the kennel to encourage Sally to come out.

"Come on, Sally. You can do it. Don't be scared."

Sally cautiously sniffed the air. She ventured one paw out of the kennel and then another until she finally emerged all the way. Though she was visibly shaking, Sally examined every corner of the stall, her nose to the ground, sniffing.

Jean picked up the empty plastic kennel. "I'll bring the next dog."

"Sounds good. I want to watch Sally for a moment and make sure she's settling in all right."

"Okay. I'll be right back."

Damon entered the stall with a bowl of water just as Jean left. He set the bowl in front of Sally, and after a thorough sniff, she lapped the water greedily. He got down on his haunches to stroke her.

"You were thirsty, weren't you, girl?"

He was such a compassionate man. The trauma in his past could have made him hard and bitter, but instead he did everything he could to alleviate suffering, in people and in animals.

He rose and faced her, his face tense. "I don't want us to have any awkwardness between us. What happened this morning was…" He shook his head.

"Awkward?" She so wanted to lighten the self-consciousness between them.

Damon gave her a relieved smile. "Yeah, awkward. Do you think we can move past it?"

Relief flooded through Charlotte. "Yeah, I think we can."

"Charlotte?" Jean called from outside the stall. "I've got Lucy here. Where do you want her?"

"I'll be right there."

There was so much more she wanted to say to Damon, but now wasn't the time. And even if it was, she wasn't sure she could put her feelings into words. "Thanks."

He nodded. "I've still got water bowls to distribute. I'd better get going."

He left the stall and held the door open for her. With one final look at Sally, Charlotte followed him.

We're going to be okay, girl. You'll see.

Chapter Eleven

Chris basted a chicken in the oven while Damon washed and chopped vegetables for a salad. He'd spent part of the day acting as Chris's sous chef since the first two veterans were scheduled to arrive at the farm in time for dinner.

Damon felt a combination of excitement and nervousness. He'd read the veterans' medical files and learned they'd both seen active duty in the Middle East. They'd both experienced the loss of members of their units and witnessed the aftermath of horrific crimes perpetrated on civilians. Damon was confident a combination of talk therapy as well as the peaceful setting on the farm and the work they'd do here would help ease their PTSD. It was also possible that medication would be beneficial.

In truth, Branson Farm needed the veterans as much as they needed Branson Farm. With the arrival yesterday of the dogs, the monumental task of looking after them had begun. It had only been a day, but he already recognized they needed help to care for the dogs' many needs.

The crunch of gravel told him a vehicle had driven into the farmyard. Damon dried his hands on a towel.

"It's showtime, Chris."

Garrett must have heard the vehicle as well, because as they made their way out onto the porch, he was walking toward them from the barn. A driver and two passengers emerged from a large black SUV. As the driver opened the back hatch and began removing luggage, Damon approached him and extended his hand.

"Hi. I'm Damon Greyson. This is Chris Redwick and my brother-in-law Garrett Saunders. Welcome to Branson Farm."

The driver shook their hands. "Thank you. I'm Pete Mathews with the VA Hospital in Minneapolis."

"Good to meet you."

"There's been a change in personnel," Mr. Mathews said. "Corporal Stewart, can you please introduce yourself?"

A woman in fatigues stepped forward, her gaze somewhere over Damon's left shoulder. "Corporal Des Stewart, sir."

"Welcome, Corporal Stewart." Damon extended his hand in a shake, doing his best to keep his expression neutral while his mind raced. The VA had thrown him a complete curveball. He knew nothing about this woman or the status of her mental health.

Pete Mathews handed him a folder. "These are Corporal Stewart's medical records. Unfortunately, Corporal Johnson, who was scheduled to come here, had to be readmitted to the hospital and was deemed ineligible for the program at this time."

Damon's heart sank. The marine must have had serious problems to necessitate more time in hospital. If his building hadn't been so delayed, maybe he could have helped him before his pain reached a crisis point.

"And this is Lieutenant Michael Bates," Mathews continued.

A tall man wearing civilian clothes stepped forward to shake his hand. "Mr. Greyson, sir."

"Please, call me Damon. While you're here at Branson Farm, there are no ranks. We go by first names, and we don't stand on ceremony." He wanted everyone to feel comfortable enough to talk and share with each other, no matter if they were a private or a general. He turned to Des Stewart with a smile. "And you can wear your civilian clothes. I guess you didn't get the memo."

"No, sir. I mean…Damon."

She couldn't have looked more uncomfortable. He wondered how having a woman in the mix would affect the dynamic of the group. They'd have to figure things out because there was no way he was turning Des Stewart away.

"Damon and I are getting dinner ready," Chris said. "Why don't we get you settled in your rooms, and then you can help. The others will be joining us for dinner at six."

"I still have some work to finish in the barn," Garrett said. "Charlotte had to run into Bismarck for medication for one of the dogs."

"Charlotte?" Des asked.

"My sister," Garrett said with a smile. "It was her crazy idea to have us look after all these dogs when the local shelter couldn't handle them. You'll meet her and my wife Blair at dinner."

Des nodded. "Mr. Cunningham told me about the dogs when the space opened up. It was one of the reasons I wanted to come here."

"I'm glad to hear it. It takes a lot of people to look after them. I'll see you at dinner."

With a wave, Garrett headed to the barn. Pete Mathews handed Damon his business card. "I have to get back to Minneapolis. If you have any questions or concerns, please give me a call."

Damon shook his hand. "Thank you for your help."

After he said his goodbyes to Des Stewart and Michael Bates, Mathews got into the SUV and drove away.

"Let's show you the rooms," Damon said.

The four of them walked up the stairs to the second floor. Damon showed them the bathroom. "All five of you will be sharing this bathroom. You'll have to work out a schedule amongst yourselves. The bathroom on the main floor is solely for the use of Garrett and Blair. They own the farm."

"Since you two are first to arrive, you get the pick of the rooms. There are three bedrooms on this floor and two more in the attic." Chris pointed to the bedroom at the end of the hall. "Personally, I think that's the best room. My wife and I stayed in it when we lived here."

"You used to live here?" Michael asked.

"Yeah. Garrett and I are old friends. We served together in Afghanistan."

Michael looked at Chris with new respect. "So you're both veterans."

"Yeah. So is Damon."

Michael and Des turned to look at him. Damon was never comfortable talking about himself, but he knew it was important to establish creditability.

"I signed up with the army at eighteen and served four years. It was a great experience and I learned a lot, mainly that I'm not cut out to be in the army."

Even Des cracked a smile at that. Damon continued. "I never served overseas, but I did meet veterans who had, and I saw that several of them needed help. I believed I could better serve by educating myself so I could help people affected by trauma, especially veterans."

At eighteen he'd been desperate to get far away from St. Paul and his parents, especially his mother. Grandfather Greyson offered to send him to an Ivy League college, but Damon didn't want to be beholden to him or to his parents. He'd seen the pressure they'd put on Ben, and he wanted no part of it. And aside from that, he hadn't been ready for college. He had no idea what he wanted to do with his life. He only knew he needed to get away. And to somehow heal himself. The army allowed him the time and space to begin that process.

He'd benefited from the structure and discipline of the army. While in the military, he took his first tentative steps to get help for the abuse that had destroyed his childhood. He'd made friends and was still in touch with many of them.

But after four years, he decided it was time to move on. With a combination of savings and student loans, he paid for his tuition at the University of Michigan for both his Bachelor and Masters degrees. It was a point of pride to have financed his education himself.

"Can we look at the attic bedrooms?" Des asked.

"Sure." Damon pointed to the stairs. "Right this way."

They climbed the stairs to the third floor, and Des entered the first room. "This looks new."

"It is new," Chris replied. "New drywall, new paint, new air conditioning, new bed. The only thing that's old is the wooden furniture."

"Which has been newly refinished," Damon added. Charlotte had put a lot of effort and love into the furniture.

"I'll take this room, if it's okay with you, Michael," Des said.

"Fine with me."

Des's glance darted toward Damon. "Is that okay?"

"Of course." He could see it would take a lot of effort to gain her trust.

"I'd like the room on the second floor nearest the bathroom," Michael said.

Chris grinned. "Good choice. Like I said, my favorite room. I did a lot of healing there. I hope it does the same for you."

"Yeah, I hope so." Michael's face was tense, his hands clenching and unclenching. "I have trouble sleeping sometimes. Am I allowed to smoke?"

"Yes." Sleep disturbances were common with PTSD. "But no smoking close to the house or in the barn. And of course, no smoking in your room, or anywhere in the house."

Michael expelled a breath. "Understood. I'll try not to wake anyone."

"I appreciate that." He'd work on getting Michael off the nicotine over the next twelve weeks. "We'll let you get settled in. When you're ready, come downstairs, and you can help us get supper on the table."

Des nodded. "Yes, sir...um, Damon."

In the kitchen, Chris turned to Damon and quietly

asked, "What do you think?"

He wasn't sure how to answer. "We'll do everything we can for both of them."

"Yeah, but a woman changes things. I don't know if the other men will be comfortable talking in front of her. Or maybe she won't feel comfortable talking in front of us."

Group sessions were important. Damon wanted them to benefit from each other's experiences, to see they weren't alone with their struggles. When he'd found a support group for survivors of childhood sexual abuse, it had changed his perspective. Until then, he'd felt very alone, like he was the only person in the world who'd been abused as a child. He'd found that was far from the truth. Learning how many other survivors were out there had both comforted Damon and angered him.

"I promise you, we'll figure it out. This is too important, to all of us."

Chris nodded, but still looked concerned. Damon picked up Des Stewart's file from the kitchen table and slipped it inside a drawer. Later tonight he'd study it and try to come up with some kind of game plan.

A vehicle drove into the yard. Damon looked through a window and saw Charlotte's Jeep head toward the barn and park there. He watched as she walked into the barn carrying a package, presumably the medication for one of the dogs.

Damon's body tightened at the thought of seeing her walk out of the bathroom wearing nothing but a towel. Her image would likely be burned into his memory for eternity.

She'd been right to walk away from him that

morning. Even if Charlotte wanted to pursue a relationship, she was likely better off without him. He'd never been able to hold on to a relationship with a woman longer than a few months. After dating a woman for a while, he'd convince himself he wasn't right for her, that he didn't feel a connection to her the way he believed he should. Once, a woman he'd been dating broke up with him because she said she needed someone to commit to her one hundred percent, and she knew that person wasn't Damon. She'd been right.

Would he ever be able to commit to a woman completely? Would he ever have a normal relationship?

Physician, heal thyself. He was a lot better helping others than helping himself.

Des and Michael joined them in the kitchen and Damon gave them the task of putting an extra leaf in the table and setting it for seven. Future meals might occasionally include Chris's wife Alison and their two daughters, and of course the three other veterans. Damon made a mental note to purchase more chairs, and perhaps a folding table.

Blair arrived home from work, and when Garrett and Charlotte came into the house, introductions were made all around. Damon noted that Des appeared relieved to see the two other women. He was curious to read the story in her medical file.

They gathered around the table and began to eat. Blair passed a plate of roast chicken to Des. "Where are you from, Des?"

"A small town in Indiana you've probably never heard of."

There was a pause as they waited for her to name the town. Instead, Des looked down at her plate and remained silent. Blair smiled and continued the conversation. Damon was glad she was perceptive enough to avoid an awkward silence that would point to Des.

"Damon and I grew up in St. Paul, Minnesota. I went to school in Rochester, Minnesota to become a vet tech. What about you, Michael? Where are you from?"

"I'm from Georgia, near Atlanta."

"Is your family still there?"

"Yes, my parents are in Decatur, and my two brothers are in Atlanta." He smiled in Blair's direction. "In my family, my father is Michael. My friends call me Mike."

Garrett lifted his glass of water in a salute. "In that case, Mike it is."

Everyone lifted a glass. "To Mike."

"What about you, Des?" Charlotte asked. "Is Des short for something else?"

"It's Desiree." She smiled shyly at Charlotte. "But I've been Des for a long time."

"So is everyone here from someplace else?" Mike asked.

"Everyone except Garrett and Charlotte," Chris said. "They're the only ones who grew up in North Dakota."

"On the next farm over, to be exact. Our parents still live there," Garrett said. "Which reminds me, Char. Mom wants you to come over soon. She's got a bunch of vegetables in her garden she wants to give us. You know how she grows enough to feed the entire state."

Charlotte grinned. "I sure do. I'll give her a call tomorrow."

"When Blair and I and our older brother Ben were

kids, we'd spend summers here on the farm with our grandparents, Everett and Anna Branson." Damon's memories of his grandparents made him smile. "That's why we call this place Branson Farm."

Garrett continued the story. "And since Charlotte and I and our younger sister Lauren lived only about a mile away, we hung out with the Greyson kids during those summers."

"Actually, Garrett and Ben hung out together, and once in a while they'd let me tag along," Damon said.

Charlotte laughed. "Blair and I would tag along whether they wanted us to or not."

He shared a smile with Charlotte. He remembered her from those summers, first as a sunny young girl who trailed behind their big brothers, not taking no for an answer. Later, when they were both in their teens, he'd had a huge crush on the beautiful, vivacious Charlotte Saunders who was so far out of his league she was practically in another zip code. He'd been awkward and self-conscious, barely able to speak when she was around. The secrets he'd carried back then had weighed heavily on his soul. But Charlotte had been kind and always tried to draw him into conversation and include him in activities.

The woman he saw today was still beautiful, still kind, but she was far more cautious and subdued than the teenaged Charlotte. It made him sad to think that a light had gone out in her.

It made him angry, too. Someone had done that to her.

After dinner, everyone helped with the cleanup. Damon made it clear to Des and Mike that they wouldn't be waited on or coddled. They all had to pull together to make Branson Farm work.

Once the leftovers were put away and dishes washed, Charlotte led the group out to the barn, with Blair's dog Frisco hopping beside them on his three legs. She told Des and Mike the story of how the seizures from the puppy mill and the animal hoarder house had resulted in the overcrowding at the shelter, and how all the dogs at Branson Farm had nearly been euthanized, even the pregnant ones.

"Without Blair and Garrett, and now you, it wouldn't have been possible to save them."

As they entered the barn and turned on the overhead lights, a cacophony of barking began. Charlotte spoke over the noise.

"It takes a lot of effort to care for this many dogs, especially when most of them have medical needs." Charlotte pointed to one of the stalls. "Six dogs with serious skin infections are in that stall. We're trying to keep them separated from the others. And in four of the other stalls, we have the pregnant and nursing dogs. Only Hope has given birth so far. She has six puppies."

Garrett picked up the story. "We can't let them all out at the same time, at least not yet. We don't want them to fight or run away, and I'm concerned they could chase our horses. So we're taking them out on their leashes, a few at a time, as many times a day as we can manage. That's going to be part of your jobs. Our ultimate goal is to get them healthy and well-socialized so they can be adopted, or at least fostered in someone's home."

"Another goal is to have them all spayed or neutered over the summer," Blair added. "That's another good reason we can't have them running around loose. And it's a requirement for adoption."

"It must cost a fortune to feed them all," Mike said.

"It does," Charlotte agreed. "We're supplying most of the food, but some is coming in from the community. One of the volunteers at the shelter started a funding page online and people have been donating. Which reminds me, Sheila Martin will be here tomorrow to take pictures and videos of the dogs for social media. Especially the puppies."

"That's a good idea," Damon said. Eventually some of the money they'd receive from the VA could be used to feed the dogs, but right now money was tight. They'd need the community to help. "We want people around here to be aware of this story."

"Do you think they'll all be adopted?" Des asked quietly.

Garrett shrugged. "All I know is that the majority of the dogs will have to be out of the barn by winter. It'll be cold, and the horses will need to be housed in here."

"What if they're not all adopted?" she asked.

The silence that followed Des's question was an answer in itself. No one wanted to consider what would happen if that were the case.

"We'll cross that bridge when we come to it. We have enough to deal with right now." Charlotte smiled brightly and touched Des's arm. "Come see Hope's pups. You too, Mike."

They followed Charlotte into Hope's stall. Blair slipped on a pair of latex gloves. "I'm going to check on the pregnant dogs and then see about the quarantine dogs. Do they need to go out for a walk, Garrett?"

"Yeah, they do."

Damon donned gloves and helped Garrett put collars and leashes on the quarantine dogs in preparation for their outing. There was a good possibility some of the dogs wouldn't be adopted before winter. Some could still be lost.

Having to euthanize even one dog would kill Charlotte. So it simply couldn't happen.

Chapter Twelve

Within a week, the three other veterans arrived at the farm. Corporal Ray Kosloski had been leading a convoy in Iraq when one of trucks hit an IED, killing everyone on board, including his best friend. Corporal Trey Jeffries was part of an army checkpoint that mistakenly killed an Iraqi family, including an eight-month-old child, believing they were insurgents. In Staff Sergeant Thomas Kelfield's case, there was no single incident that triggered his PTSD. But during his time as a medic, he'd seen trauma and blood and ruined lives over and over again. Eventually it had become too much for him to deal with.

Damon had only twelve weeks to make a difference in their lives, and there was a lot of ground to cover. He established a schedule to keep them on track. The first thing he did each day was to take everyone out for an early morning run through the pasture. Getting in better physical shape would help the vets' mental outlook. After a breakfast of healthy foods, another of his priorities, they took turns looking after the needs of the dogs while Damon held individual counseling sessions with each vet. Later in the day, they got together for a group session. Sitting at the picnic table under the shade of the cottonwood trees, the men slowly began to tell their stories.

Chris's story was particularly poignant. He told

Damon about seeing two little Afghan girls on the side of the road as his convoy drove by. As the Humvee he and Garrett and their friend Tommy Carmichael were in approached the girls, the explosives strapped around them were detonated. Garrett lost part of his leg, and Tommy was killed. Chris couldn't get the faces of those little girls out of his head. When he returned home to his wife and children, every time he closed his eyes, he saw his daughters on that dusty Afghan road. The vision had driven him to the edge of suicide.

Only Des remained silent. In individual counseling sessions, she talked about everything except what was really bothering her. In group sessions, she listened and sympathized with the others, but she only shook her head when they asked what had brought her to Branson Farm.

After reading her file, Damon understood why. In her job as a communication specialist, she had been repeatedly sexually harassed by her commanding officer. When, after months of harassment, she had finally complained to the higher-ups, she hadn't been believed. They'd taken her commanding officer's word that Des was a troublemaker and had left her under his command where the harassment only increased. She asked for transfers, but because she'd been labeled as difficult, her requests were denied. Despondent, Des attempted suicide by taking a bottle of pills given to her by a doctor for her anxiety. She only survived because her roommate came home early and called 911. Once in the VA hospital, she was finally believed. But Damon noted that there'd been no consequences for her commanding officer.

It was no wonder Des felt uncomfortable speaking

to a group of men, including him. He did his best to draw her out in one-on-one sessions, but Des proved a hard nut to crack. He wasn't ready to give up, but he worried he wouldn't be able to reach her.

****

The next morning when Charlotte went into the barn, she discovered that Peppermint Patty had given birth to four puppies. They nursed while a tired Patty lay on her side, her eyes closed. Charlotte sat on the straw next to the whelping box and stroked her head.

"You did good, Patty. Your puppies are beautiful."

Ten puppies, with ten more scheduled to arrive soon. Charlotte wondered what she'd gotten Branson Farm into with her crazy scheme. How could they possibly find homes for all these dogs? Maybe she was simply delaying euthanasia rather than saving them from it.

She shook off her anxious thoughts and got to work. After changing the towels in Patty's box, she fed the pregnant and nursing dogs and put fresh hay in their stalls. She'd just finished taking Hope out for a walk when Des entered the barn.

"Hi. Do you need some help?" she asked.

Charlotte grinned. "Always. You want to see Patty's puppies first?"

"She had her puppies? Yes, for sure!"

After cooing over the puppies for a few minutes, Des straightened. "What do you want me to do first?"

"Let's take out all the dogs, and then we'll feed and water them."

They each leashed three dogs and walked them to a grassy area away from the barn. The dogs quickly relieved themselves and set about to sniff their new home, noses to the ground. Charlotte noticed that Des appeared more relaxed around the dogs than she did with people. She knew exactly how she felt.

"You really love dogs, don't you?"

Des smiled. "I do. I had a part-Terrier mutt when I was a kid. Buddy was the best dog ever. When I heard about the dogs and what you were trying to do here, I jumped at the chance to come to Branson Farm."

"How do you like it here?"

She looked away and shrugged. "I love the dogs, of course, and I love looking after them. I'd like to get to know the horses at some point, too."

"And the people?"

Des shrugged again. "They seem nice." She looked up at Charlotte. "I'm glad you're here. I'm not as comfortable with the men."

Charlotte wondered what had happened to her, though she could guess. "I can certainly vouch for Garrett. You won't find many better men then my brother. I haven't known Chris as long, but I work with his wife Alison, and I know they're devoted to each other and their kids." She told her about working as a nurse in Bismarck and about her leave. It reminded her how quickly her time off was passing.

"What about Damon? What's his story?" Des asked.

Charlotte answered without hesitation. "Damon is sincere in everything he does, especially in making Branson Farm a place of healing for veterans. He's a good man, Des. You can trust him."

"Chris told me that Damon is living at your house. Are you together?"

"No. We're friends. Like he said, we've known

each other a long time. He's only staying at my place until his own apartment is ready."

Her feelings for Damon were complex, and a little confused, but she knew he was more to her than a friend. Especially since they'd kissed. Charlotte couldn't stop thinking about kissing him.

What would have happened that morning outside the bathroom if, instead of running, she'd dropped her towel? If she'd found the courage to bare herself to Damon, physically and emotionally, could she have made love to him?

Making love. Not simply having sex or scratching an itch, not something that was forced on her. It would have been the first time for her.

A part of her longed for that depth of connection with another human being. No, not just anyone, she amended. *With Damon. Only Damon.*

The realization came as shock. And it frightened her. Making love with Damon would leave her vulnerable and open to heartache.

Maybe she needed to trust Damon as much as she encouraged Des to.

****

Damon hit the bag with two quick jabs followed by a right cross. He practiced the move over and over, mixing in a few uppercuts and a hook for good measure. No matter how hard he hit the bag, the image of Charlotte soaking wet and covered only by a towel was burned into his memory. He'd relived that moment over and over the last few days. Maybe he needed to rethink their living arrangements, because sleeping down the hall from Charlotte was slowly driving him mad.

He couldn't remember being so tempted by a woman before. But his feelings for Charlotte went well beyond sex. He liked her, cared about her, and when he thought about it, he realized his feelings for her went all the way back to their teen years. In those days he'd believed she was perfect, his ideal. He still did.

With a start, he wondered if his inability to connect deeply with another woman all these years was because he still had that ideal picture of Charlotte Saunders in his head and no one else could measure up. How messed up was that?

His phone rang, and he welcomed the distraction. Damon tugged at the Velcro closure of his gloves and pulled them off.

"Hello?"

"Damon, it's Dad. Do you have a minute to talk?"

"Sure." He dropped to the mat and began unravelling the cotton wrap binding his hands. "What's up?"

"I've quit drinking. Again." Peter's voice was barely a whisper. "I'm going to AA."

Damon went still. "Really?"

"I've been sober for nearly a month this time. It's a start."

It was a month longer than he'd ever known Peter to go without a drink. "Does Victoria know you're going to AA?"

"No. She wouldn't be happy if she knew. I'm tired of the alcohol controlling my life, and I'm sick of Victoria using the alcohol against me."

For a lot of years, Damon's mother kept Peter compliant by controlling his access to alcohol. She wouldn't like Peter not dancing to her tune anymore.

He carefully posed his next question. "Are you planning to leave her?"

"I know I have to, but I can't leave until I figure out what Victoria is scheming. I know it has something to do with you."

He'd said as much in his last call. "Dad, maybe it would be best if you left now. Don't worry about what Victoria is planning."

"I owe this to you, Damon." His voice broke. "I owe you much more."

"Dad—"

"I have to go. Be careful, son."

The line went dead. Damon stared at his phone. It was a little late for his father to express regret for what happened to him as a child, but it was something.

He wondered if he should be concerned for Peter's safety. Victoria wouldn't actually hurt him, would she?

Damon realized he didn't have a definitive answer. That was the thing about sociopaths. You could never underestimate their capacity for cruelty. But would she resort to violence?

He was too tired to think about it right now. He needed a shower and then his bed. Leaving his gloves and his hand wrap on the mat, he made his way upstairs.

To his surprise the lights were still on. Charlotte was curled up on the couch reading a book.

"Hey. I thought you were in bed."

She set down the book. "I couldn't sleep. Thought I'd read for a while."

Damon sat in the upholstered chair across from her. Her long blonde hair was unbound and flowed down her right shoulder. She wore a blue terrycloth robe over her night clothes, and her bare feet with their pretty pink toenails were resting on the coffee table. Every day she grew more beautiful to him.

He closed his eyes in misery as he massaged his temple. Maybe it would be best if he moved into Ben and Jamie's basement. Being this close to Charlotte without being able to touch her was killing him.

"Damon? Are you okay?"

He opened his eyes and saw the concern on her face. It was getting harder and harder to hide his feelings, but he couldn't tell her the complete truth.

"I just got a call from my dad. He's planning to leave my mother."

"Oh. I'm sorry, Damon."

He gave a tired shake to his head. "Don't be. It should have happened years ago. It's not like we were ever a happy family. Quite the opposite."

"I got that impression from Blair. Last summer when you were all here for your grandfather's funeral, I felt the tension between the three of you and your parents. Actually, it was more than tension. There's real animosity there, isn't there?"

"Yes." He sighed and rubbed his hand over his face. "My father is an alcoholic, and my mother is a sociopath."

Her eyes widened in disbelief. "A sociopath?"

Damon hated talking about his mother. Sociopaths were people in movies and crime novels. They weren't housewives in the suburbs.

"Unfortunately, it's true. Victoria is incapable of feeling empathy. She's ruthless in pursuing her own agendas. She craves money and power, and she doesn't care who she has to destroy to get what she wants. The pain she's inflicted on all of us…" Damon had to stop and look away from the sympathy he saw on Charlotte's face.

"I'm so sorry, Damon."

He didn't want her pity. He didn't want anyone's pity. But she was the only person he could talk to about his family. His siblings were finally in a good place in their lives and he didn't want to do or say anything to change that. He didn't want to remind them of their shared painful past.

He trusted Charlotte. Despite the tension between them, he knew he could talk to her and she wouldn't judge him.

"Peter, my dad, said he's heard Victoria talking to someone on the phone. He's heard her say my name, and he thinks she's planning something that involves me. He wanted to warn me."

"Warn you? About your mother? What does he think she'll do to you?"

It hurt to see the incredulity on her face. He knew how difficult it was for normal people to wrap their heads around the actions of someone as abnormal as Victoria. Now that he'd given her a glimpse into the deep dysfunction in his family, he wouldn't blame Charlotte if she asked him to leave her house.

"I don't know. My father comes from a rich family with political power. For years, Victoria has enjoyed the money and status the Greyson name gave her, even though my father's drinking meant he didn't rise high enough in political circles to suit her. But recently, Grandfather Greyson cut off Peter and Victoria financially. Without any money coming in, Victoria is probably desperate. There's no telling what she'll do."

"But she wouldn't do something to actually hurt you, would she? I mean, she's your mother."

He didn't want to tell her Victoria had never harbored any maternal feelings for him.

"She's never been overtly violent before. She's probably looking for some way to swindle money from me, the way she tried with Ben."

"What do you mean? What did she do to Ben?"

"She tried to blackmail him. She told him she would testify against him in court and say he was an unfit parent unless he gave her half a million dollars. Ben was afraid he'd lose his children."

Her eyes went wide with shock. "Blackmail?"

"She seems to know what's going on in our lives. Someone here must be feeding her information."

Charlotte shook her head as if what he was telling her was too bizarre for her to take in. Damon closed his eyes. No one else's mother blackmailed, threatened, and spied on them. He didn't want any of Victoria's sickness to touch Charlotte. Tomorrow he'd find someplace else to live.

"I'm sorry, Charlotte. I shouldn't have told you. You don't need to worry about my crazy family."

"No, I'm sorry." She set her feet on the floor. "I'm sorry your mother is the way she is. I'm sorry she's made life for you and your siblings such a hell. And I'm sorry you've had to go through this alone."

"I appreciate that, Charlotte, but I think it would be best if I moved out. Ben's got a room in his basement I can use."

Charlotte shook her head. "If you really think your mother is planning something, it's probably best if you weren't living at Ben and Jamie's. They've got kids in the house, and with Jamie being pregnant, maybe you don't want to get them involved."

She had a point. "Then I'll find someplace else, someplace on my own."

"There's no need for you to move."

"I don't want you to get mixed up in this mess."

"I can take care of myself, Damon. You've seen it."

He knew she could handle herself in a fair fight. But Victoria rarely played fair.

"Charlotte—"

"I don't want you to leave." Charlotte's gaze dropped to her hands clasped tightly in her lap. "Despite the bathroom incident, I like having you here. I want us to be friends. Am I still your friend, Damon?"

Her last words were said on a whisper. She lifted her gaze, and Damon stared into her hazel eyes, fisting his hands to keep from reaching for her.

"Always."

Chapter Thirteen

Charlotte tossed a couple of cloth bags and a basket into the back of her Jeep before closing the tailgate. She was off to her parents' farm to pick some of the bounty from her mother's garden. It would give her the opportunity to see her mother. She'd been feeling guilty for neglecting her parents, but she'd been so busy with the dogs there hadn't been time. But now that they had five helpers, the workload was more manageable.

Damon walked across the yard toward her. He had an easy, confident stride, and moved with a grace that was a pleasure to watch.

"Hi," he said when he reached her. "Are you leaving?"

"I'm going over to my mom's to pick vegetables from her garden. She always grows more than they can use."

"Please thank her for us. With all the people we're feeding, we can sure use the food."

Charlotte tilted her head and smiled. "Why don't you tell her yourself? Come with me."

He hesitated before answering, and Charlotte turned away. She'd thought after their talk last night that maybe their relationship was on a new footing. But perhaps she'd been wrong.

"You don't have to—"

"I want to come with you. Are you sure?"

There wasn't anything she wanted more than to spend time with him. "I'm sure."

He gave her a smile that warmed her heart. "Okay, I've got some time till my next session. Let's go."

The drive to her parents' farm took less than five minutes. As they drove into the yard, Grace stepped out the front door and waved. Charlotte parked and jumped out of her vehicle.

"Hi, Mom." Charlotte hugged her mother. "I brought reinforcements."

"Damon, it's good to see you."

"It's good to see you, too, Mrs. Saunders." He extended his hand to her. "Thank you for offering us fresh vegetables."

"Please, call me Grace." She grasped his hand with both of hers. "You're more than welcome. I tend to plant more than Robert and I can use."

Charlotte laughed. "She's not kidding. Wait till you see her garden."

Grace looped her arm through Damon's. "Come on. I'll show you."

After retrieving her bags and the basket, Charlotte followed Damon and her mother. Damon leaned toward Grace as they walked, listening avidly to her talk about the number of different vegetables she'd planted. Charlotte thought of their conversation about *his* mother. She couldn't imagine growing up without the love and security her parents had provided. To know Damon had been damaged so profoundly by the actions of his parents hurt her heart. And it made her angry.

They crossed a grassy lawn and then walked through a break in the caragana hedge. Damon stopped in his tracks when they reached the other side.

"Whoa."

Charlotte chuckled. "Impressive, isn't it?"

"This is all vegetable garden?"

"It is," Grace said with a satisfied smile. "My pride and joy. About an acre and a half of land planted with every vegetable you'd ever want to eat."

"And some fruits, too. Right, Mom?"

"That's right. We have strawberries, raspberries, rhubarb, and several apple trees."

"Amazing." Damon shook his head. "This has got to be a tremendous amount of work."

"It's a labor of love. But it's much more than Robert and I can use, so I try to give away as much as I can to friends, people at church, colleagues at work. In the fall we take a load of potatoes and carrots to the food bank in Bismarck."

"Do you preserve any of the vegetables for the winter?" Damon asked.

"Oh, yes. I find canning and freezing very satisfying."

"You should see the jars and jars of dill pickles she makes," Charlotte said.

"Don't forget the pickled carrots," Grace said with a wink her direction.

"Oh, I love those. You have to make some for me this fall."

Grace put her arm around Charlotte's shoulders. "Even better, I'll teach you how to pickle them yourself."

Charlotte hugged her back. "Fair enough. So what are you giving us today, Mom?"

Grace walked between the rows. "My second planting of lettuce, spinach, and kale is perfect right now. So is the radish. You can make yourselves a nice salad."

"Sounds great." Damon rubbed his hands together. "What do you want me to do?"

Grace handed him a knife from her basket. "Follow me."

They went on ahead to cut the greens for salad while Charlotte checked one of the early ripening cherry tomato plants for fruit. She listened to the conversation between Damon and her mother as she popped a tomato in her mouth. Grace explained to Damon that the lettuces would grow again from the root after they were cut down. She talked to him about how they rotated the crops each year and supplemented the soil with compost they made from garden and kitchen waste. She demonstrated how she thinned the row of carrots to give the remaining plants room to grow. Damon listened attentively and asked questions while he worked. Charlotte knew there was nothing her mother liked better than teaching, and Damon was an eager student.

She remembered her mother giving her and her brother and sister similar lessons when they were kids. At the time, all three of them complained about the work. But she wouldn't give up those memories for anything. She'd learned so much from her mother, from both her parents, about hard work, commitment, and love.

Damon hadn't had that opportunity to learn those simple lessons from his parents. He'd missed so much that she took for granted.

Charlotte walked toward her mother with her basket of tomatoes. "Is there anything else you want to give us, Mom?"

"Why don't you check the raspberries and strawberries? I picked the raspberries the other day, but there might be enough to give your group dessert tonight."

"Sure." Charlotte took a plastic container with a lid from her mother and went into the raspberries. She hadn't been picking for a minute when she scratched her arm on a spiny raspberry cane.

"Ouch! Dammit!"

"You okay?"

Charlotte whirled at the sound of Damon's voice. "You startled me. I didn't know you were behind me."

"Sorry. Your mom sent me over to help you." He took her arm in his hands and examined it. "That looks nasty."

Charlotte's skin tingled under his touch. "It's just a scratch."

"Why don't I take over the raspberries? You can take the strawberries. They don't look quite as lethal."

"Are you sure you want to tackle them?"

"I'm sure." He rolled down his shirt sleeves and buttoned them at the wrist. "At least I've got some protection."

Charlotte waved as she walked away. "Have fun."

As she searched through the strawberry patch for ripe berries, she kept one eye on Damon. He stuck his arm into the middle of the patch, braving the barbs to get the succulent fruit. When her mother joined him, Charlotte listened to their easy conversation. It made her feel good to know they liked each other.

When they were done, they walked back to her Jeep and put their bounty in the back.

"If you come back in a couple of days, the green beans and peas should be ready to pick," Grace said.

"Are you sure?" Damon asked. "I don't want to take so much you don't have enough for yourself."

"Damon, did you see the mile-long row of beans? I think Mom has plenty."

"She's right," Grace said. "If you don't take them, they'll just go to waste. So you have to come again."

"Waste is a terrible thing," he said, his lips curving into a smile.

"It is," Grace said solemnly. "We'll see you in a couple of days?"

"You will. I might bring some of the people from my retreat, if you don't mind. I think they'd enjoy your garden."

"That would be wonderful. I look forward to it."

"Thank you."

Damon kissed Grace's cheek. The unexpected gesture caused a lump to form in Charlotte's throat.

On the short drive back to Branson Farm, Damon was quiet until they turned the corner off the main road and drove into the farmyard.

"I always liked your mom. When we were kids and Garrett took Ben and me over to your house, she'd give us fresh-baked cookies and lemonade. Back then, I wondered what it would be like to have a mom who baked cookies for me."

"It's pretty great." Charlotte stopped the Jeep in front of the house.

Damon's smile was wistful. "You're lucky."

She nodded. If she had the power, she'd go back in time and give Damon a mother who baked cookies for him. He deserved that and so much more.

****

Ray's face was a picture of tension as Damon approached the picnic table under the cottonwood trees where they were meeting for a counseling session. He'd had him fill out cognitive worksheets since he arrived at Branson Farm, like the rest of the veterans. The worksheets were meant to help Ray identify his thoughts about events and his feelings associated with them. By writing down what he was thinking and feeling, he could begin to recognize the thoughts running through his head.

When Damon examined Ray's worksheets, he saw that one of the strongest feelings associated with the IED blast in Iraq was guilt. Ray had been in the lead truck of the convoy when it broke down. As he and his men worked feverishly to fix the truck, he'd waved the second truck around them, putting them in the lead, so the convoy could keep going. About 200 yards down the road, the lead truck hit an IED and exploded. Everyone in the truck was killed, including Ray's best friend Joe.

The guilt was killing him. Since he'd left the military and come home, Ray had been self-medicating with alcohol, and as a result had trouble holding down a job. Worse, he reported feeling depressed and disconnected from his wife and children. Damon knew getting to the heart of his guilt was key to helping him.

"How are you doing today, Ray?"

"I'm okay." His fidgeting told Damon he was far from okay.

"We're going to get right into it. I've been reading your worksheets. Can I ask you about this thought you recorded—'I should have had them wait instead of going ahead.' "

Ray clutched his hands together in his lap, his head down. "Sure."

"Help me understand. What does protocol say about what should happen when the lead truck breaks down in a convoy?"

Ray took a deep breath before speaking. "The convoy has to keep moving. Protocol says the lead truck should wave the next truck through so they can lead. We fix our truck as quickly as we can and rejoin them."

"Okay," Damon said. "But if the protocol says you should wave the next truck through, why did you say you should have made them wait?"

"Because if I'd made them wait, this wouldn't have happened." Ray's mouth twisted and tears filled his eyes. "They'd still be alive. It's my fault they're dead."

Damon waited while he cried. Ray bowed his head, his shoulders shaking with his sobs. Eventually his tears subsided, and Damon handed him a tissue.

"It's a tragedy those men died." Damon waited until Ray blew his nose and looked up at him. "I want us to think about the idea that you should have made them wait. Not from the perspective of what we know now, nearly five years later, but what you knew at the time. When you were in the lead truck and scanning the road, did you see anything that made you think there could be an IED ahead?"

"No."

"So, prior to the second truck taking over, you hadn't seen anything suspicious."

"No."

"When the second truck took over as lead, what

was their responsibility at that point, and what was yours?"

"The truck that Joe and my other friends were in became lead, and they were to keep the convoy moving. My responsibility was to fix my truck so we could join them."

"Does that mean the responsibility for scanning ahead for danger fell to Joe and your other friends?"

"Yes, but I should have been able to see ahead to warn them," Ray insisted.

"Before we determine that, tell me something. How far ahead of you was Joe's truck when the explosion occurred?"

Ray sighed. "Probably about two hundred yards."

"Two hundred yards. That's about two football fields, right?"

"Yeah, I guess so."

"Can you tell me if there are IEDs that you wouldn't be able to detect at two hundred yards?"

"Yes, absolutely."

"What about an IED ten yards away? Can you always detect it?"

"No, not always."

"Ray, did you consider Joe and the others on that truck to be good soldiers?"

"Of course I did."

"If they'd been able to detect the IED, do you think they would have done something different?"

"Of course they would have! They would have stopped or gone around it."

Damon nodded in agreement. "So, at the time, you couldn't see anything from two hundred yards away, and they obviously couldn't see anything from ten yards away. Protocol said you should wave the next truck through so the convoy could keep moving and wouldn't be sitting ducks on the road. In light of all that, can you help me understand why you wouldn't have waved them through? And remember—based on the information you had at that time."

Ray stared at him. "I guess I hadn't thought about Joe and the others not being able to see the danger in front of them."

"How does that make you feel?"

"Maybe a little less guilty."

"It's important to consider what was actually going on at the time and what you knew," Damon said. "You had to assume there were insurgents in the area, and now we know that was true because they were planting explosives. If you'd stopped the convoy, it could have resulted in an even bigger tragedy. Did you ever consider that you did exactly the right thing in waving Joe's truck forward?"

Ray shook his head. "I…I hadn't considered that either."

"You said your friend Joe was a good soldier. Knowing that you followed protocol and potentially saved others from being hurt, do you think Joe would hold it against you that you waved him through?"

"No." Fresh tears filled Ray's eyes. "He'd probably tell me I did a good job."

"It's possible to grieve for your friends and still know you did the right thing."

Ray nodded, and Damon could see it was the first time he'd considered that perhaps all the blame for the deaths of his friends didn't fall on him. He hoped this was a first step for Ray. Maybe now he could begin to emerge from the mountain of guilt he'd buried himself under.

****

The next day, Damon's phone rang while he was in the middle of a counseling session with the whole group. When he saw Clayton's name on his phone, his heart sank. He never called unless it was bad news.

"I'm really sorry. It's my contractor. I've got to take this." He walked away from the picnic table and put the phone up to his ear.

"Clayton? What's going on?"

"I'm afraid I've got some news for you, and it's not good."

Damon's heart fell. "What is it now?"

"It's the electrical. When we budgeted for the new electrical system, we assumed we could tie into the existing system since we'd been assured it was upgraded. But when we dug into it, we discovered old knob-and-tube wiring in the walls."

"What? That can't be."

"I'm sorry, Damon, but it's true. I can send you pictures. The former owners did upgrade electrical outlets but without changing the wiring in the walls, the electrical service in the building is not only inadequate, it's dangerous. With all the modern appliances and computing devices that are going to be used, the old knob-and-tube will be easily overloaded. There's a definite danger of fire."

Damon rubbed his temple where a headache was beginning to form. "So how do we fix it?"

"We rip out all the old knob-and-tube and replace it with new wiring."

"How much are we talking to fix it?"

"We need new wire, cables, electrical panels, and the labor to install them. By the time we repair the walls that we have to open to make the change, it could be upwards of a hundred and fifty thousand."

Damon hung his head. *Granddad, what kind of building did you saddle me with?* "I've already sunk everything I have into this building. I don't have that kind of money. Before I try to borrow that much, I want to get a second opinion about the electrical system."

"I figured you would. I've already talked to a commercial electrical expert. He's the one who gave me the quote. I'll send it to you."

Damn. Damon could see his dreams turn to ash as they spoke. If it only affected him, he could deal with it. He'd convinced Blair and Garrett to go in on this venture with him. They'd worked hard to make it happen, and he knew his sister was counting on the income from the retreat to allow her to rescue more horses. Worse, a need in the veteran community would go unmet.

Clayton cleared his throat and continued. "We can carry on with work on the rest of the building until you come up with the money."

Damon wasn't sure if there was any point. Would a bank even loan him the money?

"All right. I'll talk to you later."

"I'm sorry I had to deliver such bad news. But it can be fixed, I promise you."

Not if he couldn't find the money. "Yeah. Bye, Clayton."

He ended the call and walked back to the picnic table. Chris gave him a worried frown. "What's wrong with the building this time?"

157

Damon relayed Clayton's news. He did his best to put a positive spin on events. "The work will get done, and the building will open. It's just going to take longer than we planned."

"In the meantime, there are worse places to be," Mike said. "I like it here. It's peaceful."

Des smiled shyly. "I think Branson Farm is a special place, too."

Damon steered the conversation back to them and their problems, but inside he felt sick. How was he going to make the retreat work?

Chapter Fourteen

The next afternoon, Charlotte arrived back at the farm after picking more vegetables in her mother's garden. She dropped off a bag of salad greens in the kitchen where Chris and Trey were starting dinner.

"Where's everyone?" she asked.

Chris mixed dressing into his potato salad. "Damon went into town to talk to his banker. Tom, Ray, and Mike are weeding Blair's flower beds and cutting the grass. I'm not sure where Des is."

"She's likely in the barn with the puppies," Trey added. "I saw her headed that way a while ago."

"Do you need any help with dinner?" Charlotte asked.

"No, everything's ready. All we have to do is wash the lettuce, and I can handle that." Chris put the bowl of potato salad in the fridge. "Tell your mom thanks for the fresh veggies. We really appreciate it."

"You should come with me next time and tell her yourself. I know she'd love to meet you."

"Yeah, I'd like to meet her, too. I've been thinking it might be nice to start a small kitchen garden here at Branson Farm next spring. Thought I'd run the idea past Blair and Garrett. I figure your mom could give us some pointers."

It was good to hear Chris talk about the future. Charlotte knew he'd come very close to ending his life last year. But now he was working at Branson Farm, officially in charge of food. He still had work to do on his own recovery from PTSD, but Alison had told her that the purpose the work had given him, as well as the counseling he'd received, had gone a long way in helping him heal.

"There's nothing Mom likes better than talking about gardening."

"Let me know when you plan to visit her again, and I'll tag along."

"I'll do that," Charlotte said with a smile. "If you don't need me, I'm going to check on the dogs before dinner."

In the barn, Charlotte made sure all the dogs had water in their bowls inside their kennels. She wished the dogs didn't have to be caged for so much of the day, but right now there was little alternative. Mike, Ray, and Tom had erected a temporary dog run out of snow fencing that Garrett borrowed from a neighbor, but unfortunately, it wasn't as secure as they would have liked. A couple of the dogs had already figured out they could escape by tunnelling beneath the fencing. And there was no way to make a secure and easy-to-use gate with the fencing. Until they found the funds to create a permanent dog run, the dogs would have to stay in their crates except for their walks. They kept the doors of the barn open much of the day to bring in fresh air, but without giving them a lot of exercise outdoors, she wondered if the dogs were much better off than they'd been with the hoarder.

Her rational brain knew they were much better off, but she'd still like to give them more freedom. Finding a way to let them roam outside was a big hurdle to cross. But it would have to wait for another day.

After satisfying herself that the kenneled dogs all had water, she made her way to Hope's stall to visit the puppies, always the highlight of her day. When she opened the stall door, she saw Des curled in a ball next to Hope's box, a couple of puppies sleeping next to her, her arm protectively around them.

"Des? Are you okay?" Charlotte went down on her knees beside her, touching her head and her arm to check for abrasions. "Are you hurt? Did something happen?"

"He called me," she whispered. "He wasn't supposed to have my new cell number. But he found it. He always finds me."

"Who called you?"

"My commanding officer." A tear rolled down her cheek. "I told the VA he harassed me, but it was more than that. He raped me. Over and over again. And I let it happen."

"Oh, honey, I'm so sorry." Charlotte stroked Des' hair. Memories rushed back, buffeting her with pain.

Des pushed herself to a seated position, and, wrapping her arms around her knees, rocked back and forth. "I've never told anyone he raped me."

"Why not?" Charlotte was afraid she knew the answer.

"Because I let it happen. It was easier to give in than to keep fighting. I was so tired of fighting him off."

"He was your commanding officer. He was in a position of power over you."

"He threatened to have me demoted, or worse, if I didn't sleep with him. At first, I refused, but he kept after me until he wore me down. I didn't have the strength to fight anymore. So I said yes. How could I then complain about him, when I'd consented?"

"I suppose he explained that to you very carefully, didn't he?" Anger boiled through Charlotte's veins. "He told you that you had no right to complain. And even if you did, no one would believe you. They knew you were nothing but a whore."

You asked for it. The words pounded through her head like a drumbeat. It was the line Clayton had used to keep her quiet, the words that had haunted her dreams for ten years.

Des lowered her head to her knees, her voice almost inaudible. "Yes."

"That bastard."

Charlotte wanted to hit something, to scream at the top of her lungs. But that wouldn't help Des.

Des lifted her gaze to Charlotte's. "You know, don't you? You know what it's like to be raped."

Charlotte squeezed her eyes shut and bowed her head. This was the moment she'd dreaded for so long. Confronting her rape and acknowledging what happened to her was painful, but there was also a sense of relief. For the first time she could speak about the rape with someone who knew firsthand what she'd been through. Someone who wouldn't judge her.

She opened her eyes. "Yes. I know exactly what it's like."

"I'm sorry to make you relive it," Des said.

Charlotte grasped her hand. "Don't be sorry. Maybe it's time I faced it, too."

"You've never talked about it with anyone?"

"No." She'd done her best to pretend it never

happened, but of course that didn't work. The rape had been with her every day for ten years, in every decision she made. In every invitation she refused, in every sleepless night. In the negative self-talk that streamed through her head.

It was your fault.

"Why didn't you tell anyone?" Des asked.

"Because it's too painful, too shameful. I drank too much, and I dressed provocatively. I flirted and teased until someone took me up on my offer. If my parents knew…" She shook her head, unable to finish the sentence.

"When did this happen?"

"Ten years ago, in college."

"You must have been very young."

"Nineteen." When Charlotte thought back to the person she'd been at nineteen, it was like looking at a different girl. Back then, she loved to dance and go to parties. She was up for any adventure with her many friends. She loved to laugh and have fun. She was happy.

Des took her hand. "My commanding officer manipulated me, twisted my head around until I didn't know which direction was up. I was a grown woman when this happened to me. If I could be so controlled at my age, how can you blame yourself when you were just a kid?"

Charlotte stared at her. One other thing she'd been at nineteen was naïve. She'd never imagined she could be raped, never imagined anyone would harm her. Her idyllic childhood and adolescence hadn't prepared her for the possibility. Rape didn't happen to good girls from Masonville.

Except when it did.

"Have you told Damon?" Des asked.

"No." Charlotte imagined the disappointment in his eyes. He thought she was somebody else, somebody good. She wanted him to continue to think that. "What about you? Will you talk to Damon about what happened to you?"

Des sighed and let go of her hand. "I don't know."

"I'd say tell him, but that would be a case of do what I say but not what I do. That would make me a hypocrite." Charlotte lifted a sleeping puppy and cuddled it close, nuzzling its head with her chin. "Talk to him, Des."

Des shook her head. "Why should I tell him when you won't?"

Charlotte set the puppy down beside Hope. He immediately crawled to his mother's belly and began to nurse. "My rape is ten years in the past. There's nothing to be done. But your commanding officer is still a threat to you. He's still calling you. At the very least, we need to put a stop to that."

Des looked away. "Maybe I'm afraid."

"Of course you're afraid. I understand better than anyone. But if you say nothing, he wins. Good men, like the ones we have here, need to know so they can stand up for women and tell other men it's not okay to hurt us." She blinked as her eyes filled with tears. "Maybe talking will help you. I hope you can be braver than me."

Des put her arms around her and hugged. "I believe you're braver than you realize."

Charlotte closed her eyes and hugged her back. She wished she could believe that, but after ten years of

164

silence, she knew what a coward she was.

****

When Damon returned to the farm after his meeting with his bankers, Des was sitting on the front porch. She rose and walked down the steps toward him as he approached the house.

"Do you have a few minutes to speak privately?" Her body language and facial expressions were tense, as if she were readying for battle.

"Of course. How about we walk in the pasture? I do some of my best thinking out there."

She nodded, and they walked past the barn. Damon remained silent and waited for Des to tell him what was on her mind in her own way.

Finally, she spoke, her voice soft but unwavering. "My commanding officer did more than harass me. He raped me."

Damon wished he was surprised by this news, but sadly he wasn't. "Tell me what happened."

As they walked, Des told him how she'd been coerced and bullied into providing sex. Anger on her behalf made him want to hit something, but for Des's sake he stayed calm.

"He called me the other day and told me to stay quiet," Des said. "He said no one would believe me."

"He called you here?" He couldn't believe the man's audacity. "He was wrong, Des. People believe you. *I* believe you, and I'm going to make sure this harassment stops. First of all, give me your phone. We're going to block his calls."

Des reached into her back pocket for her phone and handed it to him. "I've blocked his calls before, but then he calls from a different number."

Damon stopped walking to change the settings. "If he calls from another number, we'll block him again. And again and again until he gets the message." When he finished, he handed back the phone.

"Do I have your permission to call the VA and tell them he's continuing to harass you?"

Des gave him a dubious look. "I don't know. I just want the calls to stop. If he knows I've told someone, he'll be angry, and it'll be so much worse."

"We won't do anything you're not comfortable with."

Des blew out a breath, her eyes on the ground as they continued their walk. "Can you make the calls stop?"

"I'll do my best. As an extra precaution, we'll contact your service provider and make sure he can't reach you from this latest number he's using. Maybe we'll get you a new number."

"All right."

"If at some point you want to make an official complaint against him, or go to the police, I'll stand behind you all the way. But you don't have to make that decision today, or ever. It's totally up to you."

Damon let the silence settle between them as they began walking again. Making a complaint was a big step, one he wouldn't take unless Des was ready.

"I don't think I can do that," she whispered at last.

"That's okay. For today, speaking up and telling your truth is enough. I know it wasn't easy. You should be proud of yourself."

He saw her smile, though she continued to look down at the ground. "I'm glad I talked to you. Charlotte said you could help."

"Charlotte said that?"

"Yeah. I told her what happened to me and she urged me to talk to you. She said I should speak to the group, too. I haven't decided if I can do that yet."

"We'll take it one step at a time. Are you ready to head back? It's almost time for dinner, if you're up to it."

"Yeah, I'm ready. And for the first time since I got here, I think I'm hungry." She looked up at him with a smile. "I feel like a weight's been lifted from my shoulders."

"Good. At some point, you might want to speak to a female counselor, one who's experienced in counseling rape survivors. I don't want you to feel you only have me to talk to."

"I think I'm good. I trust you."

"I'm glad, but we'll keep that door open." He weighed his next words carefully. "For what it's worth, I understand the feeling of violation you must be experiencing because I've been there. I was sexually assaulted by a pedophile when I was a child."

Des looked up sharply. "Oh, my God! I'm so sorry."

He shook his head. "I didn't tell you to get your sympathy, only to let you know I understand."

"You seem so together, so strong. How did you get past all the pain and anger? The feelings of worthlessness?"

"Believe me, I have my moments when all that stuff comes roaring back. It took a lot of years of therapy and a lot of great counselors to put me back together. Becoming a counselor and helping people like you is more rewarding than you can imagine. But the

167

thing that helped most was standing up to my abuser and testifying in court. I told everyone exactly what he did to me and how it affected my life. I refused to be silent. I wasn't the one with a shameful secret. He was. But it took me years to get to that point, so I understand where you're coming from."

Des nodded but remained quiet on the walk back. As they passed the barn, Charlotte emerged from inside. She glanced from Des to him and back to Des. Without saying a word, she looped her arm through Des's and the three of them walked to the house together.

Chapter Fifteen

Later that night, Charlotte set the kettle on the stove to boil and brought out her teapot. She found the nightly ritual of a cup of herbal tea with Damon calming. They talked over the events of the day, or sometimes they simply sat together quietly. He was an easy person to be around, she realized.

She carried the tea into the living room and set a cup in front of Damon. "How did things go at the bank today?"

"Okay, I think." Damon stirred milk into his tea. "They sounded optimistic about the loan. Despite all its problems, my building is still a valuable asset, so they're willing to use it as collateral."

Charlotte sat on the sofa and sipped her tea. "I'm sorry the renovation has been such a challenge."

"It's been frustrating, for sure." He sighed and shook his head. "My granddad was a shrewd investor. It doesn't make sense that he would have left me a building with so many problems."

"He probably didn't know how bad it was."

"It looks that way. Morley said he and Granddad knew and trusted the previous owner. He assured them the building was in good shape, so they never had it inspected."

"An inspection may not have found the problems anyway. Three months after I bought this house, I discovered the sewer line was plugged with tree roots. My inspection didn't catch that," Charlotte said.

"Morley spoke to the previous owner again today. He told him he was sure the electrical was upgraded a few years ago. If it wasn't, he said he'd been defrauded because he knew he paid for it. He was going to speak to his contractor and get back to Morley."

"Wow, that's crazy."

"I know I need to let it go and concentrate on fixing the building so we can move on. But I can't get past the feeling that Granddad let me down. I hate feeling that way, because he was one of the few people in my life who was always there for me."

"Your grandfather wanted the best for you. Whatever ends up happening with the building doesn't change how much he loved you."

"You're right." Damon closed his eyes and nodded. "It doesn't change the fact that Granddad was the best man I've ever known, either. He's the person I've always tried to emulate."

He looked so tired, and so disappointed. It broke Charlotte's heart to see him defeated.

"Everett Branson was a man of integrity and honor, and so are you, Damon. You're very much like your grandfather."

He met her gaze, his eyes wide with surprise. Then he smiled. "That's about the nicest thing you could say to me. Thank you."

"You're welcome."

A comfortable silence settled over the room as they drank their tea. Charlotte meant every word. Damon was the best man she knew. Always would be.

He finally broke the silence. "I talked to Des today.

Really talked. She told me she confided in you about the rape and that you urged her to speak to me."

"I'm glad she came to you." Maybe Des had a chance to start healing now.

"She said the two of you had a good talk."

Charlotte looked up sharply. Had Des told him about her rape, too?

"Did she?"

"You're a good friend, Charlotte. You listened when she needed someone to talk to."

She prayed Des hadn't betrayed her confidence. "Maybe it was easier for her to talk to another woman."

"It probably was. It was the breakthrough I needed with Des, and I have you to thank for it."

Charlotte set her empty teacup on the coffee table and looked away, uncomfortable with his praise. "I didn't do anything."

"You did more than you know. She hasn't decided if she'll talk to the group about her rape, or if she wants to press charges. Whatever she wants to do, I'll respect her wishes."

Charlotte clasped her hands in her lap, her palms sweaty. She was a fraud, a coward. Des was brave enough to come forward with the truth, yet she continued to remain silent.

"Des felt responsible for the rape, so she didn't think she had any right to complain," Damon said. "Abusers count on silence. But as soon as victims speak their truth, abusers lose their power."

Charlotte clutched her hands together in her lap. She wanted so badly to tell Damon the truth, to unburden herself. The words were on the tip of her tongue.

He'll hate me if he knows the truth.

She couldn't do it. She couldn't tell Damon what she'd done. He'd blame her, the way she blamed herself. And she couldn't bear it.

Because I'm in love with him.

Her heart jumped into her throat at the sudden realization. She rose abruptly to her feet, knocking over her empty cup. "I have to go."

Damon rose as well, confusion in his eyes. "Where are you going?"

Charlotte stumbled toward the door, the dogs following her. "I need to take River and Daisy out."

"I'll come with you. It's late."

"I'll be fine. We're only going for a quick walk."

"Charlotte, come on. It's dark. I'll go with you."

"No!"

At her shout, Damon stopped in the middle of the living room. The confusion on his face quickly turned to concern. "Charlotte, if I said something to upset you, I'm sorry."

She couldn't look at him. "You did nothing wrong. I need to be by myself for a while, that's all."

Charlotte quickly attached the dogs' leashes and hurried outside. No matter how hard she tried to do the right thing, she always failed. The smart thing to do, the kind thing, would be to tell Damon to move to his brother's house. He didn't need someone in his life as messed up as she was. If she really loved him, she'd do what was right for him.

But how could she let him go?

****

Damon spent half the night wondering what he'd done wrong. Last night, after Charlotte had been gone for nearly an hour, he'd been on the verge of searching for her when she finally returned to the house with the dogs. She didn't explain why she'd been out walking for so long, and he didn't ask.

The next morning, Damon took a quick shower. By the time he dressed, let the dogs out into the back yard, and made coffee, Charlotte arrived in the kitchen.

"Good morning." Damon poured her a cup of coffee, adding a splash of milk the way she liked it before handing it to her.

"Good morning." Charlotte's gaze skittered past his, landing somewhere over his left shoulder.

"I'm making eggs and toast. You want some?"

She shook her head. "No, thanks. Coffee's fine."

She let the dogs back into the house while he made toast, his appetite for more deserting him as well. When Charlotte came back to the kitchen with the dogs, she put her coffee in a to-go cup.

"Would you mind picking up Chris? I'm going to the shelter in Bismarck, and I need my own vehicle."

"Sure. I can pick up Chris."

"Good. Thanks."

Charlotte slung her purse over her shoulder and grabbed the leashes. "I'll see you later."

Damon watched her clip the leashes to the dogs' collars. In a moment she'd be gone. He couldn't let her leave. Not like this.

"Charlotte, wait." He laid his hand on her arm. "Are you angry with me? What can I do to make this right?"

She stared at his hand on her arm. "I'm not angry at you. Not at all. But I've been thinking it might be better for you if you stay with your brother."

His heart plummeted at her words. "Better for me? Why?"

She lifted her gaze, her hazel eyes staring unflinchingly into his. "Because there can never be anything between us."

Panic gripped him. She was sending him away. He grabbed both of her arms.

"Don't say that. I want to be with you. I want to be more than simply your friend."

Panic filled her eyes. She shook her head in denial. "No. You deserve someone better. Someone good."

He gripped her arms. "Are you saying this because you were raped? I don't give a damn about that."

"How did you know?" she whispered. Her face went deathly white. "Did Des tell you? I've never told anyone before."

"Des didn't tell me. I guessed." He loosened his hold on her arms. "Maybe I have a sixth sense when it comes to spotting someone who's been abused. I don't care what happened to you in the past. I only care about your future. About our future."

"No." Tears filled her eyes. "We don't have a future."

Desperation clawed at his throat. "You're wrong. I love you."

He loved her. He hadn't consciously let himself even think it, but it was true. Maybe it had always been true.

Her eyes widened in alarm at his admission. Shaking her head once more, she pulled away. "I have to go."

If he'd had a plan about the way he wanted to tell her he loved her, this wasn't it. A declaration of love should include candlelight, or a long walk on a beach. But it was clear those romantic fantasies were never going to happen. Because they were only fantasies, and real life didn't work that way. At least not for him.

"Charlotte—"

"I have to go," she repeated.

She grabbed her dogs' leashes and left the house. Damon stood in the doorway and watched River and Daisy jump into the back seat of her Jeep. When she saw him watching, she hesitated, standing completely still as she stared back at him. Damon held his breath, praying she'd walk back to him and tell him it was all a mistake.

But she didn't. She opened the door and climbed behind the wheel. A moment later she was gone.

Damon stepped back inside the house and closed the door. After texting Chris to tell him he'd be a few minutes late, he washed the breakfast dishes and tidied the kitchen. As soon as he finished, he walked back to his bedroom and packed his things into the two bags he'd come with.

****

Charlotte drove to Bismarck to the shelter and left her dogs with Michelle at the front desk before heading to the hospital. There, she spoke with Angie in Human Resources and arranged to go back to work five days earlier then she'd originally planned. She couldn't be at the farm and see Damon every day and not have her heart break in two.

When she went back to the shelter to pick up her dogs, Gina was in the front reception area. She smiled when Charlotte walked in.

"Hey, how are you? I haven't seen you in a while."

Seeing her friend's smiling face, Charlotte's composure began to crack.

"I'm good." She swallowed the tears that hovered on the edge of her composure.

Gina and Michelle exchanged a look. "Why don't you come into my office for a cup of coffee?"

Charlotte didn't want coffee, but she wasn't ready to go to the farm either. "Sure."

She and the dogs followed Gina to her office. Gina put a pod in her one-cup coffeemaker and closed the lid. The scent of fresh-brewed coffee soon filled the small office. Gina passed her the cup and made one for herself. She held up a packet of sugar.

"I'm out of creamer, but I've sugar."

"Thanks." She opened the packet and poured it into her cup.

"How are the dogs? Any more puppies since the last time I spoke to you?"

"No, but Jamie thinks Sally will have hers any day. The rest are doing pretty well. The skin diseases on the quarantine dogs are clearing up. We think we should be able to put them with the rest of the dogs in a week or two. Hope's puppies are growing, and they're adorable."

"I'm confident we'll find homes for the puppies. It's the rest I'm concerned about. But that's not what I want to talk about today. How are *you* doing?"

"I'm…fine."

Gina didn't look convinced. "Really?"

Charlotte slumped in her seat. "No, not really. But I will be. I'm going back to work soon, and things will start getting back to normal."

She wrapped her hands around her warm cup. After

Damon, nothing would be normal in her life ever again. The thought of him moving out caused an ache in her chest, as if her heart had been ripped out. But there was no choice. He deserved better.

"Charlotte, I don't know what's going on with you, but if you want to talk, I'd be happy to listen."

"You're a good friend, Gina. You really are. But I'm fine." She got to her feet, and River and Daisy rose as well. "Thanks for the coffee. When you get a chance, come out to the farm and see how all the dogs are doing."

"I will. And remember, my offer to listen is always open."

"Thank you." Gina's kindness humbled her. But she couldn't take her up on her offer.

She was in this alone.

After saying goodbye to Michelle, Charlotte and the dogs got back into the Jeep. With a sigh, she started the vehicle and put it in gear. She couldn't put off going to the farm any longer.

The first thing she noticed when she pulled into the farmyard was that Jamie's car was parked outside the barn. Charlotte's heart rate accelerated as she got out of the Jeep. Jamie hadn't mentioned visiting today. She let River and Daisy out of the back seat. They immediately joined Frisco and ran toward the house.

As Charlotte approached the barn, Des emerged from inside and came toward her. "Des, what's going on? Why is Jamie here?"

Des grasped her hand. "I'm so sorry, Charlotte. It's Sally. All her puppies were born dead."

Charlotte couldn't speak. Her mind couldn't comprehend what Des was saying. *Dead?* How could

177

they be dead?

Finally, she found her voice. "I want to see them."

"Charlotte—"

"I need to see them."

Des took her hand and they walked into the barn together. "When Mike and I went out to the barn first thing this morning, one of the puppies had already been born. We tried to revive it but it was already dead. We called Jamie right away."

They approached Sally's stall. The door was open, and Garrett and Damon were both there with Jamie. Six dead puppies were laid out on the straw close to Sally. She sniffed at one of them and licked its head. Damon looked up when she and Des walked in. He said nothing, but his eyes conveyed his sympathy. Jamie held her stethoscope to Sally's abdomen and listened for a moment, before removing the earpieces.

"I'd like to take Sally to the clinic and watch her for a day or two," Jamie said quietly. "We'll give her some time with the puppies first so she realizes what happened and has a chance to grieve."

"Will she understand the puppies are dead?" Garrett asked.

"Yes, she'll figure it out from the temperature drop and the fact they're not moving. I've seen mother dogs become aggressive if a dead puppy is taken away too soon, so we don't want to rush her."

Charlotte couldn't stop staring at the dead puppies. Her thoughts detached from her body. While she stood in the barn, her mind whisked back in time ten years to a clinic in Minneapolis. She was covered with a thick flannel sheet and was looking up at a ceiling with bright lights. She was drowsy. Someone placed a mask over her face. *Breathe in and count backwards from one hundred, Charlotte. When you wake up, it will be over, and you can go home.*

Garrett knelt beside Jamie and stroked Sally's head. "Why do you think this happened?"

She shook her head. "Could be any number of things. We knew Sally wasn't in good physical condition when she came here. She could have been infected with a bacteria or virus that passed to the puppies."

Charlotte heard their conversation but couldn't respond. She was back in the clinic, waking up, the flannel sheet tucked securely around her. As she gained consciousness, a battle began to rage inside her between relief and emptiness.

She sensed Damon's approach. "Des, why don't you take Charlotte outside?"

Charlotte felt Des's arm around her waist as she led her outside into the sunshine. River ran to her, tail madly wagging. She scratched him behind his ears and he leaned against her, his eyes closing in bliss. River had had a rough start in life. He'd been born in a puppy mill and had been rescued when the mill had been raided by animal protection officers. But River didn't care about the past. He only cared about today. As long as he had a full belly and an occasional scratch behind the ears, he was happy.

How she wished such simple pleasures would be enough for her. It would be such a relief to forget the past and live in the moment. To live without ghosts.

But life wasn't like that. At least hers wasn't.

Charlotte did her best to shake off the gloom. "Have the dogs been taken out for their walks?"

"We started but didn't finish," Des said.

"Okay." She took a deep breath and blew it out. "Tell me where you left off, and I'll look after the rest."

"We'll do it together."

Charlotte spent the rest of the day walking dogs, cleaning cages, and changing straw, doing her best to stay too busy to think. It mostly worked, except when Garrett carried Sally's kennel to Jamie's car. Jamie gave her a hug before she left. She didn't see anyone leave with Sally's puppies, but when she found the courage to look inside the stall, they were gone. Damon must have taken them out the back way. Using a wheelbarrow and a pitchfork, Charlotte removed all the straw and hauled it away. Then she swept the stall and washed it with bleach.

Life went on.

How she hated that phrase.

By five o'clock, she was exhausted, physically and mentally. She only wanted to go home with her dogs and curl into a ball. Tonight, she didn't want to be around anyone.

Charlotte walked up the front porch stairs and entered the kitchen where Chris was busy getting dinner ready. He looked up when she approached.

"Charlotte, hi. Garrett told me about the puppies. I'm really sorry."

"Thanks." She swallowed. "Listen, I'm going to head home. I'll see you tomorrow."

"You don't want to stay for dinner?"

The thought of food made her ill. So did the idea of making polite conversation. "No, I'm not hungry. You can get a ride home with Damon, right?"

"Sure, no problem." Chris put down his paring

knife. "I'm the last person who should give advice, but I'm going to give it anyway. If there's one thing I've learned, it's that if you keep stuff bottled up inside, pretty soon it's going to explode. Talk to someone, Char. People here care about you. Damon cares about you."

As Charlotte stared into his sincere blue eyes, panic filled her chest. She backed away, shaking her head. "I have to go. I'll see you tomorrow."

She ran out of the house as if a thousand ghosts were chasing her.

Chapter Sixteen

After dropping Chris at his house, Damon considered parking his truck and going to his brother's house next door. He'd called Ben that morning and asked about staying with his family for a few days. He had his suitcases in the back of his truck, ready to move.

But something in the haunted look in Charlotte's eyes as she stared at those dead puppies stopped him.

Chris told him how she'd bolted from the kitchen after he urged her to talk to someone. Once again Charlotte was keeping secrets. But he was afraid that this time her secrets were more than she could handle. She needed him.

Damon turned his truck around and headed for Charlotte's house. Standing at the side door, he took a deep breath before using the key she'd given him. He paused with the key in the lock. She wouldn't appreciate him intruding on her privacy, but she needed him. He could feel it.

Damon turned the key and went inside the house. All the lights were off. The dogs greeted him at the door with friendly barks, tongues lolling and tails wagging, but Charlotte was nowhere to be seen. Her Jeep was parked outside, so she had to be home.

He bent to stroke the dogs, then straightened as he called out. "Hello? Charlotte?"

There was no reply. He turned on the kitchen lights and walked to the living room, the dogs at his heels. Charlotte was on the couch, and she sat up taller as he approached. Had she been sitting here alone in the dark since she left the farm?

"What are you doing here?" She pushed her unbound hair off her face and tried to smooth it.

"I was worried about you." He slowly moved closer, trying not to scare her. "I wanted to see if you're okay."

"I'm fine."

"Are you?"

Her gaze jerked to his briefly before skittering away. "I'm upset about the puppies, but I'll be fine."

Damon stepped around the coffee table to sit next to her. "Have you eaten? You didn't stay for dinner."

"I'm not hungry."

He touched her hand. "I can make you a sandwich. I think we have tuna—"

She jerked away from his touch. "No! I told you. I'm not hungry. Quit trying to fix me!"

Damon gently tucked her hair behind her ear, and when she didn't slap his hand away, he cupped her cheek, caressing the delicate skin beneath her eye with his thumb. "I only want you to be happy, Charlotte."

She stared at him, her brow furrowed. "Why are you being so nice to me? I've been horrible to you."

"Because I love you."

She searched his eyes before looking away, her mouth twisting in misery. "I should have saved them."

The statement took him aback. "The puppies? There was nothing you could have done. They were already dead before they were born. You heard what

Jamie said. Sally was probably too weak or sick to carry them to term."

She pulled away from him and shook her head. "Maybe if I'd given Sally better-quality food, they could have survived. I should have had Jamie check on her every day. I should have had her run tests. It's my fault."

"No one's at fault, least of all you." She was starting to scare him. "You did everything you could for them, but some things aren't meant to be."

Charlotte seemed to deflate, all of the fight leaving her body. Damon grasped one of her ice-cold hands and rubbed it, trying to give her some warmth.

"No, some things aren't meant to be." Tears filled her eyes and threatened to spill down her cheeks. "They didn't get a chance to take a single breath. They didn't get a chance at anything."

Sobs wracked her body, and she doubled over as if in pain. Damon pulled her onto his lap and held her, his heart breaking at the sorrow he heard in her cries. He knew she was upset about the death of the puppies, but her grief outstripped even that sadness. He had to wonder if she was grieving another loss as well. Her silence frustrated him. If she would talk to him, he could help her.

Damon breathed deeply, trying to control his frustration. He couldn't make her talk, not if she wasn't ready. As a counselor, he knew that. He had to be patient and hope that someday she'd come to trust him.

Until that happened, he'd stay close to her. There was nowhere else he wanted to be.

****

Charlotte cried until she couldn't cry any longer.

As her sobs subsided, she became aware of Damon's arms around her, holding her securely. He caressed her hair with gentle, calming strokes. With her ear pressed against his chest, she listened to the strong, reassuring beat of his heart. The sound comforted her, and reminded her that, like his heartbeat, Damon was steady and true.

She loved him. How did she imagine she could send him away? She was so tired of fighting her feelings, so tired of trying to be some kind of paragon of virtue. She only wanted to *be*. To live and to love.

"Did you mean it when you said you loved me?" she whispered.

Damon tightened his hold. "Of course I meant it."

Charlotte wished she could find the courage to tell him she loved him, too. "I thought I could send you away, but I can't. I want to make love with you, Damon."

His hand stilled on her hair. "Are you sure?"

"I'm very sure." She twisted in his arms to look up into his face. "Do you want me?"

She felt a shudder rush through his body. "You have no idea how much I want you. But you've had an upsetting day. We need to slow down."

"No! I don't want to slow down. I want to live, Damon. I want to feel alive."

"Charlotte, sweetheart—"

"Don't say no. Please."

He stared unblinkingly into her eyes. Then with a suddenness that took her breath away, he crushed her against his body and brought his mouth down on hers. Charlotte sighed, relieved.

He wants me. She hadn't thought anyone would

ever want her.

He swept her mouth with his tongue, stroking her tongue over and over until she thought she'd die of the pleasure. Finally, he broke the kiss, and they stared at each other, both breathing heavily. Damon threaded her hair through his fingers, the look on his face full of wonder.

"Charlotte. Beautiful, beautiful Charlotte."

The way he said her name made her feel special, like she was something good and worthwhile. Charlotte hadn't felt that way for a long time.

Damon set her on her feet, and then, taking her hand, led her to his room. After closing the door, he turned to her.

"Can I undress you?" he asked.

Charlotte swallowed and nodded. As much as she wanted Damon, she was afraid. Would her fears stop her from going through with this? Would she disappoint him? The last thing she wanted was to make him believe he was somehow to blame for her nervousness.

Damon seemed to sense her apprehension. "What if we undress each other? We can do it as quickly or as slowly as you like." He brought her hand to his mouth for a kiss. "Do you want the lights on or off?"

She thought for a moment. Though she was nervous about baring her body to him, she trusted him. And more than anything, she wanted to see *him*. "Let's put the bedside lamp on."

Damon reached over to click on the lamp. A small pool of light illuminated the bed.

"I'll give you the first turn," he said.

Nerves danced along Charlotte's spine. "All right."

She moved closer to unbutton his shirt. Her fingers

felt stiff and awkward, and her hands shook as they tried to work the first button.

"Take your time, sweetheart. We've got all night."

Charlotte looked up into his eyes at his quietly spoken words. He smiled reassuringly at her. He was so kind. It couldn't have been easy for him to let her set such a slow pace, but he was willing to put aside his own needs for her. It only made her love him more.

And the knowledge somehow chased away her fears.

With renewed purpose, and steadier hands, Charlotte unfastened the rest of the buttons. She pushed the shirt off his shoulders, allowing her hands to flow over the smooth, warm skin of his powerful shoulders. His muscled chest and abdomen tempted her to touch and caress. The contrast of smooth skin over hard muscle was intoxicating.

"Obviously, your workouts on the bag have paid off." She traced the corded muscles of his shoulders down to his biceps.

He chuckled. "Glad you approve."

She definitely approved. "It's your turn now. You get to take off one piece of my clothing."

"All right. Your T-shirt has to go."

Nerves mixed with excitement as she reached for the hem of her T-shirt. Damon covered her hands with his.

"You got to take off my shirt, so I get to take off yours. Fair's fair."

Charlotte let it drop, her hands no longer steady. "Right. Fair's fair."

Damon grasped the bottom of her T-shirt and lifted it a few inches to expose her belly. His eyes were fixed on hers, but with a light in them she hadn't seen before.

Then he knelt on one knee in front of her and trailed a line of light kisses across her bare abdomen. Her belly quivered in response, and moisture pooled between her thighs. Her breath came out in little pants.

Dear God, what would she do when he *really* touched her?

She rejoiced in her arousal. She'd been afraid she would never experience this kind of feeling again, that she'd never be normal again.

But with Damon, everything felt right.

He inched the T-shirt up her body, kissing her bare skin as it was revealed. When he lifted the shirt over her breasts, he stood and kissed his way across the top of her breasts. And then, using his tongue, he licked at the lace covering her nipples. Charlotte grabbed his thick hair in both hands, nearly orgasming on the spot.

Damon lifted his head and kissed her face, his light kisses across her cheeks and her closed eyes leaving fire in their wake.

"What do you need, Charlotte?" His honeyed whisper aroused her further. "Tell me what you want, what feels good."

In her limited experience with boys before the rape, none of them had ever asked her what she wanted. She'd accepted their fumbling hands and awkward kisses because she thought that was what sex, or at least the lead-up to sex, was supposed to be.

But Damon blew all her expectations out of the water. With simply a few kisses and some whispered words, he'd shown her what love and sex should be. He'd shown her what trust should look like. Still, she had fears.

Charlotte cupped his face between her hands and looked into his eyes. "I want all the barriers to be gone between us. I want to see you and touch you, and I want you to touch me. I want that, truly, but I'm afraid. What if I don't like it when you touch me…there? What if I don't react the way I'm supposed to?"

Damon softly kissed her lips. "There's no 'supposed to,' Charlotte. However you feel is totally right for you. We'll take it slow, but if gets to be too much, just tell me and we'll stop. Okay?"

"Okay." Knowing she was in control made things easier. And so did being with Damon. She couldn't imagine doing this with anyone else.

"First, let's get rid of this."

With one quick move, he pulled her T-shirt over her head and tossed it to the floor, surprising Charlotte.

"Oh!"

Instinctively, she drew her arms across her breasts to cover them. She shivered and looked away. As goosebumps skittered across her bare skin, she chastised herself for her reaction.

"Charlotte, I'm sorry. I didn't mean to scare you or rush you."

The consternation on Damon's face made her drop her arms. This was Damon. She knew she could trust him. The knowledge emboldened her.

"I was just surprised, that's all." She pulled one bra strap down, letting it dangle loosely on her shoulder. "I'm fine. Maybe you can help me get rid of this. You know, to even things up."

She pulled down the other strap and then lifted her face. His eyes were fixed on her left bra strap. "Maybe you can unfasten the hooks for me."

His gaze jerked to hers. "Are you sure?"

She smiled, doing her best to reassure him. "I'm very sure."

As she said the words, she realized how much she meant them. She wanted this. She wanted *him.*

Damon reached behind her and released the hooks of her bra, letting it fall to the floor. Charlotte pushed aside the urge to cover her breasts again as Damon stared at her.

This is Damon. I can trust him.

"You are so damn beautiful."

His words came out on a moan, and she realized how much it cost him to go this slow and be this careful with her. It made her love him even more.

His hand visibly shook as he reached out to touch her left breast. With reverent fingers, he traced the edges of her breast, then rubbed his thumb over the nipple. Charlotte's breath caught. She hadn't expected the spike of desire that rushed to her core at his tender caress.

"You like that?" he asked, repeating the gentle assault on her other breast.

"Yes." Her breathing became ragged. "Yes."

He had both hands on her breasts now. "Will you let me kiss your breasts?"

Charlotte closed her eyes. She couldn't imagine anything more heavenly than Damon's mouth on her breasts.

"Yes."

"I'm going to take you to the bed, sweetheart."

She felt like putty in his hands as he led her to the bed, then turned her and gently lowered her until her head made contact with the pillows.

"I'm going to kiss you now," he whispered.

He trailed kisses down her neck, across her collarbone, and down to the V between her breasts. Charlotte's chest rose up and down with her labored breath. He kissed each breast, giving special attention with his tongue to the underside. She clutched the sheets as desire rose.

"I'm going to put your nipple in my mouth now. Is that okay with you?"

"Yes! Hurry!"

She heard Damon's deep chuckle, felt him smile against her skin. "We don't want to rush, sweetheart."

"Speak for yourself, Greyson."

And then he took her nipple in his mouth, and her brain stopped functioning. All she could do was feel the exquisite sensation of Damon's tongue swirling around her extended nipple. He suckled and licked and gently nipped until she thought she would die of the pleasure. Then he lavished the other breast with the same attention and covered the first breast with his hand and kneaded gently.

Charlotte felt herself reaching for something, for somewhere she'd never been before. It was almost within her grasp, but she wasn't quite there.

Damon lifted his head to look into her face. "I want to take off your shorts and your panties." He set his hand at the apex of her thighs, over her clothes. "And then I want to put my mouth here and kiss you like I kissed your breasts. Will you let me?"

Charlotte shivered, doing her best to push back any lingering fear. "I…I've never done that before."

"I promise to make it good for you. I promise I won't hurt you."

She stared into his sincere gray-green eyes, her mind racing. She wanted this and she could no longer let fear—and the past—stop her.

She wanted to live. To love.

"Okay."

Damon nodded. "Okay."

He slid her shorts and panties down her legs and tossed them to the floor. Charlotte lifted her head to look into Damon's face. She was completely naked and exposed. She should have been anxious or nervous. This was, after all, the stuff of her nightmares. And yet she wasn't. The light of desire in his eyes made her feel powerful and beautiful. And totally unafraid.

This is Damon. I can trust him.

She silently lifted her arms to him, needing him to hold her, to kiss her. He understood, even without any words being spoken. Damon wrapped her in his arms, and kissed her, his mouth somehow communicating his ardor and his need for her.

He needed her? She'd never before considered that Damon could need her, that she could be important to his happiness. No one had ever needed her before, not like this.

Somehow it made all the difference.

When they broke the kiss, she put both hands on the sides of his face and smiled up at him.

"You are a fantastic kisser."

His grin brought out the dimple in his cheek. "Glad you enjoyed it."

"I enjoy *you*. You're amazing."

The smile left his face. "I...you're the amazing one, Charlotte. I don't know what to say."

She ran her hand through his thick hair. "Just say

you'll make love to me. That you'll teach me how to make love to you."

Damon solemnly nodded. "I will."

At her nod, he kissed her lips one last time before slowly moving down her body. Once again he kissed his way down her neck and chest, taking her nipples in his mouth and teasing them until she writhed on the bed and moaned his name.

He moved his exploration lower, kissing her lower belly and then the insides of her thighs. His hands were everywhere at once, on her breasts, running up and down her legs, and beneath her, kneading her buttocks.

At last he positioned himself between her legs and parted the sensitive folds of her sex with gentle fingers. Then he licked the folds with his tongue. The sensations were so intense, so mind-blowingly *good*, Charlotte nearly rocketed off the bed. She clutched the blanket covering the bed and inhaled sharply.

Damon licked her again, once, twice, before gently suckling. The sensation was intense but so exquisitely wonderful that Charlotte nearly wept with joy. Again, she felt herself reaching for that unseen something just beyond her grasp. She was so close she could feel it. So close…

And then he inserted his finger inside her, curling his knuckle to press on a sensitive knot of nerves that pushed her over the edge. Her body bucked and writhed, and she moaned Damon's name again and again. But he stayed with her, suckling and licking, his mouth wringing every last ounce of pleasure from her.

Eventually, the trembling in her body eased and she lay limp, totally sated. Damon pulled her into his arms and held her as her heartrate and breathing returned to a more normal pace. Both her body and her soul had been moved by Damon's tender lovemaking. Nothing had ever felt like this before. She'd flown so high she swore she could see heaven.

When she could finally speak again, she could think of only one thing to say.

"Wow."

She felt Damon's chuckle rumble through her chest, and it made her smile.

"Will it always be like that between us?" she asked.

"I hope so."

"Good," she said. Again, she felt his laugh, and she laughed with him. Peace and joy and happiness flowed over her. She wanted to give Damon pleasure too. If she could give him even a fraction of the pleasure he'd given her, she'd be satisfied.

She placed her hand on his chest and caressed the warm skin. "Tell me what you like, Damon. Tell me where to touch you, how to make you happy."

He stilled. "I want that too, Charlotte. But I don't have any protection."

It took her brain a moment to catch the meaning of his words. No protection equaled no means of birth control. Which equaled no lovemaking. Disappointment swamped her.

"Oh."

"I'm sorry I'm unprepared. You took me by surprise."

She'd taken herself by surprise, too. And her next thought surprised her even more. She lifted her head to look into his face so she could see his reaction.

"What if we did something else till you can get

some condoms?"

His brows drew together. "Something else?"

"I could do to you what you did to me."

"Charlotte, you don't have to."

"I want to." She hesitated, examining his face, worried that she'd disgusted him. "Unless you don't want me to."

"My God, Charlotte. Just the thought of you…" He closed his eyes, and she felt a tremble roll through his body. "Yes, I want you to."

"Good."

Damon stood and quickly removed his remaining clothes before lying beside her once more. She kissed him and then, just as he had done, she moved down his body, kissing, licking, teasing, touching. She loved the feel of him, the smooth, warm skin, the springy hairs on his chest, the hard muscle. And she loved his scent. It was warm and earthy and utterly *him*.

At last she arrived at his engorged penis. Charlotte was intimidated by what she proposed to do, but she wouldn't back down.

This is Damon. I can trust him.

She positioned herself over him and tentatively kissed his shaft. When she heard his sharp intake of breath, she grew bolder. She placed featherlight kisses on his penis again, then ran her tongue up and down, whirling it around the tip. Damon moaned as he gripped the sheets.

"Oh, my God, Charlotte. Don't stop, please."

Taking a deep breath, she took him into her mouth. She sucked and slid her mouth and lips and teeth up and down his shaft, taking him deeper and deeper.

"Charlotte!"

He pulled out of her mouth, his seed spilling over his stomach. The rapturous look on his face made Charlotte glad she'd set aside her fears. And she realized now how far she'd go to please him.

As far as Damon wanted to go.

Chapter Seventeen

The next day was the Fourth of July. Everyone at Branson Farm decided as a group not to participate in festivities in town. None of the veterans felt ready to mingle with people they didn't know, and Damon didn't want to push them. Blair and Garrett planned a small celebration on the farm with plenty of food and games like horseshoes and corn hole toss, and a bonfire after sundown. Chris's wife Alison and their two girls arrived in the afternoon, bringing a piñata and a pin-the-tail-on-the-donkey game with them. Everyone made an extra effort to ensure the children had fun.

Damon guessed by Charlotte's smile and her frequent laughter that she was more at peace today, though he knew she was still grieving the death of Sally's puppies. He hoped he was a small part of the reason for her contentment, because she certainly made him happy. Last night had been the happiest of his life.

After lunch, Damon made a quick trip to Bismarck on the pretext of buying more soft drinks. He found one of the few businesses open on the holiday, a pharmacy downtown, and purchased the soft drinks along with a large box of condoms. Maybe he was being optimistic about the number of condoms in the box, but he didn't care. After the previous night, he had reason for optimism. Or at least he hoped so.

Simply the thought of Charlotte's mouth wrapped

Jana Richards

around his shaft, and the remembered feel of her taking him deep into her throat, gave him an erection. If he didn't get inside her soon, he was going to spontaneously combust.

He hoped Charlotte hadn't changed her mind since last night about making love with him. He'd wanted to sleep with her last night, but she'd insisted it would be too difficult being that close and not being able to touch. He couldn't help thinking she wasn't ready for such intimacy.

He'd have to be careful with her, even more careful than yesterday. The oral sex had been new to her, so she didn't associate it with her rape, at least not as much. But penetration would likely bring up all kinds of unpleasant memories, even if she trusted him.

He remembered his first few fumbling attempts at sex with a girl as a teenager. For a time, he'd been confused about which gender he preferred, because Victor Campbell had repeatedly told him that he liked sex with men. After hearing it so often at such a young age, it had taken him a while to discover the truth for himself.

Damon pushed the old, bad memories aside. Today was all about Charlotte and, hopefully, their future. He wanted a future with Charlotte more than anything he'd ever wanted in his life.

After a late supper followed by a bonfire, they drove back to Masonville. Damon pulled his truck into the driveway behind Charlotte's Jeep and turned off the ignition while Charlotte let out the dogs. Before getting out of the truck, he reached under the front seat for the bag containing his earlier purchase. She grinned as he approached.

"What ya got there, Mr. Greyson?"

He opened the bag for her to see. "Something essential to my happiness, Ms. Saunders. And yours, too. At least I hope it will make you happy."

Her demeanor sobered. "I want this, Damon. Very much."

He gave her a reassuring smile. "Come on. Let's go inside."

Once inside the kitchen, Damon turned her in his arms and kissed her. She opened eagerly to him, their tongues tangling, stroking. Charlotte broke the kiss and clutched his shoulders.

"I love kissing you."

He kissed the end of her nose. "I love kissing you, too."

"Will you take me to bed?"

"Yes."

He scooped her into his arms, surprising her and making her laugh. He started toward his bedroom, making sure he still had the bag with the condoms in his hand. Once in the bedroom, he set Charlotte on her feet and pulled back the covers on the bed. He was disconcerted to see that his hands shook as he removed the box of condoms from the plastic bag and set it on the night table. He stared at the bed. What if he blew this chance with Charlotte? What if his awkwardness, his immense need for her, scared her off? She meant everything to him.

Charlotte touched his arm. "Hey, I'm the one who's supposed to be nervous."

Damon bowed his head, avoiding her gaze. "Sorry."

"You have nothing to be sorry about. You're the

most wonderful man, Damon." She began unbuttoning his shirt. "I couldn't do this with anyone but you."

Damon met her eyes. "I don't want anyone but you either. I want to make this good for you." So good that she'd stay with him. So good she'd want to make love with him again and again.

"You will." She spread open his shirt and kissed his chest. "You already have."

She smiled up at him, and his nervousness evaporated. He loved her so much his heart threatened to burst.

Damon lowered his head and kissed her again. They undressed each other slowly, carefully. There was no need to hurry. He wanted to savor this moment, to rejoice at each inch of creamy skin revealed to him. Charlotte was a precious gift, and he cherished her.

"You are exquisite, Charlotte." He kissed her neck, then trailed kisses down her collarbone. "So beautiful."

He felt the shiver of desire that raced through her body as his lips touched her warm skin.

"So are you, Damon. So beautiful."

He'd never considered himself anything special. Growing up with an older brother as handsome as Ben and a baby sister as pretty as Blair meant he'd often been overlooked. And expendable. His mother had certainly never thought of him as anything special. He wasn't worth her time.

No. Damn it, he wasn't going to bring his mother into bed with them. She had no place there. She had no place anywhere in his life. He pushed her forcefully away.

He guided Charlotte to the bed and lay next to her. Once more he kissed his way down her body to the apex of her thighs. This time he knew exactly where to kiss her, where to touch her, how to give her the most pleasure. Damon spread her legs wider, giving him better access, then lowered his head to touch the most intimate part of her. With his mouth and tongue and lips he suckled, licked, and kissed her, inserting his tongue to touch the spot he'd learned drove her wild. Charlotte bucked and moaned and writhed on the bed. He stayed with her, spreading the folds to insert his tongue even deeper.

And then he inserted a finger inside her and she came undone. Her body stiffened with her release.

"Damon!"

The taste of her was sweet, as exquisite as the rest of her. He eagerly took her in, loving everything about the way she smelled and the way she felt. As he rode the wave of her orgasm, his own desire built to almost painful heights.

Gradually, her orgasm eased. Damon kissed her inner thighs and felt her shiver before he left the bed in search of a condom. He ripped open the box, tearing off a piece of the cardboard in his haste. He made himself breathe in slowly. If he wasn't careful, this could be over before it began.

He pulled a condom from the box and tore the package open. As he rolled the condom over his erection, he saw that Charlotte watched him, her eyes wide. He couldn't tell if she was afraid, but he wanted to reassure her.

"We'll go as slowly as you need to go. And if you tell me to stop, I'll stop."

"I won't tell you to stop."

He prayed she wouldn't. He longed to be inside

her, to feel her warmth. "Okay, but I want you to know it's an option. You only have to say the word."

She gave a brief nod. Damon approached the bed and positioned himself between her spread legs. Bit by bit he lowered himself until he touched her soft opening. Damon's whole body trembled. How long would he be able to hang on?

"I'm going to enter a little at a time. Tell me if I'm hurting you."

Charlotte wrapped her arms around him. "You're not hurting me."

He sank a little deeper into her, closing his eyes and savoring the feel of flesh against flesh. *So, so good.* Then he withdrew and plunged back again, careful not to go too fast or too far.

But it was killing him.

Then Charlotte wrapped her legs around his waist and whispered his name. "You won't hurt me. You'd never hurt me, Damon. I know you wouldn't."

Her trust in him was humbling. As he sank into her the next time, he came apart in her arms. Wave after wave after wave of pleasure washed over him, taking him someplace he'd never been before.

She took him home. For the first time in his life, here, with Charlotte, he was home.

****

The next week was the happiest of Damon's life. He and Charlotte spent their days working at Branson Farm and their nights making love. Every day he fell a little more in love with her. He could no longer imagine his life without her in it.

She still hadn't talked about her rape. He knew her, and he knew that until she talked about what had happened to her, until she truly dealt with it, she couldn't move forward. She couldn't be happy. He wanted happiness for Charlotte more than he wanted it for himself.

Each day, after working at the farm, they drove back to Masonville with Chris and dropped him off at his house. Anticipation would soar in Damon's chest as they drove to her place. This was his favorite time, not only because he knew he and Charlotte would make love, but because he got to spend time with her. She spoke freely about her happy childhood and her relationship with her parents and siblings, and about her work as a nurse. But whenever he asked about college, she gave only the briefest of descriptions. She'd taken her nurses' training in Grand Forks, at the University of North Dakota. After she graduated, she got a job at the hospital in Bismarck and purchased her house in Masonville so she could be close to family. End of story. Damon knew there had to be much more. She trusted him with her body but not with her secrets.

Today, Charlotte parked her Jeep in the driveway. They entered the house with the dogs, and Damon pulled her into his arms as soon as they entered the kitchen.

"I'll put on the kettle." Damon kissed her, lingering against her lips and drinking in her sweetness. "You want peppermint or decaf Earl Grey?"

Charlotte looped her arms around his neck and grinned. "Surprise me."

He grinned back. "Be careful what you wish for."

"I'm not worried. I know I can trust you."

"Do you really?" He hadn't meant to say the words aloud, but they slipped out, and it was too late to take them back.

Charlotte's smile faded. "Of course I do."

He really wanted to ask why she didn't trust him enough to talk to him about her rape. But he'd settle for a partial truth. "Then why don't you want to tell anyone that we're together?"

She dropped her arms from around his neck. "It's no one's business."

"Even our families?"

Charlotte stepped away, distress clearly written on her face. "It's too new. Is it so wrong to want to enjoy what we have together without others intruding?"

"No, it's not wrong." He approached her and kissed her forehead. "But I think people have already guessed. Ben, in particular."

She looked at him in alarm. "You didn't tell him, did you?"

"No, of course not. But he's not stupid. I told him I was going to stay at his place, and then I didn't show up. When he asked me what was going on, I said we had a change of plans. I'm pretty sure he figured things out."

Charlotte's forehead wrinkled in worry. "If Ben knows, that means Jamie knows, too."

"Has she said anything to you?"

"No."

"She's not likely to. Jamie wouldn't intrude on your privacy."

Charlotte nodded. Damon looped his arms around her waist. "Let's not worry about it. Let's enjoy being together. Okay?"

She nodded. "Okay."

He kissed her forehead again and pulled her close.

He tried not to let her reticence to talk about their relationship get to him, but an insecure part of him couldn't help wondering if she was ashamed to be with him. Ashamed of him.

Damon did his best to push the fear away. He held Charlotte at arm's length and forced himself to smile at her.

"How about I make the tea and you feed the dogs?"

A relieved smile lit her face. "Deal."

A short time later they were in the living room with their tea. Charlotte sat next to him on the sofa.

"How did your meeting go this afternoon?" she asked.

"Pretty well. For once I didn't hear about a lot of problems." Damon had borrowed Charlotte's Jeep in the afternoon to meet with his contractor at his building.

"Have you heard anything from the bank about the loan?"

"Not yet."

"Are you worried?"

Strangely, he wasn't. "The manager was optimistic. He gave me the impression the loans committee would rubber stamp my request. In the meantime, we're carrying on with the work we can at the building. We're getting close to the drywall stage in some areas."

"It's exciting."

"Yeah. I had a look at my apartment. It's coming along."

Charlotte sipped her tea. "Do you know when it will be ready?"

"Are you anxious to get rid of me?"

Damon watched her face. Her answer, and especially her expression, would tell him a lot about the way she felt about him. Was she only interested in a brief affair, or did their relationship mean something more to her?

"I'm not anxious to get rid of you at all." Charlotte lifted sincere eyes to his. "It's been wonderful having you here."

"For me, too." The best time of his life.

She grinned at him. "I'd be okay if the building took another six months to finish."

Damon groaned. "Good grief, I hope not. Clayton promised me six weeks, tops."

"Clayton?" She sat up a little straighter.

"My contractor, Clayton Brown. He owns Brown Construction. The company came highly recommended. Clayton took over the business from his grandfather a few years ago."

She nodded but said nothing more. She carefully set her cup on the coffee table and reached for his hand.

"Let's go to bed, Damon."

"You haven't finished your tea."

She plucked his cup from his hand and set it aside. "I don't care."

She kissed him, and in it he felt her need for him. His own desire rose up to meet hers. They hurried to the bedroom, kissing and shedding clothes along the way, anxious to touch bare flesh.

In the bedroom they stripped off the remainder of each other's clothes. Charlotte ripped one of the buttons off his shirt in her haste. Damon grinned.

"Hey, I know you're wild for my body, but there's no rush. We've got all night."

Instead of laughing the way he thought she would, she reached for the zipper of his pants.

"Maybe I don't want to wait." She pushed his jeans down his legs. "Maybe I want you right now."

Their coupling was fast. Damon totally lost control. He was usually so careful with Charlotte, but this time he pounded into her, hard, fast, deep. And Charlotte was even more wild, her body writhing with abandon, her hips rising eagerly to meet his. There was an almost desperate quality to her lovemaking.

Desperate?

Damon didn't have time to analyze his odd feeling. When he came, his orgasm seemed to come from the tips of his toes. It spread through his whole body until it burst uncontrollably out of him. The sensation was remarkable, and unlike anything he'd ever experienced before. As his trembling subsided, he lay on top of Charlotte, their bodies still joined.

"I should move. I must be crushing you."

She tightened her arms around him. "No, don't go. Stay. Please."

Something in her voice alarmed him. He lifted his head to look into her face. "Charlotte? You okay?"

She avoided his eyes. "Yes, of course. I just want to hold you a little longer. Okay?"

He wrapped his arms around her. "Of course, it's okay. Always."

She pressed her face against his neck and sighed. Damon held her, his mind racing. Was she feeling vulnerable because they'd talked about his leaving? He didn't realize that talk about his new apartment would affect her so profoundly. It wasn't like he was moving far away.

He rejected the idea. He knew Charlotte well enough by now to understand she was okay on her own.

Something else was bothering her.

He wished she'd talk to him. Not only about the rape, but about anything that concerned her, anything that hurt her, no matter how big or small. Again, the thought assailed him that she'd let him touch her body but not her secrets. Not her heart.

Damon sighed. All he could do was love her and hope that someday she'd be able to love him back.

Chapter Eighteen

Charlotte parked the Jeep and stared at the Fletcher Building across the street, her heart pounding in her chest. It didn't have to be him. Brown was a common surname. There could be any number of Clayton Browns in the world. In fact, when she'd Googled his name, several Clayton Browns came up, none of them the man she knew.

She was kidding herself. Clayton was in the area, and she remembered that he'd bragged about his family's construction company and how much it was worth. The website for Brown Construction listed him as the current owner, though it didn't show any pictures of him. But it was him. She could feel it.

The question she wanted an answer to was whether Clayton was being completely honest with Damon about the condition of the building. Charlotte knew exactly what he was capable of. It wasn't a big stretch to believe he could be dishonest in his business dealings.

First things first. She had to confirm that Damon's general contractor was the same Clayton Brown she knew.

Charlotte entered the coffee shop directly across the street. At one-thirty in the afternoon, lunch was over and afternoon coffee breaks hadn't begun, so the shop was empty. After ordering coffee, she bought a newspaper and sat at a table in front of the large windows facing the street. From here, she had a perfect vantage point. She sipped her coffee and pretended to read the paper, the knot in her stomach growing by the second.

After nearly forty minutes and a second cup of coffee, her patience finally paid off. Clayton emerged from the Fletcher Building, wearing a hard hat. There was no doubt. The Clayton Brown who'd raped her in college and the Clayton Brown who was Damon's general contractor were one and the same.

Now what did she do? Did she go to Damon with this news? Other than a gut instinct, she had no proof Clayton was cheating Damon. For all she knew, the building really had been in bad shape. But Damon had been confused and upset by the condition of the legacy his grandfather left him. She'd known Everett Branson all her life, and he'd been no fool. He would have made sure the building was a sound investment before he purchased it. Clayton was behind the problems. She could feel it.

Yet...

Damon knew she'd been raped, but she hadn't provided any details, and he hadn't pushed. The idea of opening up to the man she loved terrified her. If he knew the whole story, would he look at her differently?

As she stared out the window, Clayton began crossing the street, and Charlotte suddenly realized he was heading to the coffee shop. Grabbing her purse, she ran to the women's washroom, shutting the door behind her just as Clayton entered the shop. She locked the door and sagged against it, her heart racing. In the mirror across the room, she saw the face of a frightened, cowering woman. It was the same face she'd seen in the mirror the morning after her rape. She hated that after all this time Clayton still held the power to reduce her to a quivering mess.

After ten minutes, Charlotte cautiously opened the door a crack. The bathroom was located down a short hallway and had a direct view of the front door and the tables in front of the window where she'd been sitting. Clayton wasn't sitting at the tables. Perhaps he'd taken his coffee to go.

Charlotte opened the door wider and stepped into the hallway, preparing to make her escape. Suddenly Clayton came into view carrying a tray of coffee as he headed to the door. She turned and re-entered the bathroom, locking the door once more. Had he seen her? He'd only needed to glance to his left to see her retreat into the bathroom. Charlotte leaned against the door and wiped her sweaty palms against her denim shorts, feeling sick to her stomach.

She stayed in the bathroom a full fifteen minutes before daring to open the door again. Thankfully, no one was outside waiting to use the facilities when she emerged, and Clayton was nowhere in sight. She ventured out of the bathroom and cautiously made her way to her table. Taking her seat once more, she scanned Damon's building across the street. Construction workers came and went from behind the chain-link fencing that had been erected at the front of the building, but there was no sign of Clayton. Perhaps he'd left.

Charlotte grabbed her purse and hurried to her Jeep. As she entered her vehicle and turned it on, it occurred to her that Clayton had seen her Jeep that day in the parking lot of the supermarket. It was bright yellow and everyone in Masonville knew it was hers. What if he'd recognized it sitting in front of the coffee shop? What if he knew she'd been watching him? Did he know of her connection to Damon? Masonville was a small town. A few inquiries would reveal they were working together at Branson Farm. And that he was living at her house.

Ice cold fear travelled down her spine as she drove away.

****

Late in the afternoon, Damon saw Charlotte drive into the farmyard and park her Jeep in front of the house. She'd left after lunch, saying she needed to run some errands. But the nervous tension he'd detected in her since the morning made him wonder about the nature of her errands.

He chastised himself for being suspicious. Charlotte didn't have to answer to him for anything. Still, he couldn't shake a sense of dread.

Damon approached her as she got out of the Jeep. "Hi. Did you get your errands done?"

She turned away to close the door, not looking at him. "All done."

"You okay?"

Charlotte swiveled sharply to face him. "Yes, of course I am. Why wouldn't I be?"

"I don't know. You seem nervous."

"I'm fine, Damon. Stop fussing." She softened her sharp tone with a smile. "I know you mean well, but please. Stop."

Damon stepped closer and touched her arm, trailing his fingers from her upper arm to her fingers.

"Sweetheart, you can talk to me. You can tell me anything. I promise you can trust me."

"I know."

He wondered if she really understood that. So far, he hadn't breached her defenses, and he didn't know if he ever would. But he loved her too much to stop trying.

"Charlotte—"

She abruptly pulled her hand away and stepped back. "Des is coming."

Damon winced. Charlotte's refusal to let the others know they were together was like a slap to the face.

Des hurried to them, her excitement evident. "Guys! You have to come see! Lucy had her pups!"

Charlotte and Damon fell into step beside Des as they headed to the barn. "When did this happen?" Charlotte asked.

"Sometime this afternoon. After I finished cleaning kennels, I went to check on Lucy and three of the pups had already been born. The fourth came soon after."

"Are they okay?" Damon heard the trepidation in Charlotte's voice.

Des smiled at her as she opened the door to Lucy's stall. "They're perfect. See for yourself."

Lucy lay on her side in the whelping box, her four tiny pups curled next to her, asleep. Charlotte got down on her knees on the straw in front of the box.

"Oh, they're beautiful," she whispered. "They look just like Lucy. Some kind of retriever cross."

She looked up at Damon with a smile as she stroked the head of a puppy with one finger. The joy on her face took his breath away.

He crouched next to Lucy's box, but all he could

see was Charlotte. "Yeah. Beautiful."

They admired the puppies until they heard Chris ring the dinner bell on the front porch. Dusting the straw from their clothes, they headed to the house.

The old wooden table was loaded with food. Trey had become Chris's right-hand man in the kitchen and had proven to be an excellent baker. He'd told Damon that his fondest dream was to open a bakery in his hometown.

Over the last few weeks, Trey and the others had become more comfortable with Damon and each other, more willing to share their secrets and private pains. Even Des had begun communicating more in their group sessions.

If only Charlotte could do the same.

"When do you go back to work, Char?" Blair asked over dinner.

"Next week. It's going to be strange not coming out here every day."

Damon lifted his head in surprise. "I thought you still had a couple of weeks of leave left."

She avoided looking at him directly, pretending to concentrate on the food on her plate. "It's time I head back to the hospital. My co-workers have been picking up the slack long enough."

Damon looked down at his plate as well, his appetite deserting him. Another secret she was keeping from him.

"We'll miss you," Des said.

"I'll miss you, too. There's no way I'd feel comfortable going back to work if I didn't know you and Mike were here to look after the dogs."

Des and Mike had taken over most of the dog

214

duties, while Tom and Ray gravitated more to the horses and other outdoor work. Ray pointed his fork at Damon.

"Tom and I have been thinking that what we really need for the dogs is a permanent fenced run, something they can't tunnel underneath and escape from. That way they could get out of their kennels more, and we wouldn't have to worry about them chasing the horses."

"I agree." He and Garrett had talked about a run since the dogs arrived. "We'd like to build some kind of pen for the dogs, but we're tapped out financially."

"If the money becomes available, Tom and I would be happy to build it," Ray said. "I've got some experience with chain-link fencing."

"I'll help, too," Des said.

"Me, too," Mike added.

Damon was touched by their offer, and it got him thinking. A portion of the money they'd received from the VA had been designated as salary for his counseling services. If he reallocated all or a portion of that money to purchase chain-link fencing, they could build the pen. "Thanks. If money becomes available, you'll be the first to know."

Damon's phone vibrated in his pocket. He pulled it out and saw that his bank was calling.

"Excuse me. I have to take this."

He rose and went out on the porch, answering the phone as he did so.

"Hello?"

"Hi, Mr. Greyson. This is Sam Johnson from the loans department at First Dakota Bank. I'm happy to let you know that the committee has approved your loan."

Damon's relief was profound. He was one step

closer to his dream.

"Thank you. That's wonderful news."

They spoke a few minutes about signing papers and other details before saying goodbye. Damon returned to the kitchen.

"I got the loan," he announced. "We can finish the work on the Fletcher Building."

Everyone cheered and offered congratulations. Everyone but Charlotte, Damon noticed. She smiled, but he knew her and her smiles, and this one was forced. Did that mean she wasn't happy about the loan? She'd been a cheerleader for the veterans' retreat from the beginning. What had suddenly changed?

****

Charlotte's mind raced as she drove home with Damon and Chris. What was she to do? Damon was about to commit to a large debt, a debt that would affect his financial future for years to come. What if Clayton was somehow tricking him? She wished she had proof instead of simply a bad feeling.

She couldn't keep Damon in the dark. He deserved to know who he was dealing with. But the idea of telling him the truth, of seeing disappointment, or even disgust in his eyes, stopped her.

They dropped Chris at his house and headed home.

"You're quiet tonight," Damon said.

Charlotte glanced at him briefly before turning her attention back to the road. "Just tired, I guess."

"You didn't seem excited about the bank coming through with the loan."

She stared straight ahead. "I'm very excited about the veterans' retreat. You know that."

"Do I?"

"Yes! You're going to help a lot of people and a lot of animals. You're doing important work."

"Then why do I feel like you wish the bank had said no?"

They pulled into her driveway, and she turned off the ignition of the Jeep. She came up with a version of the truth. "I'm concerned about the debt you're taking on. A hundred and fifty thousand is a lot of money."

Damon reached over to grasp her hand. "I know. It scares me too. But it's going to be worth it. I want to make a difference, Charlotte. Think of all the veterans we're going to be able to help. That's what I came to Masonville to do."

"You're definitely going to make a difference," she whispered.

"I hope so. The retreat wasn't the only reason I came to Masonville. I want a home here. I spent a lot of years moving from place to place, not knowing where I belonged, but now I need to put down roots. I want to be close to my brother and sister and their families." He squeezed her hand. "And now that I've found you again, I want to be close to you, too."

He was such a good man. And an intelligent man, too. And so was Morley Walker. Damon had told her Morley had recommended Clayton's construction firm based on its reputation. Maybe she should trust that Clayton was on the up and up. At least as far as his construction company was concerned.

Charlotte brought his hand to her lips for a kiss. "I want to be close to you, too."

****

Three solid days of rain made taking the dogs out for their walks much more difficult. Pools of water

217

dotted the landscape and turned the farmyard to mud. Despite wearing rubber boots and a raincoat, it was impossible for Charlotte not to get wet and muddy. Worse, both dogs and humans were trailing a muddy mess into the barn. She and Des and Mike decided to close the doors of the barn and let the dogs run around inside instead. They could clean up any accidents by hosing down the concrete floor later.

Charlotte was feeding the dogs when her phone rang. Pulling it from her back pocket, she saw Gina was calling from the shelter.

"Hey, Gina. What's up?"

"For a change, I've got some good news for you. Remember the photos Sheila took of the puppies?"

"Sure. She came back twice to take more pictures."

"Well, you're never going to believe it, but once those pictures got on social media, the story went viral. People really connected with the story of Branson Farm and how veterans with PTSD are looking after dogs and horses that might otherwise have been put down. Every single puppy has already been adopted."

"What?"

"All the puppies have been spoken for. Once they're old enough, they'll go to good homes. Isn't that great?"

"That's amazing. We always figured the puppies would be adopted, but I didn't expect it to happen this quickly."

"Each new owner has agreed to pay for the first shots. But that's not even the best part!"

Charlotte heard the excitement in Gina's voice. "Okay, I'll bite. What's the best part?"

"There's a lot of interest in the mother dogs as

well. Someone has already spoken for Sally. Once she's completely recovered, she can go to her new forever home."

Charlotte was suddenly weepy. After everything Sally had been through, she deserved a good home where she'd be loved and cared for. "That's such great news, Gina."

"Sheila thinks that if we do profiles on each of the remaining dogs on social media, we'll be able to drum up interest for them too. And not just here in North Dakota. Apparently, the article the local paper wrote about Branson Farms and the rescue dogs was picked up by news agencies all over the country. People have been really struck by what you're trying to do. You need to check the online funding page. It's gone crazy."

She hadn't given the funding page a second thought since she heard it had been set up. "Really? Hang on, I have to see this for myself."

Charlotte ran to the other side of the barn where Des and Mike were changing the straw in Hope's stall. "Guys, can you get out a phone? We need to see this."

Gina read out the page's address while Mike punched it into his phone. When the page came up and they saw the number, none of them could speak. Over two million dollars had been raised.

Charlotte's first thought was that she had to tell Damon. He deserved to know how much people supported Branson Farm. How much they supported *him* and his ideas for veterans. Finally, Mike broke the silence.

"Holy cow!"

"We could build that dog run," Des said.

Charlotte shook her head in wonder. "We could

219

build a hundred dog runs!"

"See?" Gina exclaimed over the phone. "I told you it was amazing! Technically, the money was raised in the name of the shelter, but since Branson Farm is our satellite shelter, you can have money for whatever you need. We never would have been able to raise this kind of cash on our own. It's Branson Farm's story that has sparked such an outpouring."

"Thanks for letting us know, Gina. Keep that good news coming!"

She laughed. "I'll do my best. Talk to you soon."

Maybe this was a turning point, for the dogs and for her. Despite Clayton's presence in Masonville, he couldn't hurt her. He didn't want the truth to come out any more than she did. "Let's finish up here and tell the others the news. They're going to be blown away!"

Donning rain jackets, they ran laughing through the puddles and the pouring rain to the front porch and left their muddy boots outside on a rug. When they walked through the door, Charlotte was surprised that it was reserved Des who was first to blurt out their news.

"Guys! You're never going to guess what happened!"

Des and Mike excitedly told the others about the online fundraiser and showed them the amount on the website.

Damon looked at Mike's phone, then stared at Charlotte in confusion.

"Is this for real?"

"Totally and completely for real," Charlotte said. "People are behind what you're doing here, Damon. They want to help."

He shook his head in disbelief. "This is amazing."

"Does this mean we can build the dog run?" Ray asked.

"It sure does," Charlotte said. "It's going to be the most awesome dog run ever."

"And that's not even the best part," Des said. "All the puppies have been spoken for. And Sally, too."

Everyone cheered. Charlotte laughed. The excitement in their voices lifted her heart.

Garrett rubbed his hands together. "I think this calls for a celebration. Trey, do we have any cookies left?"

"You bet!"

"I'll put on some coffee," Chris said.

While the others were busy putting together an impromptu celebration, Damon took Charlotte's hand and looked into her eyes. "You're amazing."

"Me? You're the one who dreamed up Branson Farm. And everyone here has worked so hard."

"That's true, but you're the soul of this place. I'm glad you're here, Charlotte."

She loved him so much. Maybe now that things were beginning to look up, she could tell him how she felt. If she was brave enough.

"There's no place else I'd rather be."

They joined the others at the table and made silly toasts and clinked their coffee mugs together. It was so good to laugh, to have fun. It felt like forever to Charlotte since she'd had fun.

Damon's phone rang, disrupting the party. He frowned when he looked at the screen.

"What is it?" Charlotte asked.

"It's my contractor." Damon pushed back his chair and stood. "I have to take this."

The table went silent, the mood abruptly changing. They listened somberly to Damon's conversation.

"Hi, Clayton. What's up?"

He paced in a small circle, the phone to his ear. Finally, he stopped, his head bowed and shoulders slumped. "How are we just noticing this now?"

Charlotte heard the irritation in his voice, and the frustration, and knew there had to be another problem. From his dejected posture, it had to be a big one.

"How much to fix it?"

Charlotte glanced at her brother. Garrett appeared as concerned as she was. He reached over and squeezed her hand.

Just when they thought things were looking up.

Damon let out a defeated sigh, his head bowed. "If that's the case, I'm not sure the bank will loan me any more money."

He held the phone to his ear and listened as Clayton spoke. Damon straightened his back, anger etched on his face. "I'll be right over to have a look." He ended the call and swore.

Charlotte waited, along with the others, for Damon to tell them what was going on. He stood silently, rubbing his temple, then sighed and resumed his seat beside her again.

"There's about six inches of water in the basement right now. The leak only became apparent with all this rain. Clayton says there could be a number of causes, and they're trying to find the source."

"What does this mean for the completion of the building?" Mike asked.

"I don't know," Damon answered. "Worst-case scenario, the basement needs waterproofing around the exterior perimeter. That means they'll have to dig all the way around the outside of the building right down to the bottom of the foundation. They'll repair any cracks, then apply a coating of tar and a waterproof membrane to seal it. Once that's done, they can install new weeping tile in the trench to take away any groundwater, then refill it with dirt."

"Wait. Does that mean you'd have to dig up the sidewalk in front of the building?" Chris asked.

"Yeah. And the lane on the west side and the paved parking lot in the back. It was in good shape. I wasn't going to touch it."

Garrett asked the question on everyone's mind. "How much would this worst-case scenario cost?"

"It's too early to know for sure, but my contractor estimates it could be as much as two hundred and fifty thousand by the time we do all the repairs to the parking lot and the town property."

They sat in stunned silence. Finally, Des spoke.

"What are you going to do?"

"Right now, I'm going to town to see for myself. If the entire foundation needs to be dug up, I guess I'm going back to the bank. There's nothing else I can do. I'm in too deep to quit now." Damon got to his feet, his jaw clenched. "Granddad got taken. The seller took advantage of a sick old man who didn't understand what he was buying."

"I don't know, Damon." Garrett shook his head. "Blair and I were with Everett until the end, and if he lost a step mentally or intellectually, I didn't see it. He was as sharp as ever. You saw the video he made for his Will."

"Yeah. But then how do you explain all the

problems with the building?"

"I don't know. Maybe the previous owner didn't know about the problems either. Maybe they only became evident during renovation."

Or there could be another explanation, Charlotte thought. It could be that Clayton Brown was a crook.

Chapter Nineteen

Damon's heart dropped as they descended the basement stairs. The damp, musty smell and the humidity hit him first. The sound of a running motor grew louder. Then at the bottom of the stairs he saw the water covering the entire basement floor.

"How deep is it?" he asked.

"About six inches, maybe eight in low areas," Clayton replied.

Damon saw a hose snaking down from an open basement window and into the water. "So you've started pumping out the water."

"Yeah. We're pumping it directly into the town's storm sewer. We have to get the water out of here before it does some serious damage."

Damon glanced at one of the furnaces which sat in a pool of water. "It might already be too late."

Clayton nodded. "We'll have to get the furnaces inspected once the water is gone."

Damon followed Clayton into the basement, the water rising halfway up his rubber boots. "Why didn't the sump pump take the water away?"

The sump pump was supposed to automatically take away any excess water in situations like this, but it obviously hadn't in this case.

"We don't know yet. I have someone coming to take a look at it."

Dollar signs went off in Damon's head. "How much is that going to cost?"

"I can't say yet," Clayton replied. "All I know is that we don't have a choice but to fix it. Follow me. We think we found the source of the leak."

He followed Clayton into a storage room in the back corner of the basement. Clayton turned on his flashlight and illuminated one of the original block walls of the basement. A shelving unit stood in front of it.

"What am I looking at?" Damon asked.

Clayton moved closer to the wall and pointed out an area between two of the shelves. "See that crack there? That's the source of our leak."

Damon bent to examine it. A narrow crack ran down the wall, following the mortar between the old concrete blocks of the foundation in a stair-like pattern.

"I think the crack is growing," Clayton said. "There's tremendous pressure against this corner. If we don't dig out the perimeter of the foundation and make some repairs quickly, there's a possibility this corner could collapse."

"So now you're saying that not only is the foundation leaking, there's danger of a cave-in?"

"It's a definite possibility. We won't know for sure until we dig down and assess the damage."

"Maybe I should get a second opinion, perhaps a foundation expert."

Clayton shrugged. "Suit yourself. But if you're balking at the cost of sump pump repair, you're not going to be happy about what it's going to cost to hire a foundation expert."

Damon blew out a breath. He was between a rock

and a hard place. "How much is left of the money I last gave you, the money from the bank loan? Maybe we can divert some of it to this repair."

"Sorry, I've already spent that money on electrical repairs."

Damon made a quick decision. "Once the water's pumped out, all work on the building has to stop. I don't have the money to do the foundation work right now, and if you're saying there's danger of collapse, I can't have anyone working in here."

"Wait a minute—"

"That's my final word. Until I talk to the bank again and see if they're willing to loan me more money, I can't complete the work. I don't have any more money. Like I said, I want you to pump out the water and then leave the building."

"What about me and my crew? Are you planning to pay us?"

"You'll be paid for your work up to and including today, but that's it."

Clayton stepped toward him. Damon could see the anger in his eyes, even in the dull light of the storage room. "None of this is my fault. It's this damn old building."

Damon stood his ground and stared directly into Clayton's face, refusing to be intimidated. "Work stops on this building as soon as the water is pumped out. Is that clear?"

Clayton's jaw worked. "Crystal."

With that he pushed open the storage room door and left. Damon exhaled a pent-up breath, his senses on high alert. He wasn't sure he could trust his contractor any longer.

****

The following Monday Damon pulled up in front of the farmhouse and turned off the ignition. For a moment he sat behind the wheel and closed his eyes, not moving. His meeting with the bankers had been exhausting. They'd asked a lot of questions, mostly about his finances and his contract with the VA, but there were some questions that bordered on the personal. Why did he select Brown Construction? What was his relationship like with his general contractor? Had he conducted his own inspection of the building? Damon came away wondering if the loan officers suspected he was trying to somehow scam the bank.

Or did they suspect Clayton was trying to scam him?

The thought made him uneasy. And it made him feel stupid. He should have had an inspection done before he started work on the building.

With a sigh he got out of his truck. His heart lifted when he saw Charlotte walking across the yard toward him. She lifted her hand in a wave, and he waved back. God, he loved her. He wished she could feel the same way.

As Charlotte reached him, he resisted the urge to pull her into his arms and kiss her. The others were close by, and she'd made it clear she didn't want anyone to know they'd been sleeping together. Her denial of their relationship was a hurt to his soul. Did she not want anyone to know because of the sordid things that had happened to him as a child?

He dismissed the thought. Charlotte wasn't like that. Despite years of therapy, he still had a tendency to attribute the way people treated him to the sexual abuse perpetrated on him. Sometimes Damon felt like he wore a sign in flashing neon lights proclaiming "Victim" or "Unclean." It was something he'd been trying to get past for years.

"Hi," Charlotte said. "How did your meeting go?"

"Okay, I guess, though I couldn't get a read on whether they would extend another loan."

"It's so much money." Her brow was wrinkled in concern. "I hate to see you in so much debt. I know your grandfather didn't want that either."

"I know. Don't worry. It's going to be okay."

"So till you find out whether the bank will come through with another loan, you've stopped all work on the building?"

"Yeah. The crew's left." He allowed himself a brief touch to her hand. "Tonight, when we get home, will you come to my bed?"

"Yes, of course."

She answered without hesitation, her eyes clear. He knew she cared for him and wanted him physically.

If only it could be more.

****

On the pretense of going to Bismarck to buy dog food, Charlotte drove to Masonville instead and parked her Jeep around the corner from the coffee shop and walked to Damon's building. She wasn't sure what she could accomplish by coming here. She knew nothing about construction. Unless Clayton left a sign of cheating so obvious that even she could detect it, her trip here was pointless.

But she had to see the place for herself. She could look around at her leisure since all work had stopped on the building until Damon came up with more money.

If only she knew what she was looking for.

Charlotte walked around the building to the back door. The small parking lot at the back was empty, and no one was in the alley. She hoped Damon was too busy in counseling sessions this afternoon to notice that she'd "borrowed" his keys. Trying each key on the ring, she finally found the right one. She quickly slipped inside and locked the door behind her.

The back door opened to a small, dimly lit vestibule. There was a light switch next to the door, and she assumed the building had power, but she decided not to turn on the lights. The last thing she wanted was to have a concerned citizen alert the police that someone was lurking in the Fletcher Building when there wasn't supposed to be anyone there.

As her eyes grew accustomed to the dim light, Charlotte examined her surroundings. To her left she saw a door she believed led to the basement. On her right was a hallway leading to the front entrance of the building at street level. The staircase to the upper levels was opposite the front door. Charlotte decided to begin her exploration on the upper floors. Checking first to make sure no one was looking through the glass front doors, she hurried up the stairs.

She walked to the second floor on a wide staircase with beautiful wooden handrails and treads. Though new drywall had been hung in most of the rooms and hallways, it was nice to see that at least some of the original millwork remained. Charlotte loved the high ceilings and the tall windows that let in natural light.

This floor held community space with several large rooms that could be used for group counseling meetings or socializing and recreation. Another space fitted with partially assembled cabinets looked like it was going to be a communal kitchen. Nothing seemed out of place or wrong. She wasn't sure what she expected. If Clayton cheated Damon, it wasn't like he was going to tack up a note that said, "This is how I screwed over Damon Greyson."

With a sigh Charlotte returned to the stairs. The third floor was set up as a sort of dormitory with individual rooms, each with its own small bathroom. There was a larger space, overlooking the street, that was likely meant to be Damon's apartment. It wasn't huge, but the high ceilings and large windows made it appear bigger. Damon would be comfortable here.

The thought of Damon leaving her house unsettled her. She couldn't bear the thought of being alone again. Lauren had lived with her for a time after moving back to Masonville. Charlotte had loved having someone to cook with, spend evenings with, laugh with. After Lauren married Cole, learning to live by herself again had been difficult.

But when Damon moved out, it was going to feel like having her heart ripped from her chest. She couldn't breathe just thinking about not having him close.

What if you asked him to stay?

She wanted to, more than anything. But asking him to stay, committing to him, meant being honest. She'd have to tell Damon everything and let him decide whether he wanted to be with her. Charlotte wasn't sure she was brave enough to be that honest.

Mentally shaking herself, Charlotte headed for the stairs once more. She had a job to do. There was only one more space to check out—the basement. She descended the stairs and retraced her steps to the door that led to the basement. When she tried the knob, it turned in her hand and opened with a creak. Charlotte took a deep breath and began to descend the stairs.

The basement was dim, the only light from a couple of small windows at street level. Again, she opted not to switch on the lights. She pulled out her phone and activated the flashlight.

A musty smell permeated the basement, which made sense since Damon said there'd been six inches of water on the floor a couple of days ago. Charlotte shone her light on the floor. All the water had been pumped out, leaving only a few damp spots in the concrete.

She aimed her beam of light around the room. The basement mostly contained the building's mechanical components like the furnaces and hot water heaters. Exposed plumbing on the basement's old block wall looked like hookups for laundry equipment. Pipes of copper and plastic in different diameters ran along the ceiling joists. Several large black pipes ran vertically from the ceiling and disappeared into the concrete floor. Charlotte assumed they were sewage pipes, taking waste from the building and connecting to the town's main sewer line beneath the street. They looked new, which made sense since Damon had had to replace all the plumbing infrastructure in the building.

She moved her exploration into the interior of the basement. A motor suddenly came to life and Charlotte jumped, startled by the noise. *It's only the air-conditioning fan*, she told herself. Willing her heart to stop racing, she kept walking forward.

While the rest of the basement was wide open, in this area six storage rooms had been built. Charlotte opened the door to one of the rooms, shone her light inside, and saw that the walls were lined with empty shelves. She hadn't researched the history of the Fletcher Building, but as far as she remembered, it had always had businesses at street level and apartments on the second and third floors. The six storage rooms corresponded to the six businesses on the main level. The basement probably provided extra storage for those businesses.

Charlotte opened the door of the other storage rooms and peeked inside. All were empty and most were about the size of a small bedroom. Only the one in a corner of the basement appeared larger. She opened the door and stepped inside, shining her light around the room. This storage room was mostly the same as the others, aside from being larger and having two solid block walls instead of one like the rest of the rooms. She was about to leave when her attention was caught by something on the floor, in the corner. It looked like dirt, which wouldn't be terribly surprising in an old, musty basement. But on closer examination Charlotte realized the dirt had chunks in it. She picked up a tiny piece and shone her light on it. It appeared to be made of concrete or some such manmade material. And was that a fleck of white paint, the same color the block walls were painted?

Charlotte lifted her phone to illuminate the wall just above the debris. Behind the shelves she saw a large crack running down the wall in a staircase shape as it followed the grout between the old block foundation. She ran her fingers over the crack, measuring the size. Probably enough to let in water when it rained, though again there was no water on the floor.

The question was, had this crack occurred on its own because of the building's age and other natural causes, or had it been helped along by human intervention? Charlotte had no idea, but maybe she could bring her concerns to someone with expertise.

She took pictures of the crack and the dirt on the floor and left the claustrophobic confines of the storage room. There was only one space left, a small room in the opposite corner of the basement. The door to this room was unlocked. When she went inside, the door immediately closed behind her, plunging her into darkness and causing her heart to beat in alarm. Charlotte blew out a breath and forced herself to realize that the spring-loaded hinges of the door made it close so quickly. No one was trying to trap her in here.

She shone the light of her phone around the tiny room and realized this was where the sump pump was housed. Damon said the sump pump had failed to take away the water that had leaked into the basement, causing the flood.

Charlotte saw some tools on the floor. A hammer, a chisel, and three different kinds of wrenches lay next to the sump pump. Was someone trying to fix it? Why would they leave their tools?

After taking some pictures, she was anxious to leave. Being in the Fletcher Building alone, especially in the basement, gave her the creeps. She left the dark confines of the room, hurried across the basement floor, and ran up the stairs. Just as she was about to open the back door of the building and escape to the safety of her Jeep, it swung open, revealing a man on the other side. Charlotte suppressed a scream.

"Charlotte Saunders? What are you doing here?"

Clayton Brown entered the building and closed the door behind him. He carried a large black toolbox in his left hand. She did her best to keep her voice level and sound relatively calm.

"Just looking around."

"How did you get in?"

"I borrowed the key. My brother and sister-in-law are part of this venture. We wanted to see how much progress has been made."

Clayton blocked her only escape route. "This is a small town, Charlotte. I heard you and Damon Greyson are sleeping together. Did he send you here?"

He put a sneer in his voice that made her relationship with Damon sound dirty.

"Of course not." She shone the flashlight of her phone in his face. "How did *you* get in? And why are you here? Work has stopped on the building."

"I'm the general contractor. I have a key, of course. I wanted to check on the basement. If it rains again, there could be another flood."

On the surface it sounded reasonable. But she knew better than most that Clayton couldn't be trusted. She took a step forward.

"Get out of my way, Clayton."

He stood his ground and gave her a leering grin. "What's your rush? Why don't you stay a while? We could grab a drink and get reacquainted, for old time's sake."

His words caused the anger she'd bottled inside for ten years to explode out of her. "Old time's sake? You raped me, Clayton. You held me down and forced yourself into my body while I screamed at you to stop.

You're nothing but a rapist."

With one hand, she pushed hard at the middle of his chest, making him stagger back a step and causing the toolbox to crash against the wall behind him. The move surprised him enough for her to open the door. But she wasn't fast enough to make her escape. Before she could get out the door, he grabbed her wrist with one hand and squeezed.

"If you start spreading that story, no one is going to believe you. I'm a respected businessman, and you're nothing but a tramp who sleeps around. Why would anyone believe a whore like you?"

For one moment Charlotte was nineteen again and Clayton was looming over her, telling her she wanted it, and if she didn't it was her own fault for teasing him with her short skirts and lowcut shirts. She was asking for it. She was nothing but a whore.

No! No, not again. I won't let him put the blame on me again.

Charlotte broke Clayton's hold on her wrist with a quick thrust and fled through the door. As she ran across the parking lot, she dared a glance behind her to see if he was chasing her. She almost fainted with relief when he wasn't. She continued to run down the street, not stopping until she got to her Jeep. When she was safe inside with the doors locked, she started shaking. Her heart hammered, the beats reverberating inside her head.

It wasn't until her breathing calmed that she realized Clayton's truck hadn't been in the parking lot behind the Fletcher Building. If he'd come to the building to legitimately check on leakage, as he claimed, he'd have no reason to hide the fact. Instead, he'd parked a distance away—for the same reason she had. He didn't want anyone to know he was there.

As Charlotte put the Jeep in gear and drove away, she considered what that meant. Clayton was up to no good, and she couldn't be silent any longer.

Her stomach flipped over at the thought.

****

By the time Damon got to Charlotte's house after dropping off Chris, her Jeep was already parked in the driveway. He parked behind the Jeep and turned off the ignition. Something was wrong. He'd sensed it when she returned to the farm this afternoon. He'd asked where she'd gone, but only got a vague answer about running errands. He hadn't pressed her on it. He had no right to question where she went or what she did.

Was she getting ready to ask him to leave?

Damon squeezed his eyes shut, trying to block the question from his mind. But if she no longer wanted him, there was nothing he could do. With a sigh, he opened the truck door and headed to the house.

Charlotte was waiting for him in the living room. She stood as he entered the room, her hands clasped in front of her, her face pale and tense.

"I need to tell you something."

He nodded, his heart sinking. "Whatever you want to say, it's all right."

She exhaled, and began, her voice barely above a whisper. "When I was nineteen and in my second year of college, I was raped."

Damon's legs turned to jelly, and he abruptly sat. This wasn't what he'd expected her to say right now. Sure, he'd known, but hearing her say the words was another thing entirely. He called on all his training as a counselor to stay calm and listen, because this wasn't about him. This was Charlotte's story.

"Can you tell me what happened?"

She began pacing. River paced with her, then stopped and looked up at her with a whine as he picked up on her anxiety.

"I was a party girl," she said. "I was away from home for the first time, and I was determined to fully experience college life. That meant going to parties and flirting with guys and drinking too much. I wanted to have fun."

"There's nothing wrong with wanting to have fun."

The look she gave him was bleak. "I was too stupid and naïve to know that flirting had consequences."

"This isn't on you, Charlotte. Rape is about power and control. The rapist is at fault, not you."

She attempted a smile. "I know that in my head, but my heart is still having trouble with that idea. The truth is, I enjoyed the attention I got from men. My parents had kept a close watch on me at home, so when I went away to nursing school, it was like I'd been set free.

"I went to parties with friends most weekends, mostly on campus. I'd run into this one guy a few times, and I flirted outrageously with him because I thought he was cute. He flirted back. But he never asked me out. I thought it was because he was on the university hockey team and they often played out of town. They had curfews their coach expected them to follow, so he and his friends had to leave the parties early sometimes.

"Then one weekend my friend and I were invited to a party off campus. Turns out the party was thrown by someone on the hockey team. It started off the same as most parties. There was music and dancing and a lot of drinking. I admit I did my share. I was thrilled when the cute guy I'd been flirting with showed up. I thought he was finally going to ask me out.

"At first, he seemed nice, and I let him kiss me, touch me. But as the night wore on, he became more aggressive and demanding. He started to scare me. I told him I wanted to go home, and I called a cab. He got angry and grabbed me. He said I'd been teasing him for weeks, and he was going to give me what I was asking for. I wish I would have been so drunk I couldn't remember."

Damon had to touch her, to comfort. He rose and put his arms around her. She leaned into his embrace for a few brief moments before pulling away.

"I…I have to finish my story before I lose my nerve."

Damon nodded and sat once more. Why was she telling him this story today? What had happened?

"I told him no. I tried to fight him, but he was too strong, and he didn't care that I didn't want this. He pulled up my skirt, ripped off my tights, and raped me."

The pain and humiliation he saw on Charlotte's face nearly undid him. Telling him this story was unbearable for her. Cold, calculating anger took over. He wanted to make that nameless man pay for what he did to her. He wanted to hurt him. He wanted to hurt him bad.

"I never told anyone. Not my friends, my sister, my parents. You're the first person I've ever told any details."

He had to calm himself. She needed him to be

strong for her.

"I'm glad you told me. I hope you can get some measure of relief by speaking about it."

Her face twisted as she held back tears. "I didn't tell you this to give myself relief. If it only affected me, I would have gone to my grave with this secret. But there's something you need to know. The man who raped me was Clayton Brown."

Damon stared at her, stunned, uncomprehending. Clayton Brown? His contractor, Clayton Brown, raped Charlotte?

"With all the problems at your building, I was afraid he was responsible, but I had no proof. So this afternoon I went over there to look around."

"What? How did you get in?"

"I, hmm, borrowed your keys." She waved her hand. "But that's not the point. I found a spot in the basement that looks like it may have been tampered with. When I was about to leave, Clayton showed up. He said he was there to check for leaks in the basement, but the basement was fine. There was no water."

Damon's head was spinning from an overload of information. "Wait. Clayton was at my building? This afternoon?"

"Yes. He wasn't supposed to be there, since all work has stopped, right?"

"Did he touch you?"

She avoided his eyes, bending to scratch Daisy's ears instead. "I can look after myself, Damon."

"Charlotte, did he touch you?"

She sighed. "He grabbed my wrist and told me not to tell you about the rape. He said you wouldn't believe me anyway. It was nothing—"

"Like hell it was nothing!"

Rage roared through his body. He'd make him pay. He'd damn well make him pay.

I'll kill the bastard.

Damon rose and headed to the door.

"Damon, what are you doing?"

"I'm going to have a few words with Clayton Brown."

Charlotte pulled on his arm. "No! I don't need you fighting my battles for me."

He shook her off. "This is my battle now." No one hurt the woman he loved.

"No! Stop! Damon, listen. I told you this story because I think he may be cheating you. We have to catch him in the act and stop him."

Damon reached for the doorknob. "I don't care about the damn building." All he wanted was the satisfaction of beating Clayton's face to a bloody pulp.

"No!"

The next thing he knew, his feet were pulled out from under him and he was flat on his face on the floor. Charlotte sat on him and twisted his arm behind his back.

"I really don't want to hurt you, Damon, but I will if you don't calm down."

He struggled, but she tightened her hold, painfully wrenching his arm. "Let me go, Charlotte."

"If you beat him up, it may satisfy you for a short time. But he'll have gotten away with raping me and cheating you. And you'll probably land in jail. Do you want that? Or do you want him to face the consequences?"

She was right. Beating the crap out of Clayton

would be momentarily satisfying for him, but it wouldn't help Charlotte.

"Okay, I'm listening. Can I get up now?"

She released his arm and got off his back. Damon dragged himself to his feet and rubbed his arm.

"Damn, girl. You don't know your own strength."

She gave him a tremulous smile. "That's what you get for being a hothead."

"I'm sorry. I guess I went a little crazy. The idea of you being hurt…" He couldn't finish.

Her smile suddenly turned to tears. "I'm sorry. I didn't want to upset you. And I was afraid you'd be hurt if you went after Clayton."

Damon wrapped his arms around her and held her close. "How do you know he wasn't the one who'd get hurt?"

She wrapped her arms around his waist and sniffed against his chest. "Yes, I should have more faith in you."

Damon leaned back and lifted her chin so he could look in her eyes. "Charlotte, I love you. You telling me this makes no difference. I'll always love you."

She nodded silently. Her eyes flooded with tears and she pressed her face against his chest once more. Damon held her, his heart heavy. She'd never said she loved him too. He wondered if she ever could.

Chapter Twenty

"Do you still want to come with me to Ben's office and tell them what you found?" Damon asked.

The previous evening he'd phoned his brother and told him he had reason to believe Clayton was cheating him. Ben suggested they get together with Morley to figure out next steps.

Charlotte hesitated, indecision in her eyes. "Do we have to tell them the whole story?"

Damon tenderly brushed her hair from her forehead. "Of course not. We can just say you knew Clayton in the past."

She closed her eyes, anguish written on her face. "I feel like such a coward."

"Not a chance. You're the bravest person I know."

"I should have told you right away, as soon as I found out Clayton was your contractor. But I was afraid."

"Were you afraid of him?"

Charlotte looked directly into his eyes. "I was afraid of you. Afraid of what you'd think of me."

"What Clayton said about me not believing you—it's total crap. I believe everything about you, Charlotte. I believe in you."

Her gaze softened as she laid her hand on his cheek. "I believe in you, too."

Damon wished they could stay together like this all

day, but they had work to do. He laid his hand over hers. "Come on. I told Ben we'd meet him at nine."

They drove the Jeep the short distance to Ben and Morley's office and parked in front. Damon turned to Charlotte. "It's not too late to change your mind. They already know I'm suspicious of Clayton because of all the cost overruns. You don't have to be involved at all."

"I want to be involved. I need to speak up this time." Her eyes were steady and determined. "Let's go."

Ben and Morley's assistant Carmen greeted them in the outer office. "Can I get you some coffee?"

"Not for me, thank you," Charlotte said.

"I'll have coffee, please," Damon said. "Where's everyone?"

Carmen poured coffee into a mug. "Ben is on the phone in his office right now, and Morley should be here any minute. Do you take anything in your coffee?"

"Black's fine. Thank you."

Carmen passed him the mug and indicated some chairs in the waiting area. "Why don't you have a seat? It shouldn't be long."

They sat, and Carmen went back to her desk. Charlotte tapped her fingers against her thigh, her body vibrating. Damon took her restless hand in his and squeezed. He wanted to let her know he was on her side, no matter what. She smiled tentatively, as if to tell him she was okay.

Damon wished he was. He was keeping it together for her sake, but it was hard. He was worried about Charlotte. No one knew better than he did the devastation of sexual assault. And he also knew that staying silent only made the toll greater. Charlotte had stayed silent for ten years. Had she been punishing herself?

Morley opened the front door and entered with a man who looked to be in his mid-thirties. Judging by the work boots he wore, Damon guessed he was in construction.

Both he and Charlotte rose from their seats. Damon extended his hand.

"Morley, thank you for meeting with us."

"It's my pleasure. I'd like you to meet Jeff Burns. His dad and I are old friends. Jeff's made time out of his busy day to speak with us."

Damon shook Jeff's hand. "I appreciate your help."

Jeff grinned. "Morley has helped me and my dad with company business on numerous occasions, so I'm happy to repay the favor."

Damon put his hand on the small of Charlotte's back as he introduced her. "This is my friend Charlotte Saunders."

As they were shaking hands, Ben opened his office door and stepped out. "Sorry to make you wait. Why don't we go into Morley's office and talk?"

Once chairs had been found for everyone and more coffee poured, Morley sat behind his desk. "Jeff, I know we were a little vague about why we asked you here. We need your expertise. We're concerned that Damon's contractor may be fabricating problems with his building as a way of extorting money from him. Damon, can you give Jeff a rundown of what's happened since you began renovations?"

"Sure." Damon went through the whole saga, from hiring Clayton's construction company on Morley's recommendation, to the constant problems and cost overruns. He finished with Clayton's last bombshell, the need to waterproof the basement by digging around the entire foundation and the threat of a cave-in. "When Clayton told me about the leak, I went over there. There was at least six inches of water in the basement. I had to stop work on the project because I don't have the money to carry on. And if the building really is dangerous, I can't have workers in it."

Jeff nodded. "I know this building. It's over a hundred years old, so it's possible it has multiple problems."

"True," Morley said, "but when Damon's grandfather purchased the building, he was told the electrical and plumbing had been upgraded. I just heard from the building's former owner. He swears he upgraded plumbing and electrical systems five years ago and is prepared to produce invoices to support that claim. It seems clear Brown lied about those repairs, and it makes me question whether other repairs he made were legitimate. We need someone with your expertise to look around and tell us if Damon was gouged."

Jeff shook his head. The expression on his face appeared skeptical to Damon. "It might be difficult to determine at this point. Changes could have been made to cover up any wrongdoing. I specialize in residential construction, but if you want me to, I'll take a look. I've heard rumors about Brown Construction lately. Things haven't been the same since Oliver Brown died. He was known for his company's high standards. But since his grandson took over, I've heard those high standards have slipped."

"I wish I'd heard those rumors before I

recommended the company to Damon," Morley said, shaking his head.

"It's not your fault, Morley. The company had a stellar reputation at one point. I checked it out myself," Damon said.

"I should have warned Damon earlier." Charlotte spoke quietly as she clutched her hands in her lap, her head down. "I knew Clayton in college. He's not someone who can be trusted."

It killed him that she was blaming herself. "Charlotte—"

"I went to the building yesterday and looked around. I don't know anything about construction, but I did see a crack in the foundation block wall." She pulled out her phone and scrolled to the pictures she'd taken before passing it to Damon. She'd shown him the pictures last night after making her confession. He glanced at the image of the foundation wall once again before passing it to Ben, his blood boiling all over again.

"Clayton showed this crack to me the day before yesterday, but it was much smaller then. Does this mean the wall is crumbling?"

"Hard to say." Jeff turned to Charlotte. "Was there still water on the basement floor?"

Charlotte shook her head. "No, it was musty-smelling, and the floor was damp in places, but the standing water was gone. Maybe someone fixed the sump pump. There were tools near it when I was there."

"No, Clayton used a portable gas pump to get rid of the water in the basement because he said the sump pump wasn't working. A repairman is supposed to take a look at the sump pump in the next few days. No one should have touched it, and there shouldn't be any tools lying around," Damon said as he passed her phone back to her. "Can you show everyone the pictures you took yesterday?"

"Yes." Charlotte scrolled through her pictures once again before handing her phone to Damon. "That's what I saw."

Damon enlarged the picture with his thumb and forefinger. "I'm no expert, but why would you need a chisel to fix a sump pump?"

"You wouldn't. Can I see?"

Damon handed the phone to Jeff, and he looked through Charlotte's photos. "This doesn't make much sense. A chisel wouldn't be of much use unless you were trying to *destroy* the sump pump."

"My money's on Clayton Brown being a crook," Ben said. "Too many things happened that shouldn't have."

"He was there." Charlotte's face was pale. "Clayton showed up as I was leaving."

"Did he say why he was there?" Ben asked.

"He said he was there to make sure no more water got into the basement."

"I suppose that's reasonable," Jeff said.

"He didn't park his truck in the lot behind the building or on the street in front. He didn't want anyone to know he was there." Charlotte looked into Damon's eyes. "I just remembered. He had a toolkit in his hand. It hit the wall behind him when I pushed him."

Damon's fist clenched. She'd had to push Clayton to make her escape. What would he have done to her if she hadn't been able to defend herself? He didn't want to think about it.

Charlotte laid her hand over his. "Maybe you should tell Ben about the phone calls you've received."

Ben's eyebrows rose. "Phone calls?"

Damon hadn't wanted to worry Ben, but maybe now was the time to bring Peter's calls out into the open. "Dad's called me a couple of times. He said he's heard Victoria speaking to someone about me, and he was going to try to get more information, but I haven't heard from him in several weeks."

Ben's face turned stony. "If Victoria is somehow involved in this…"

Morley picked up his thought. "Then it makes sense that Damon is bleeding money." Morley turned to Jeff with an apologetic smile. "Sorry. Family business. We can't wait. Do you have time right now to accompany us to the Fletcher Building and look around?"

Jeff nodded. "Of course. If there's a problem, I want to get to the bottom of it. Cheats like Brown give a bad name to the whole construction industry."

They walked the short distance to the Fletcher Building. Damon unlocked the front door and turned on the lights.

"Might as well start right here," Jeff said. He took a screwdriver from the toolbox he'd brought with him and unscrewed the cover plate. A bundle of wires was contained within the metal box behind the cover plate.

Jeff examined it closely. "The wiring is done correctly and it looks new."

"Makes sense, since I paid to rewire the whole place," Damon said. "I was shown old cloth-covered wiring and told it was a fire hazard."

"Old wiring like that *is* a fire hazard. If the work

had already been done and Brown wanted to scam you, he could have replaced the new wiring with some old knob-and-tube in one small area so he could convince you the whole building had to be rewired."

The thought of falling prey to such deception made Damon feel stupid and gullible. It made him angry, too. He'd depended on Clayton's expertise, and the man had used it against him.

"Let's check the basement," Damon said.

They headed to the door leading to the basement. Damon turned on the lights and led the way down the stairs. The musty, damp smell grew stronger with each step. Charlotte had been right. The standing water was gone, but the dampness remained. Damon hoped it wasn't breeding mold.

Jeff must have had the same thought. "You'll want to get dehumidifiers in here right away. I know a company that will rent you industrial strength dehumidifiers. I'll text you their phone number."

"Thanks. I appreciate the help."

If Clayton had been an honest general contractor, he would have offered solid advice and help, too. But it was becoming increasingly clear that Clayton was anything but honest.

At the bottom of the stairs, Jeff turned to Damon. "Let's take a look at the sump pump first."

Damon nodded and led the way to the enclosure where the sump pump was housed. Jeff went inside while Damon held open the door and shone the flashlight of his phone inside.

"The tools Charlotte photographed are gone," Jeff said.

"Brown likely took them with him when he left,"

Ben observed. "What does the damage to the sump pump look like?"

"I can't be sure," Jeff said as he shone his light over the pump, "but I think something's been jammed inside the motor. You'll need a second opinion, but it's probably inoperable."

Damon shook his head. *One more problem.*

Jeff came out of the enclosure. "Can you show me where you saw the crack in the wall?"

Charlotte led the way to the last storage room and pointed to the door.

"In this room."

They crowded inside, and Jeff shone his flashlight against the wall, then reached out to touch the crack.

"Here it is." He ran his fingers up and down its length. "The edges feel sharp, as if a tool was used to make it. But the good news is that I don't think it's deep enough to go through the whole foundation. I don't see any evidence that the foundation is crumbling, but you'd have to talk to a foundation expert to be sure."

Charlotte moved closer and touched the crack. "The crack is bigger than it was yesterday, I'm sure of it." She pulled out her phone and scrolled through her pictures. "Look. The picture's not real clear, but I think it shows a difference in size."

"I think you're right," Jeff agreed.

"And the dirt on the floor is gone," she said. "Clayton must have cleaned up before he left."

Damon took the phone from her and compared the picture to the wall. The difference was subtle, but it was there.

"If the crack doesn't go far enough through the

foundation to actually cause the leak, why bother making it bigger?" Damon asked.

"My guess is that his plan is to contact you and say he's been monitoring the foundation and the crack is getting worse. He'll tell you that if you don't act right away the results will be dire."

Ben shook his head. "How did he know it was going to rain enough to let in six inches of standing water?"

Jeff shrugged. "My guess is that it was probably a spur-of-the-moment thing. He took advantage of all that rain to create the flood. Maybe he turned off the power to the sump pump so it couldn't take the water away. His plan all along was likely to convince Damon of the foundation's instability, and the rain played nicely into that. He showed Damon the crack he'd created and told him, 'This is what caused your flood. The foundation is shot, and we have to spend all this money to fix it.' "

"He was faking it. He was faking everything." Rage poured through Damon, most of it directed at himself. How could he have been stupid enough to believe Clayton's lies? What else did he miss because his contractor took advantage of his ignorance?

"But he said he was going to dig up the sidewalk and the parking lot," Ben persisted. "If he didn't do the work, we'd certainly notice. How did he expect to get away with it?"

"There are numerous ways to cheat a client. With the electrical, like I said, he could have shown you some old knob-and-tube wiring he strung up to convince you to rewire the whole place. Same with the plumbing. Maybe he does the work but overcharges you for material and labor he didn't use, or he uses lower-grade material and unskilled labor and charges a premium for it. Maybe he doesn't pay his subcontractors and leaves you to pick up the tab. Or maybe he starts the project, but once he has most of your money, he skips town and leaves you to clean up the mess."

Morley sighed. "Let's check around some more."

They examined the entire building. Damon noted that the cupboards in the kitchen and the fittings in the bathrooms were of a cheaper quality than what he'd wanted and had paid for. When they went onto the roof, Jeff pointed out that a repair had been done to the flat roof to stop leaking, but it wasn't recent. It likely had been completed before his grandfather bought the building.

"There was water pooling up here when Clayton showed me the roof. He told me the pitch of the roof needed to be changed so the water could drain," Damon said. "I saw the damage on the ceiling below."

"Damage can be faked," Jeff said. "He likely made the water pool by plugging the scupper, the hole that leads to the eavestrough and lets water drain. Then he charged you for a full roof repair and did nothing more than patch the drywall on the ceiling below."

With every passing minute, Damon felt more and more stupid. His grandfather would be disappointed in him. Somehow that hurt most of all.

Ben took pictures of the roof. "I think we have enough evidence to break Damon's contract with Brown Construction. I don't know if it's enough to convince the police to lay charges, but it might be enough to sue Brown in civil court."

"I agree. Let's go back to the office and figure out

where we go from here," Morley said.

Outside the office, they said goodbye to Jeff, and he left with a promise to come back if they needed more help. Before they entered the office, Damon's phone rang, and he saw his father's name on the screen.

"Hang on." Damon's gut twisted as his eyes met his brother's. "Peter's calling."

Ben nodded solemnly. "Let's see what he has to say."

Damon accepted the call and put it on speaker phone. "Peter?"

"Damon, son. It's good to hear your voice."

He sounded strange, like he was barely awake, or perhaps ill.

Or drunk.

For a short time, Damon had let himself hope that Peter had changed. He was unprepared for the disappointment that swamped him at having that hope dashed.

"Why are you calling, Peter?"

"I need to warn you." There was a slur in Peter's words. "I picked up the phone when Victoria was talking to someone named Clayton. Do you know someone with that name?"

"I do," Damon said. Charlotte put her hand in his. The warmth of her touch gave him strength.

"This Clayton person said all work had stopped on your building and there wasn't any more money to be milked out of you. Victoria was furious."

Peter groaned, and then went silent. Damon could hear background noises with people talking and a low hum that sounded like an engine.

"Peter? Are you still there?"

"I'm here." The whispered reply was faint. "Victoria threatened him. She said if he didn't get her another fifty thousand in the next five days, she'd make public the evidence she has on him, and he would lose everything."

It concerned Damon that both Clayton and Victoria were growing more desperate. "What's the evidence she has on him?"

"She didn't say. Victoria told him to use his imagination to get the money. She said that you're living with a woman named Charlotte. Maybe there was some way to use her to get money from Damon."

Charlotte gasped. Ben put his hand on his shoulder. Damon swallowed back the anger.

"What did Clayton say to that?"

"That's all I heard. Victoria realized I was listening on the other line. We got into a struggle, and I fell down some stairs."

"What? Are you all right?"

"I'm…I think my arm is broken."

Peter was injured, not drunk. Damon squeezed his eyes shut, feeling guilty for believing the worst of him. "Where are you?"

"I'm on a bus, headed to Bismarck. Do you think you can pick me up? The bus is supposed to arrive there this evening."

"Yes, of course. We'll be there."

Damon saved Peter's phone number. When he looked up, Morley was shaking his head. "I never thought I'd say this, but I'm glad Everett isn't here to witness this. He'd be horrified at what his daughter's become."

Although he missed his grandfather fiercely, he

had to agree. His mother was sick, and quite possibly dangerous.

He looked at Charlotte's hand tucked into his. She didn't deserve this. She shouldn't have to be in the middle of this fight. He didn't want any of this mess to touch her.

And he was afraid for her. Somehow, Victoria knew her name and that they were living together. That made her a target. He couldn't let anything happen to her. He'd die before he'd let anything happen to Charlotte.

Ben clapped his shoulder. "Let's go inside and talk."

"Wait."

Ben held the door open, looking at him expectantly. Damon cleared his throat before turning to face Charlotte.

"It's time for you to leave."

She shook her head, confusion in her eyes. "Why? I want to help."

He dropped her hand. "No. I don't want your help. I'm moving out of your house today."

"Why? Why are you saying this?" She tried to touch him but he backed away. "Please, Damon. Don't do this."

Damon steeled himself against her pleas. Charlotte's safety was too important.

"I don't want you here." He hated what he was about to say next. "I don't have time to babysit you and worry that you'll do something stupid again, like going into an empty building on your own. Leave, Charlotte!"

She sucked in a breath, the hurt in her eyes so intense he had to look away. He told himself it was better this way, that it was for her own good.

"Go to Branson Farm or to your parents' place for the rest of the afternoon. I'll pick up my things at your house while you're gone."

She clasped her hands in front of her, her body straight and stiff and her face now devoid of expression. "If that's what you want."

Without another word, she got in her Jeep and left. Damon watched, his heart going with her.

Ben's voice broke into his thoughts. "Damon, what the hell are you doing?"

"I'm doing what I have to do to keep her safe."

Ben pulled him inside, and Morley followed. Carmen looked up in concern as they entered the office.

"You sure about that? Maybe you're protecting yourself because this whole thing suddenly got too real."

"Don't tell me how I feel." He was dying inside. *Dear God.* He'd sent Charlotte away.

"I know how crazy Victoria can make a person. I almost ran so I could get her out of my life. If I'd disappeared with my girls, I would have lost everything—my children, my brother and sister, and especially Jamie. I didn't think I had a choice, but you helped me find another way to deal with Victoria. And I know we'll find another way for you, too."

Damon looked his brother in the eye. "It's better this way. I don't want to put Charlotte in the middle of this mess. It's too dangerous. She's better off without me."

"Damon—"

"Don't." His composure hung by a thread. It was going to break any second. "Please. Don't say anything

257

more."

"Why don't we talk in my office?" Morley said. "We'll figure out what to do next."

"I have to go. I have to pick up my stuff, my truck."

"I'll come with you," Ben said. "You can stay at my house."

Damon nodded. He didn't have much choice about where to go.

"Once we get you packed up, I'll check the bus schedule and find out what time Peter gets to Bismarck," Ben said. "We'll pick him up there later."

Damon nodded again. He was glad Ben was coming with him to Bismarck, because he didn't have the strength to deal with their father right now.

They were silent as Ben drove them to Charlotte's house. Damon stared out the side window. He was stupid to have thought he could have a normal relationship with her. His damage was deep and irreparable. For a brief, happy time, he'd let himself forget that, but his parents had been only too happy to remind him.

Chapter Twenty-One

After leaving Morley's office, Charlotte picked up
her dogs at her house and drove aimlessly for over an
hour. She couldn't go to Branson Farm and face
questions from everyone there. Their concern would be
genuine, but she was afraid she'd break down in front
of them. Visiting her parents was out for the same
reason. Charlotte didn't want to cause her mother any
upset.

The only person she knew she could talk to
honestly was her sister. Having gone through a difficult
relationship with her first husband, and a rocky start to
her marriage with Cole, Lauren would listen without
judgment. After holding things inside for so long,
Charlotte desperately needed to talk. She hoped Lauren
wasn't at work today.

She pulled over to the side of the road and called
Lauren's cell phone. Her sister answered after a couple
of rings.

"Hi, Charlotte. What's up?"

"I—"

She couldn't speak. Her throat clogged with tears,
and she was overcome with anguish.

"Charlotte, honey, what's wrong?"

She tried again. "I…Damon…" Tears spilled down
her cheeks.

"Charlotte, I'm home this afternoon, and Piper is

napping right now. Why don't you come over?"

She managed a reply. "Okay."

Charlotte was at Lauren's door with her dogs in ten minutes. Lauren took one look at her and pulled her into her arms.

"Oh, honey."

For the first time, Charlotte let her pain flow with her tears. She'd thought she and Damon had something. He'd told her he loved her. If that were true, how could he leave her so easily?

She cried until she was too tired to cry anymore. Lauren handed her a couple of tissues, and while Charlotte blew her nose, her sister made tea and put a cup in front of her.

"Tell me what happened."

Charlotte told her the whole story—how Clayton was extorting money from Damon by faking problems with his building, and how Damon's father had overheard Clayton and Victoria's conversation about her.

Lauren's eyes widened. "They mentioned you by name?"

"Somehow, she found out that Damon and I were living together." Charlotte dabbed at her eyes with her sodden tissue as fresh tears started. "It didn't start out that way. I offered Damon a place to stay while his apartment was being completed. And then it turned into something more." She didn't mention she hadn't wanted to be alone after discovering Clayton was in the area.

"Do you love him?" Lauren asked gently.

Charlotte squeezed her eyes shut and nodded. "Yes."

"Did you tell him?"

"No." She wondered if it would have made a difference. "He said he loved me, but that didn't stop him from leaving me."

"Do you think he meant it? That he loves you, I mean."

Charlotte remembered the look in eyes when he told her he loved her. He'd made her believe she was worth loving. And worth forgiving.

"Yes. He meant it. That's why his leaving hurts so much."

"I don't understand. If he loves you, why push you away?"

Charlotte sipped her tea. If she pushed the hurt aside, she could see more clearly.

"I think he's trying to protect me."

"Protect you from what?"

"His family—actually his mother. She's…" Charlotte wasn't sure how to describe Victoria Grayson. "Damon calls her a sociopath."

Lauren's eyes widened. "A sociopath?"

"He has good reason to say that. He had a very difficult childhood."

"He doesn't really think she could be dangerous, does he? I mean, she wouldn't hurt you, would she?"

Charlotte had no idea what Victoria Greyson was capable of. But she didn't want to scare Lauren. "No, I think she's more dangerous psychologically than physically. She's certainly hurt her children."

"I got the impression last summer at Everett Branson's funeral that Victoria wasn't the warm and fuzzy type. She didn't seem affected by her father's death at all. Maybe Damon is embarrassed by her."

Charlotte knew Damon's feelings about his mother went far deeper than embarrassment. Had lingering shame because of the sexual abuse he'd suffered as a child caused him to pull away? He'd told her he'd worked hard through counseling to put it behind him.

Like the way you put the rape and its aftermath behind you, Charlotte? She still hadn't told him the whole truth. Her heart pounded at the thought of being completely honest with him.

Or maybe Damon had simply grown tired of her. She had to be prepared to accept that possibility. Yet when she remembered the tenderness of his touch and the passion of his lovemaking, she was sure he still had feelings for her.

"I've never heard Blair speak about her parents," Lauren said. "She must feel the same way about them as Damon does."

"Yeah." Damon's father was on his way to Masonville. She wondered what that meant for him.

Charlotte sipped her tea. Through the baby monitor, they heard Piper babbling to herself. Lauren went to check on her, leaving Charlotte alone to reflect. If Damon had pushed her away in a misguided effort to protect her, she could understand. And forgive.

She needed to be patient. Damon was worth waiting for. And fighting for.

****

Damon's knee bounced up and down, refusing to be still. He hated waiting. He and Ben sat in the Bismarck bus depot, waiting for the arrival of the bus from Minneapolis that would deliver their father.

"Do you think he'll be drunk when he gets here?" Ben asked.

Ben clasped his hands together, his face drawn. Damon put aside his own worries to concentrate on his brother. Ben had inherited their father's alcoholism, though he'd been able to keep it under control for several years. Bringing Peter into their lives meant Ben had to face the possibility he could relapse the way Peter had so many times.

"I don't know for sure. The last time I talked to him, he told me he was abstaining. He said he was going to AA as often as he could. I guess we'll see when he gets here."

Ben hung his head. "Yeah, I guess so."

"You're not Peter, Ben. You may share the same disease, but you haven't handled it the same way. You've got a great support system to help if you need us. Me and Blair and Garrett and Morley. And don't forget Jamie." It occurred to Damon that Peter didn't have a similar support system to back him up.

Ben looked up at Damon with a grin. "I could never forget Jamie. She's everything."

A sharp pang of regret hit Damon in the chest. Charlotte was his everything. Now that he'd sent her away, he had no idea how he was supposed to go on.

He stiffened his resolve. He couldn't let her be tarnished by his mother's ugliness. He'd done what he had to do to protect her, and he'd go on the way he had most of his life.

Alone.

A bus employee announced the arrival of the bus from Minneapolis on the PA system. Damon clapped Ben's shoulder.

"Come on. Let's see what kind of shape Peter's in."

Outside the terminal at the arrival lanes, they waited to one side while passengers disembarked from the bus and the staff and driver unloaded luggage. Peter was one of the last to leave the bus. At first Damon didn't recognize his father. His hair was far grayer than it had been last summer at Granddad's funeral. But it was the black circle under his left eye and the bruises on his face that made Peter hard to recognize.

"What the hell happened to you?" Ben asked.

Peter looked down at his feet, his shoulders slumped. "Like I said, I fell down some stairs."

"Fell, or were pushed?"

Damon wanted to know the answer to that question, too, but this was not the place for that conversation.

"Let's grab Peter's luggage and get out of here."

Peter identified his bag, and Ben picked it up. They walked slowly toward Ben's car, unable to move quickly because of Peter's obvious discomfort. He held his arm close to his chest as beads of sweat broke out on his forehead.

"You said you thought your arm might be broken."

Peter glanced up, and in his eyes Damon read a world of shame and pain. "It's possible."

They finally made it to the car. Damon helped Peter into the back seat while Ben stowed his bag in the trunk. When he and Ben were both in the front seat, Damon turned to look at his father.

"The first place we're going is to the hospital to have that arm looked at. Then we're heading back to Masonville to get some answers. Understand?"

The look on Peter's face was one of relief mixed with shame. What had happened to him?

He nodded his assent. "Yes, I understand. I'm sorry."

Damon glanced at Ben as he started the car. The myriad of emotions on his brother's face reflected his own turbulent feelings. Confusion, resentment, anger, but also worry and compassion. Peter had never been the father they'd needed growing up. But he was here now, and he needed their help. Whatever he'd done, or hadn't done, Peter was still their father.

At the hospital ER, Peter's right arm was x-rayed and then fitted with a cast. The ER doctor treated his various scrapes and bruises as best he could, asking a lot of questions that Peter gave vague answers to. The only thing he was clear about was that his sons had nothing to do with his injuries.

It was past nine p.m. when they left Bismarck. While they were at the hospital, Ben called Morley to give him an update, and he urged Ben to bring Peter to his house. He had plenty of room, which was fortunate since Damon would now be occupying Ben's spare bedroom. And even if he wasn't, he wouldn't have saddled Ben with the responsibility of looking after Peter.

By the time they entered Morley's house, Peter was gray with fatigue. But they needed some answers. Morley made tea and handed Peter a cup.

"How were you injured?" Morley's tone was uncompromising. "The truth."

Peter clutched the cup with his good hand and closed his eyes in exhaustion. "Victoria caught me listening on the phone extension. I ran, she tripped me, and I fell down the stairs. When she left the house, I packed a few things, grabbed whatever money I could find, and called a cab. I didn't feel safe with her anymore."

"You're saying Victoria caused your fall?" The look on Ben's face was disbelieving. "Victoria is a lot of things, but I've never considered her violent."

Peter lifted his face, the purple bruises standing out against his pale skin. "She's changed. Ever since my father cut us off financially, she's become desperate. And angry. Mostly at me."

He rose slowly and lifted his shirt to reveal angry bruises across his ribs. "A few days ago, she hit me with an antique wooden cane she bought me years ago as a birthday gift. She told me I deserved it. Perhaps I did."

"How long has this been going on?" Damon couldn't take his eyes off the bruises. Some force had been used to create them. Force fueled by fury.

"A few months now." Peter let the shirt fall and resumed his seat, his eyes not meeting theirs.

"Why did you stay with her? Why didn't you fight back?" Damon heard the anger in his brother's voice. He understood his frustration.

"Because I love her, or at least I used to." He dared a glance at Damon. "And I had nowhere else to go."

"Why did you decide to leave today?" he asked.

"I knew she'd kill me the next time. I guess I have just enough will left to survive to make a run for it."

They all went silent. Damon's mind whirled. Was Peter right? Would Victoria really kill him if she had the chance? Even knowing Victoria's history and the things she'd already done, he couldn't quite make himself believe it. Maybe he didn't want to believe it.

But the bruises on Peter's body told another story.

Morley cleared his throat. "I think we should let Peter get some rest. Tomorrow we'll meet you both at the office and figure out where we go from here."

Damon and Ben said goodnight with a promise to meet Morley and Peter at the office the following morning at ten. In the car, Damon turned to his brother.

"Do you believe him?"

Ben hesitated before turning the ignition. "I think I do. He seems sober and sane. And he was beaten. There's no denying it."

"Yeah."

"What if she comes looking for Peter? I don't want her anywhere near my family. With Jamie pregnant…" Ben stopped and shook his head.

Damon understood. Victoria knew Charlotte's name, and if she thought using their relationship gave her some sort of leverage with him, she'd use it. He went cold inside at the thought of Charlotte being hurt.

He couldn't let anything happen to her.

****

Damon and Ben arrived at the law office at ten the next morning. Carmen took one look at them and poured two cups of coffee.

"Morley called. He'll be here in a few minutes." She handed them each a cup of coffee. "I'll make a fresh pot."

"Thanks, Carmen. You're the best," Ben said.

"Thank you." Damon murmured. He'd need more than one cup to get through the day. He'd barely slept last night, his head too full of worry and what-ifs to rest.

After taking a few sips of the dark brew, he joined Ben in Morley's office to wait.

"I called a security company this morning." Ben spoke quietly as he sipped his coffee. "I'm having them install a security system at my house today. A locksmith is changing the locks, too. I spoke to Cole about Jamie never being alone at the clinic. The kids' school has been notified not to release them to anyone other than us or their grandparents the Doyles."

Damon nodded. A short time ago, Victoria had done her best to extort money from Ben. She'd manipulated and frightened him to the point that he'd nearly run away and disappeared with his children. He didn't blame Ben for taking precautions.

He wished there was something he could do to protect Charlotte. He wondered if she'd allow him to install a monitored alarm system in her house. Though, after the way he'd ended things, she'd probably tell him to go to hell.

He hoped staying away from her would be her best protection.

Morley and Peter entered the outer office, and Damon heard Morley greet Carmen. After getting coffee, they joined them. Morley shut the door behind him.

"You two look God-awful this morning."

Ben saluted him with his cup. "And a cheery good morning to you, too."

Damon observed his father from behind his coffee cup. He looked more rested and less pale this morning, though just as bruised. "You look better today, Dad."

Peter gave Damon a brief smile. "I feel better. Last night was the first decent sleep I've had in weeks. Maybe months."

With Victoria's deteriorating mental state, Peter

must have been through an incredible amount of stress, and yet, if he was to be believed, he'd maintained his sobriety.

"How have you managed to stay sober?" There was no time to beat around the bush. They needed answers.

"I joined AA. I was able to sneak out to meetings if Victoria was occupied. She didn't like the idea of me getting sober. When I couldn't get out, I kept in touch with my sponsor by phone or text. I knew if I didn't do something I was going to die."

"I go to AA meetings in Bismarck," Ben said. "I was going to go tonight, but I don't want to leave my family alone."

"I'll be there, Ben. I'll make sure everyone's okay," Damon said.

"I don't know…"

"I promise to take care of everyone." He'd die before he'd let anything happen to his nieces and his pregnant sister-in-law.

"I guess it would be okay for an hour or two." Ben turned to Peter. "Would you like to come with me?"

Peter's eyes lit with relief, and something else. Gratitude? "I'd love to."

Morley set his cup on his desk. "Now that's been decided, what's our next move? Do we file charges against Victoria for assaulting Peter? Do we go after Clayton Brown?"

"Whatever we do, we don't want Victoria to find out. She always seems to be one step ahead of us," Ben said. "She knew things about my life, and about Jamie and me, that she shouldn't have."

Peter leaned forward in his chair and whispered,

"Morley, did you call the lady in the outer office 'Carmen'?"

"Yes, I did. What of it?"

"I overheard Victoria talking to someone named Carmen. The woman was crying, and Victoria told her if she didn't come up with something good, she'd make sure the police got the information she had. I didn't know what it meant at the time, or who this woman was, but now…"

"Oh, no. It couldn't be." Morley slumped in his chair, his anguish etched on his face. He and Carmen had worked together for over twenty years. Carmen's husband Bill was Morley's close, long-time friend.

It made sense. Carmen likely heard every important conversation and phone call made in this office. She would have written up Morley's notes and letters. She knew detailed information about all of them.

Damon wracked his brain, his heart pounding. Did Carmen have information on Charlotte that she passed to Victoria?

Morley gripped the armrests of his chair and slowly pushed himself to his feet. He walked to the door and opened it.

"Carmen, could you join us for a moment?"

Carmen appeared a moment later, notepad in hand. "How can I help, Morley?"

Morley resumed his seat, the look on his face resigned. "I want you to tell me the truth. Have you been feeding information from this office to Victoria Greyson?"

She sucked in a breath, her eyes wide. "Please, Morley."

"It'll go easier on you if you tell the truth now, Carmen."

Carmen closed her eyes and nodded. "She was blackmailing us. She said as long as I gave her information, she wouldn't go to the police. She threatened to ruin us and send my husband to jail."

"What does she have on you?"

"Somehow she found out that Bill stole money from his employer to pay his gambling debts. I don't know how she found out. He plans to pay it back, I swear."

"Sweet Jesus." Morley shook his head, his eyes closed. When he reopened them, they were full of regret. "You know what this means, don't you? First, I have to fire you. Then we go to the police and tell them everything."

She nodded, her eyes shut tight. "I know."

"Hang on, Morley," Ben said. "Carmen, what was the last piece of information you fed to Victoria?"

Carmen glanced at Damon before turning her attention back to Ben. "I told her about the argument I heard between Damon and Charlotte. I told her they broke up, and Damon moved out."

Damon released a breath. "If Victoria knows we've split, maybe she'll leave Charlotte alone." If Charlotte was safe, the pain of losing her was bearable. Almost.

"We don't want to alert Victoria to the fact that we're onto her," Ben said. "So if Carmen suddenly becomes unavailable to her, she'll get suspicious. And besides, if we know what Carmen is telling her, we can influence her thinking."

"Are you saying we feed her false information?"

"Yes. At the very least we find out what Carmen

has told her."

Damon turned to Carmen. "How do we know we can trust her? Maybe she'll tip off Victoria if she thinks it'll save her husband's reputation."

Morley looked directly at Carmen, his gaze uncompromising. "We've worked together for over twenty years. I hope that counts for something."

"And yet she sold us out," Damon said.

"It won't happen again." Carmen turned to Morley, her eyes beseeching him. "I'm so sorry. I didn't know what to do, and Bill was desperate."

"You should have come to me. I would have helped you." Morley waved his hand, as if pushing the idea away. "It doesn't matter anymore. When this is over, I'll escort you and Bill to the police station myself, and you'll both make full confessions."

Carmen stared at the floor and nodded. Damon hoped they could prevent Victoria from hurting anyone else. Especially Charlotte.

Chapter Twenty-Two

It had been three days since Damon moved out of her house, though it felt like an eternity. Charlotte and her dogs spent much of those three days at Branson Farm, usually in the barn, avoiding Damon when he was there. Seeing him during meals had been excruciating for her, and uncomfortable for everyone else. But tomorrow morning at seven a.m. she was going back to work at the hospital. She'd come home early to get ready.

It was for the best. Mike and Des took great care of the dogs. They could handle things on their own. Charlotte needed to put her life back into some kind of normal order, though nothing would be truly normal again.

Not without Damon.

She understood why he'd left, or at least she thought she did. He was trying to protect her from his mother, though why Victoria Grayson would have any interest in her she had no idea. But Damon believed it. How ironic that the first man she'd trusted in ten years was the one who turned away from her.

Charlotte packed a lunch for the next day and stuck it in the fridge. River and Daisy followed her to her bedroom, where she picked out the scrubs she'd wear to work. The dogs would have to stay home tomorrow. They wouldn't understand, since they'd travelled to the farm with her almost every day. Like her, they'd need to get used to a new routine.

When would she stop missing Damon?

The doorbell rang. Hope bloomed in her heart. *Damon.* Maybe he realized his mother wasn't a danger, and he was coming back to her.

With the dogs at her heels, she hurried to the side door and opened it without checking the peephole. Clayton Brown stood on the doorstep holding a gun. Charlotte tried to close the door in his face, but he was too strong. He pushed his way in and, grabbing her arm, dragged her toward the door. The dogs barked madly, and River bared his teeth.

"Let go of me!"

"Tell your damn dogs to shut up!"

"Go to hell, Clayton."

As the dogs continued to go crazy, Charlotte struggled against Clayton's superior strength. Her brain worked overtime as she tried to free herself. Maybe if she let herself get close enough she could knee him in the groin, disabling him long enough to run away.

She wouldn't allow Clayton Brown to ruin her life a second time.

"Shut the hell up!" he yelled.

The boom of the gun reverberated in her ears. An acrid, unpleasant smell hung in the air. River yelped in pain and dropped to the floor.

"River!" Charlotte struggled to get to her dog, but Clayton prevented her, his fingers digging into her arm.

Clayton tugged. "Let's go."

"I'm not going anywhere with you. Look what you've done!" Fury and anguish roared through her head as River whined in pain and Daisy barked hysterically. "How could you shoot a defenseless animal like that?"

He aimed the gun at Daisy. "Shut up or I'll shoot the other one."

For the first time Charlotte was truly afraid. "All right, I'll come with you. Don't shoot her."

Clayton pulled her toward the door. "Good girl. It'll be much easier for you if you cooperate."

She held back tears as she glanced one last time at her dogs. Daisy looked up at her with frightened eyes as she huddled close to River, her head resting in her paws. *I swear I'll come back for you,* Charlotte silently told them. *I'll find a way.*

Clayton dragged her to an unfamiliar car, opened the driver's door, and pushed her inside.

"You drive."

He got into the passenger seat and closed the door, pointing the gun at her the whole time. "Go."

Charlotte turned the key with shaking hands and fought to stay calm. "Where are we going?"

"Just shut up and follow directions."

She dared a glance at him. Even in the dim dashboard lights she could see a sheen of sweat on his brow. Clayton was desperate, and that made him dangerous. The smartest thing she could do right now was to follow his directions and keep quiet. Make him think she was vulnerable and afraid.

And make herself believe she wasn't.

If she was going to survive this, if she was going to get back to River to help him, she had to stay strong. And think.

She followed Clayton's directions out of town. Soon they were on the Interstate going west, then north on a secondary highway and west again on a gravel road. Where the hell was he taking her, and for what purpose? She wouldn't let herself examine that question too closely.

"Up ahead, just before that bluff of trees, turn left."

Charlotte slowed the car and made the left turn. The road was barely more than a prairie trail, and she had to navigate around rocks sticking up through the ground. Tall grasses in the center of the trail made a swishing noise against the undercarriage of the car. After about a mile, the headlights picked up a makeshift campsite. A tent had been set up to one side, with a firepit to the left.

"Stop here," Clayton ordered. "There's too many rocks to get any closer."

Charlotte brought the car to a stop and turned off the ignition. With the headlights off, darkness enveloped them. The vast sky with its canopy of stars provided the only source of light.

He gestured with the gun. "Get out."

Charlotte opened her door and noted that Clayton left the car keys in the ignition when he left the car. The cool night air greeted her as she stepped from the warm confines of the car. The day had been hot, but the evening was chilly, too chilly for the T-shirt and shorts she was wearing.

"I've been camping out here for a few days," he said. "It's the middle of nowhere. No one will find us here."

As her eyes adjusted to the darkness, Charlotte examined her surroundings, trying to get her bearings and looking for a way out. She scanned the horizon but couldn't see lights that would suggest a farm or any other sign of human life was nearby. Only the yips and cries of coyotes in the distance provided proof they weren't completely alone.

The only way out was the way they came in. The car.

"I'm supposed to be at work tomorrow at seven a.m. If I don't show up, people will come looking for me."

"They won't find you." She could just make out a grin on Clayton's face as he pulled a flip phone from his pocket. "This burner phone has no GPS and can't be traced. I rented the car using a fake ID."

"Why did you bring me here?" Charlotte was disconcerted by the fear she heard in her voice.

Clayton approached, a self-satisfied smirk on his face. "Because you're going to give me everything I need."

****

"Damon." His brother pounded on the door of his basement bedroom. "I've got to talk to you."

Damon tossed aside the book he was trying to read and opened the door. Ben's expression was uncharacteristically full of alarm.

"What is it?"

"Jamie just got called to an emergency. The police brought a dog to the clinic that had been shot in a break-in. It was River. The break-in was at Charlotte's house."

Damon's whole body went cold, and he had to hold on to the door frame to stay upright. "Is Charlotte okay?"

"She wasn't there when the police arrived. The neighbors called for help when they heard the gunshot.

They saw her get into a car with a man, but they didn't get a good look at him."

Damon tried to push back the panic in his brain to think.

"A man? Does that mean Clayton Brown's got her?"

"Maybe, but to what end? To extort more money from you? He knows you're tapped out."

"I don't know. It doesn't make sense. Nothing makes sense." Damon's heart raced. "Peter heard Victoria scheming with Clayton. It isn't much of a stretch to believe they're both somehow involved in this. Either Victoria instructed Clayton to abduct Charlotte or she hired someone else."

"If that's true, then this time she's gone too far. She can't bully or bribe her way out of a kidnapping charge," Ben said.

"It doesn't matter right now. The only thing that matters is finding Charlotte." Damon grabbed his phone and a jacket and slipped on some shoes. "I'm going to Charlotte's house. Maybe the police can tell me something."

"Tell them your suspicions about Clayton."

"I will. Do you know what kind of shape River is in?" Charlotte would be devastated about her dog.

"No, but it can't be good. Jamie will call when she gets a chance, and I'll let you know."

"Thanks."

They hurried up the stairs. At the back door, Ben clapped him on the shoulder. "I wish I could come with you."

"You have to stay here with the kids. Call me if you hear anything."

"I will. I'll check with Morley, too. He has a lot of connections. Maybe he's heard something." Ben pulled him into an embrace. "She's going to be okay, Damon. I can feel it."

Damon nodded against his brother's shoulder. Shock was quickly morphing into anger, mostly at himself. This was his fault. If he hadn't been involved with Charlotte, she wouldn't have become a target for Clayton. And Victoria.

He'd never be free of his mother.

"I've got to go."

Ben released him and nodded. "Good luck."

Damon rushed to his truck and made the short drive to Charlotte's house. Two police cars were parked in front. The lights were on inside as police searched the house. As Damon approached the side door, a burly deputy sheriff appeared. "Don't come any closer. We're conducting an investigation."

"My name is Damon Greyson. I'm a friend of Charlotte Saunders, and I think I know who did this." He pulled his ID from his wallet to show the officer.

He'd do everything he could for Charlotte, and then he'd get out of her life. Forever.

****

Charlotte shivered and wrapped her arms around herself. If Clayton didn't kill her, she'd die of hypothermia.

Cut it out, Charlotte. You're going to get out of this.

She rubbed her arms against the cold. She would do everything she could to survive.

She turned her attention to her surroundings, to the tent that looked like it could hold two people, and to the firepit. The firepit was currently cold, but the amount of ash inside the circle of stones suggested it had been used for a few days, as Clayton had said.

This was no spur-of-the-moment act. He'd planned her kidnapping. But why? Was he trying to extort more money from Damon for her release? Clayton had to know he had nothing left.

There was another possibility. Maybe he meant to rape her again.

The thought caused bile to rise in her throat and panic to fill her chest. Charlotte made herself remember her hours of training, the things she'd learned. *I'm not the defenseless girl I was ten years ago. I refuse to feel like a victim again.* She repeated the words over and over in head like a mantra.

He pointed the gun at her again.

"I've got firewood in the trunk. Bring it here, and we'll get a fire going."

Charlotte walked slowly to the car. If she could get close enough to him, she could take him down. But she'd never disarmed someone with a gun. In the eight years since she'd begun her training in martial arts and self-defense, that's all she'd done, train. She'd never had to actually defend herself against someone who meant to do her harm. Could she do it?

Her heart pounded, and she willed herself to stay calm and to think. With any luck, one of her neighbors had heard the commotion at her house and called the police. But no one knew where she was, and if Clayton was to be believed, there was no way to track them.

If she was going to survive, she had to do it on her own.

She pushed away the panic that caused her hands to

shake. She wanted to survive. She wanted a life with Damon. Damn it, they both deserved a life of love together.

New resolve gave her strength. She wasn't going to let anyone take her life away from her.

Clayton walked to the driver's side of the car and hit the button that opened the trunk, then went back to the firepit, the gun still in his hand. Charlotte leaned into the trunk and lifted out a bundle of firewood. He'd come prepared. The trunk was full of such bundles, each one wrapped in green mesh and holding an armful of split logs. Even in the dark, Charlotte could tell there were few trees here. Instead, rocks stuck out of the ground with patches of grass and scrubby bush growing in between. The land here was likely only used to graze cattle, and since hundreds of acres were needed to sustain a herd, it was no wonder there were no visible signs of habitation. The nearest farm was likely miles away.

She walked back and forth from the car to the firepit, a distance she estimated to be at least thirty feet. Charlotte carried one bundle at a time while Clayton watched, the gun trained on her. She made sure to walk the same way each time, past the driver's side door.

The repetitive job gave her time to think, and plan. She had to make Clayton believe she was frightened and defenseless, the way she'd been ten years ago. She had to lull him into thinking she was compliant and of no threat to him.

"Why are you doing this, Clayton? Why have you brought me here?" She put a quaver in her voice that wasn't entirely fake.

"I need money, and you're going to help me get it."

"How am I supposed to do that? I have no money."

His grin momentarily transported her back ten years. Back then, he'd come off as charming and funny at first. Charlotte had known nothing about the darkness that lurked inside him.

But she knew now.

"You're a jackpot, sweetheart. Didn't you know that?"

What the hell was he talking about? "If you think Damon is going to pay for my return, you're wrong. He has no money left. You took it all. And besides…" She paused, taking a shaky breath for effect. "We broke up."

"So I heard. I don't give a damn about Damon Greyson's financial affairs. You, sweet Charlotte, are going to give me everything I need, and everything I want."

Charlotte dared a glance at him and saw the smug smile on his face. He wasn't just talking about money. He had her all alone in the middle of nowhere and was armed with a gun to make her compliant.

If she made a move, it had to be soon.

She made herself remember how much she loved Damon. *I'll come back to you.*

****

The police took Damon to the county sheriff's office. They asked a lot of questions, including where he'd been at the time of the break-in at Charlotte's house. He told them everything, how Clayton had extorted money from him through the renovations on his building, about Clayton's connection to his mother, and how he'd raped Charlotte in college. He told them about his mother's ruthlessness and how she'd beaten his father, and his suspicion that she was now seriously dangerous. He even told them how she'd blackmailed Carmen Miller into providing her with information.

But the hardest thing to talk about was his relationship with Charlotte. He knew the police would ask, but still he wasn't prepared for the questions.

"How long have you known Ms. Saunders?"

"Since we were kids, though I hadn't seen her for twelve or thirteen years. My grandparents were neighbors of the Saunders family, and we saw them every summer."

His mind flew back in time. He was a shy and awkward kid, prone to depression. Being on the farm over the summer gave him a respite from living with his parents, from the constant demands of his mother and his father's escape into alcohol. Damon could remember the summer he fell in love with Charlotte. He was fourteen, and she was twelve. He was far too shy to approach her, but Charlotte often sought him out to talk. They'd walk in the pasture, and she told him about her dreams to be a nurse and travel the world with Doctors Without Borders. He wondered why she'd put aside that part of her dream.

"When we checked your alibi with your brother, he told us you'd been living with Ms. Saunders for a time."

"Yes. The apartment in the Fletcher Building wasn't ready, and we needed my bedroom at Branson Farm for veterans. Charlotte offered me a room."

"Is that all she offered?"

Damon stared at him in disgust and rose from his seat. "If you're going to malign Charlotte, we're done here."

"I apologize," Deputy Crawford said. "Please sit."

Reluctantly, Damon returned to his seat. "Charlotte's the victim here."

The deputy nodded. "She is, and to get her back, we need to know everything. What was your relationship with her?"

"We were friends, and then it turned into something more."

"So you and Ms. Saunders had a sexual relationship?"

Damon nodded. "Yes."

"Yet at the time of the kidnapping you were no longer living in Ms. Saunders' house."

"I moved out and severed ties with her." Damon closed his eyes. "Once I found out about the relationship between Clayton Brown and my mother, I believed she'd be safer if they thought we were no longer together. I was wrong. I should have been with her. I should have protected her."

The officer remained silent for a few moments before asking his next question. "If Mr. Brown kidnapped Ms. Saunders, do you have any idea why?"

"I don't know. He can't extort any more money from me. He knows I'm broke. I'm afraid…" He shook his head, unable to say the words.

"You're afraid he'll rape her again?"

Damon nodded, feeling sick and powerless.

"We'll find her."

He prayed they could get to her before it was too late.

****

Charlotte dumped an armful of firewood near the firepit and walked slowly back to the car. There were only a couple of bundles of wood left in the trunk.

Clayton was still at the firepit, momentarily occupied with opening the mesh bag holding the wood. This was it. She had to act now.

She picked up her pace. As soon she reached the driver's side door, she wrenched it open, hopped inside and turned the ignition. As the engine roared to life, Clayton looked up and reached for his gun. Charlotte fumbled with the gear shift, her hands shaking as she put the car into reverse. As she backed up, a rear tire hit a stone and brought the car to a jarring stop. Charlotte's head hit the steering wheel, dazing her.

Clayton threw open the passenger door. "Get out of the car!"

He aimed his gun at her. Reaching over the seat, he turned off the motor and pulled the keys from the ignition. Charlotte blinked at him and touched her forehead where a lump was beginning to form.

"Get out now, or I swear I'll shoot!" he shouted.

She lifted her hands in surrender, her spirit sinking. "Okay, I'm getting out."

Charlotte pushed the door open and slid out of car, her legs not quite steady as she stood. Clayton waved the gun at her.

"Get the rest of the wood. And don't try anything stupid. You're lucky I still need you alive. For now." He stuck the keys into the left pocket of his jacket.

Her head pounded as she leaned into the trunk to gather another load. She wanted to give in to tears, but she couldn't let herself succumb to despair. She had to think. There had to be another way to escape. Her life depended on it.

****

Detective Crawford called a break in the interview, probably so he could verify Damon's story. Damon took the opportunity to go to a washroom to run cold water over his face. When he was done, he went out into the hallway and called Ben, even though it was past eleven now.

"Have you heard from Jamie? How's River?" he asked.

"She just called. The surgery is over, and he's going to be okay."

"Thank goodness." Maybe River's survival was a good omen for Charlotte. He prayed that it was.

"Where are you?" Ben asked.

"At the county sheriff's office. They're asking a lot of questions."

"Do you want me to come there when Jamie gets home?"

"No, I'm fine. I don't need a lawyer." At least he didn't think he did. "Have you talked to Morley? Has he heard anything?"

"Yeah, I spoke to him. He's been in touch with his police contacts. They're looking for Clayton Brown, to bring him in for questioning. He's not in any of the places he should be, either here or in Minnesota. They found his truck outside the place he'd been renting in Bismarck."

"An innocent man doesn't just disappear." Damon paced the hallway, frustration and fear eating at him. "Dammit, I wish there was something I could do."

"You've done the most important thing. You gave the police a lead. They'll take it from here."

Realistically, he knew Ben was right, but that didn't stop his worry. Or his guilt. He should have been with Charlotte. He should have stopped Clayton from taking her.

Ben read his mind. "Damon, this is not your fault. Not in any way. If Clayton kidnapped Charlotte, it's on him. We don't know his reasons."

"It's because of Victoria, I know it! If I hadn't involved myself with Charlotte, she would have been safe." The guilt of knowing he was responsible for Charlotte's abduction nearly overwhelmed him.

"If Victoria is behind this, then she'll pay." Damon heard Ben sigh. "You and I both know that nothing we do will stop her when she's determined enough. You can't control her. Whether you were with Charlotte or not wouldn't have mattered to her. She's sick, Damon. There's nothing we can do about that."

Damon again conceded that Ben was right. But that knowledge didn't help Charlotte. And it didn't alleviate his anxiety about not being able to help her. All he could do right now was trust in Charlotte's intelligence and her ability to defend herself.

Please God, give her the strength to survive.
****

Once she'd finished hauling the firewood, Clayton pulled out his flip phone. "The amazing thing about this spot is that it has excellent cell phone service. There's a tower a couple of miles from here. You and I are going to give your friend at the animal shelter a call."

Charlotte's brain whirled in confusion, her head still fuzzy from the blow she'd taken. What did he want with Gina? "Why?"

"Did you forget about the money the shelter raised? All that lovely cash. Over two million dollars! I need that money."

Clayton's expression was hard and determined. He was serious. He planned to use her to get the money raised through the online campaign for the shelter.

"Gina doesn't control that money. She can't even buy dog food without someone from the board of directors signing off on it."

Clayton aimed the gun at her head as he handed her the phone. "That's *her* problem. If your friend wants to see you again, she'd better figure it out. Phone her and make sure you don't use my name."

Charlotte tried not to look at the gun. "What should I tell her?"

"Tell her to transfer the two million electronically to an account number that you'll send her by text. If the money isn't in this account in two days, you'll be dead. And if she calls the police, you'll be dead." He waved the gun again. "Put the phone on speaker. Call her!"

Charlotte opened the phone with trembling hands and dialed Gina's cell phone number from memory. She knew Gina always kept her phone close in case there was an emergency at the shelter. Her friend picked up after a couple of rings.

"Hello?" Gina sounded cautious, probably because the phone number was unfamiliar to her.

"Gina, it's Charlotte. I need you to listen carefully. I've been kidnapped, and I'm being held hostage. My kidnapper wants the two million dollars in the shelter's bank account. I'll text you the account number where you're to transfer the money electronically."

"Oh, my God! Charlotte, what's going on?"

"Please, just do as I ask or he'll kill me. Don't call the police."

"Charlotte—"

Gina's words were cut off when Clayton grabbed the phone and ended the call. He handed her a small piece of paper. "Send this number to her. Type it exactly as it is here."

Charlotte took the phone and the paper from him and typed in the numbers. Before she could hit send, Clayton grabbed the phone and checked what she'd written against the numbers on the paper. He wasn't taking any chances.

He wasn't going to let her get away. Once the money was in his account, she'd be of no further use to him. And if Gina wasn't able to make the transfer, Charlotte knew she was a liability. She could identify him and testify against him.

Despite her fear and her pounding head, she had to make another move. It was now or never.

Clayton stuck his phone in the pocket of his jacket. In the same pocket she'd seen him stash the car keys.

"You've been a very good girl, so you deserve a reward. You can build a fire."

He looked pleased with himself. He pointed to a plastic box sitting next to the ring of fire stones. "There's kindling and matches in that box."

This is my chance. I've got one shot. "I've never built a fire before."

"Weren't you ever a girl scout?" There was a sneer in his voice. He was enjoying her distress.

"No, never." She bit her lip as she opened the plastic box and took out a book of matches. A nagging, aching need kept her from acting. "Clayton, years ago, when you met me, what did you think of me?"

He looked at her as if she was crazy. "What did I think of you? What the hell are you talking about?"

"Did you think I was smart, or funny, someone you wanted to get to know? Did you think I was a good person?"

"Build the damn fire, Charlotte." From the tone of his voice, he was growing agitated. *Good.* Perhaps that meant he would let down his guard.

Or maybe he'd simply shoot her.

She squatted near the circle of stones and spread some of the kindling in a thin layer all around the inside of the circle.

"No, not like that." Clayton waved his gun. "Put the kindling into a little pile, then put some of the smaller twigs close by, so it can catch."

As Charlotte pushed the kindling into a stack, Clayton watched her, the gun still in his right hand.

"Do you remember anything about that night, Clayton?" She took her time arranging the firewood.

"What night?"

"The night you raped me."

"I didn't rape you."

Charlotte continued as if he hadn't spoken. "I remember every detail. I remember what I wore, what you wore. I even remember the smell of your aftershave. When you've experienced a great trauma, sometimes those details stick with you. I've had nightmares about it. I've woken in a cold sweat more times than I care to remember."

"You're crazy."

She made sure to stack the twigs and firewood too far away from the kindling to be able to catch. Charlotte had been building fires in her family's firepit at the farm since she was ten years old, and she knew exactly what would and wouldn't work. She hoped Clayton did, too.

"I'd gone with friends to a party that you and your hockey team were throwing. You kept giving me drinks. At first, I thought you were simply flirting, and I flirted back. But then you started touching me in places I didn't want to be touched. When I told you to stop, you didn't. So I tried to leave, but you wouldn't let me. You pulled me into a bedroom and ripped off my clothes, and then you raped me."

"You wanted it just as much as I did."

"No, I didn't." She struck a cardboard match ineffectively against the matchbook cover, bending the match and making it useless. "I repeatedly told you to stop. You didn't."

"Shut up. You wanted it. You're nothing but a whore."

Charlotte took out another match, pushed it against the strike plate, and bent it as well. She dropped it into the fire pit. "No, I was anything but a whore. I was a virgin."

Clayton stepped closer. "You're lying."

Come a little closer. "Is that what you tell yourself to justify being a rapist?" She ruined a third match.

"Shut up!" If she agitated him enough, maybe he'd be careless.

"You need to acknowledge what you did." She ripped a fourth match out of the book.

"You're ruining them! Give me the damn matches!"

He set the gun on the stones and stepped forward to grab the matches from her hand.

Now.

Charlotte smashed the palm of her hand into

Clayton's nose, just above the lip. She was rewarded by the sound of breaking cartilage. Blood gushed from the nose. While he was reeling from the nose injury, she kneed him in the groin as hard as she could.

"I will never be your victim again!" she shouted.

Clayton fell to the ground like a sack of stones, moaning and holding his crotch. Charlotte rifled through the pocket of his jacket for the car keys and phone, then sprinted to the car and slid behind the steering wheel.

Her hands shook as she fumbled with the key in the ignition. Through the windshield she saw Clayton stumble to his feet and reach for the gun. As he lifted the gun to fire, the key slipped into the ignition. She turned it and nearly cried with relief when the engine roared to life. As she turned the car in a wide arc to avoid the rock the car had previously hit, she heard the boom of the gun and a shattering of glass as a rear side window exploded from the impact of a bullet. Charlotte stepped on the gas and kept going. She headed out the way she came, spitting dirt and grass behind her.

Freedom!

Chapter Twenty-Three

Damon rose from his seat when another deputy entered the interview room. "We just got word about a ransom demand for Ms. Saunders. A woman named Gina Watson says she received a call from Ms. Saunders. The kidnapper wants the money raised from an online campaign for the Best Friends Haven for Dogs, over two million dollars."

Damon's heart fell into his stomach. At least now they knew why Clayton had kidnapped Charlotte. But they were no closer to finding her.

"Did Ms. Watson say whether Ms. Saunders named her kidnapper?" Detective Crawford asked.

"No, she didn't give a name. She texted the number of a bank account where Ms. Watson was to transfer the money. We're checking it out now."

Deputy Crawford nodded. "Let me know if there's any further developments."

As the second deputy left the room, Damon began to pace. "What do we do now?"

"We do our jobs. We investigate the bank account. We check with car rental agencies about the car that may have been used. And we continue to look for Ms. Saunders."

It wasn't much of an answer. All they had to go on was a description of a late model car in a dark color, possibly domestic, that was seen speeding away from

Charlotte's house by the neighbor shortly after the gunshot. He knew Clayton drove a truck, so he must have rented the car.

Where the hell had he taken her?

Damon's thoughts were jarred by the ringing of his phone. The phone number on his screen was unfamiliar, with no name attached to it. He hesitated before answering.

"Hello?"

"Damon, it's Charlotte."

"Charlotte!" He had to hold onto the back of a chair to keep his knees from buckling. "Are you okay? Where are you?"

"I'm on the Interstate heading back to Masonville. I took Clayton's car and his phone."

Thank God. "How did you get away?"

"Turns out those self-defense moves actually work." The amusement in her voice faded. "He had a gun, Damon. He shot River."

"I know. Your neighbor heard the commotion and called the police. River was taken to the vet clinic, and Jamie and Dr. Waverly operated on him. Jamie says he's going to be fine. Daisy is at the clinic, too."

"Oh, thank goodness!" She was crying now. "I was so afraid. I thought I'd lost him. And I thought I'd lost you, too. All I could think about was that I wanted to see you again. I want a life with you, Damon. I wouldn't let him take that away from us."

He couldn't answer, not with Deputy Crawford listening to their conversation. He'd want to know who kidnapped her and where he was now.

As much as he loved Charlotte, he'd only bring her more pain. He couldn't do that to her.

Damon slid into the chair across from the deputy. He gestured for the phone, indicating he wanted to speak to her. "Charlotte, I'm at the county sheriff's office right now with Deputy Crawford. He needs to talk to you."

"Oh. Okay." He heard the note of disappointment in her voice.

He handed over the phone. Deputy Crawford asked her where she'd been held and how she got away.

"Okay, I see. Yes, we'll call your friend and let her know you're safe. What are you driving? Can you come straight to our office to give your statement?"

He listened for a moment. "All right, I'll see you shortly. I'm glad you're okay." The officer handed the phone back to Damon. "She wants to talk to you."

Damon accepted his phone. "I'm here, Charlotte."

"When I get back, after I talk to the police and see how River is doing, can we talk? There are some things I need to tell you."

Letting Charlotte go was going to be the hardest thing he'd ever done. But she wasn't safe around him. She could have died…

He couldn't let himself think about that. "Okay, sure."

"Will you be at the sheriff's office when I get there?"

He should go now that he knew she was free. But he needed to see her, to assure himself that she was safe and whole.

"I'll be here."

"It's not your fault. Nothing that happened was your fault, Damon. Please don't blame yourself."

Damon didn't answer. How could he not blame

himself? His mother had made Ben and Blair's life hell, but she'd always singled him out for especially horrific treatment. Victoria was a sick woman, and anyone close to him was in danger.

****

Three days later, Charlotte paced the floors of her house. She checked her watch again—one fifty-seven p.m. Damon had promised to meet her here at two. She hadn't seen him since her early morning arrival at the police station, and she'd missed him terribly.

Charlotte was afraid. There was no way of knowing how he'd react when she told him her secret. She had to be prepared for him to walk away for good.

Hadn't he already done that? He'd been putting distance between them ever since he found out that Clayton Brown was working with his mother. She wasn't sure how telling him what she'd done ten years ago would bring him back to her. She only knew she had to tell him.

The night of the kidnapping, Damon had kept his word and stayed at the police station until Charlotte arrived. She'd run into his arms the moment she'd seen him, and he held her as if afraid to let her go. As if she meant something to him.

But the embrace had been brief. Too soon, Damon pulled away. He'd guided her to Deputy Crawford and then left. After she gave her statement, the police took her to her parents' farm to spend what was left of the night. When she reached the farm and saw them on the front porch looking worried and scared and years older, Charlotte swore she was going to make Clayton pay for what he'd done.

The morning after her ordeal, the police let her

know they'd captured Clayton. Without a car or phone, he hadn't been able to get far from the campsite. He'd fired his gun at the police, a stupid move, considering how outnumbered he'd been. He was lucky they'd taken him alive. Clayton was facing some serious charges, and she would do everything she could to ensure he was punished to the full extent of the law.

A couple of days later, she got the okay from the police to move back into her home. Her dad and brother arranged for a company in Bismarck to replace her old wooden doors with sturdy new steel doors. They also had a security company install new deadbolts and a monitored alarm system. Despite the new doors and alarms, her first night back in her house had been mostly sleepless.

She visited River at the vet clinic and was relieved to see him moving about. Though he was not his normal, rambunctious self, Jamie assured her the surgery to repair the damage to his hip had gone well and they expected him to make a full recovery. Charlotte brought Daisy home with her, but it would likely be a while until her frightened dog was her old self again.

A knock sounded at her front door. Charlotte wiped her sweaty palms on her shorts.

"He's here, Daisy. Wish me luck."

Daisy followed her to the door as she first peered through the peephole and then opened it for Damon. He entered silently and avoided looking at her directly, instead bending to pet Daisy and scratch her ears.

"How ya doing, Daisy girl?"

"She misses River. She walks around the house looking for him."

Damon straightened and finally looked directly at her. "She was traumatized."

"Yeah." Charlotte walked into the kitchen and set the kettle she'd filled with water on the stove to boil. "I'm making tea. Would you like some?"

"Sure."

Damon prowled around the house while the water boiled. Restless energy rolled off him in waves. *What must be going through his head?* Charlotte was afraid the guilt he was experiencing was overwhelming him and preventing him from recognizing how much they needed each other and how good they were together.

She set the tea to steep and brought out a tray. "Why don't we have our tea in the living room?"

Damon lifted his shoulder in a shrug. "If you want."

His indifferent gesture gave her pause. Maybe she'd been wrong. Maybe his pulling away from her had nothing to do with wanting to protect her. Perhaps he was no longer interested in a relationship with her. For so long, she had pushed him away, and now he was simply giving her the space she'd demanded.

But then she thought of the other night and the way he'd held her when she arrived at the sheriff's office. She remembered how he'd murmured "Thank God," over and over. Of course, he'd been worried about her safety, but his embrace told her he felt something for her, perhaps remnants of the love he'd earlier professed.

At least she hoped so.

Charlotte gathered the tray and took it to the living room, setting it on the coffee table. She poured Damon's tea, adding milk, the way he liked it, before handing it to him.

She sat next to him on the sofa. Once again, she rubbed her hands over her shorts, her nerves on edge. "I asked you to come here today because I have a confession to make."

Damon looked up at her in surprise. "A confession? What do you mean?"

Charlotte opened her mouth to speak, but nothing came out. This was even harder than she'd imagined it would be.

Damon set down his cup. "Charlotte, whatever it is, you can tell me. Nothing you say will leave this room."

"I've never told this to anyone. But I want to tell you, so you'll understand."

He folded his hands in his lap. "What do you want me to understand?"

She couldn't help thinking he was in counselor mode, treating her the way he'd treat any patient coming to him for help. Charlotte willed herself not to cry. "I guess I want you to understand me."

His brow furrowed. "Okay."

She grasped his hand, letting the strength in it give her the courage to go on. "A couple of months after Clayton raped me, I discovered I was pregnant."

Damon didn't speak, but he gripped her hand a little tighter. She stared at their clasped hands, too afraid to look into his eyes and see revulsion.

"I was scared. I couldn't imagine having Clayton's child. I was afraid it would tie me to him forever. And the idea of telling my parents what had happened…." She couldn't finish. "I was ashamed, and I blamed myself for the rape. I know now that Clayton was responsible. It didn't matter what I wore or whether I flirted or had too much to drink. He wanted something from me and he took it. You helped me to see that."

"What happened then?" His voice was soft, gentle.

"I thought about going away somewhere for seven or eight months until the baby came, and then giving it up for adoption, but I had no money, and I didn't know how I'd explain my absence to my family or my friends at school without telling them the whole story. And I was too ashamed to do that." She wondered how much different her life would have been these last ten years if she'd found the courage to speak about the rape back then. "The only choice I could see was to go to Minneapolis and have an abortion."

Damon squeezed her hands. "That must have been a hard decision for you."

"It was the hardest decision of my life. And it went against everything I believed in. But it was the only thing I could do. I made an appointment at a clinic and took the bus to Minneapolis. After it was over, I took the bus back to my college in Grand Forks and stayed locked up in my dorm room for three days. I told anyone who came by that I had the flu."

"I'm sorry you had to go through that on your own, Charlotte."

For the first time, Charlotte lifted her gaze and met his eyes. They were full of compassion and understanding. "I finally realize I need to bring this out in the open to get past it. I have to talk about what happened with someone I trust." She laid her palm against his chest, near his heart. "You."

"Charlotte." He broke eye contact with her as he removed her hand from his chest. "I'm not who you need."

"You're wrong. You're exactly who I need." She

gripped his hand. "Don't you see? You thought you were the only one who had a past that haunted you, but you're not. We both have dark parts of our lives, histories we'd rather forget. No one will understand you better than me. And no one will love you better than me."

Damon lifted his head sharply. Panic glittered in his eyes. "You don't mean that."

"Yes, I do. I love you, Damon. I fought it for a long time because I was afraid you'd find out about the abortion and you'd hate me."

"I could never hate you."

Charlotte placed her hand on his cheek, loving the rough stubble beneath her fingertips and the warmth of his skin. "I know. I could never hate you, either. Making love with you was like being reborn. It was truly the first time I've made love with anyone. I was a virgin when Clayton raped me. Your love took away the shame and the guilt. You made me whole again, Damon."

"I…I don't know what to say."

"You don't have to say anything. I just want you to know that no matter what happened to you in the past, or who your family is, it doesn't matter. The only thing that matters is you, and the wonderful, kind person you are."

He shook his head. "My mother—"

"She doesn't matter."

"Yes, she does! She's dangerous, Charlotte. You could have died because of me!"

He rose abruptly to his feet and headed to the front door. Charlotte followed him.

"Do you love me, Damon?"

He shook his head, his eyes not meeting hers. "Don't do this, Charlotte."

She couldn't give up. "Do you love me?"

Damon closed his eyes, the look on his face so full of pain that it made Charlotte sorry to torture him like this. But she had no choice.

"Of course I love you, Charlotte. I've loved you since we were teenagers."

Charlotte sucked in a breath. She hadn't known. Her heart cried for the shy, quiet boy with the kind heart who was afraid to tell his truth.

"Then nothing else matters. Truly. We'll deal with your mother together. Don't you see we're stronger together?"

He shook his head. "You could have died. And it would have been my fault."

"No, not your fault. Never your fault." She grasped his arm. "I gave shame too much power over my life. It kept me from really living. Don't give your mother this much power. Hasn't she taken enough away from you?"

"I have to go."

He pulled away, and Charlotte let go of his arm. Her heart broke as he left her house without a backward glance.

Chapter Twenty-Four

Damon and Ben sat in Ben's office, waiting for Morley. It seemed all he did lately was wait. He hated it, and he hated being so powerless.

"Damon, try to relax. Your knee is bouncing up and down so hard you look like you're going to blast off any minute. You're giving me anxiety."

"Sorry."

Damon clamped a hand on his knee to stop the movements he hadn't been aware he'd been making. Ben's tone was gentle, but Damon caught the undercurrent of worry in his expression. Everyone was worried about him. His father wore a guilty, pained expression around him. At the farm, Blair acted as if she was afraid he was going to explode like a rogue grenade. The veterans he counseled had started asking him if *he* needed to talk. Chris and Trey cooked all his favorite foods to entice him to eat. Even Blair's dog Frisco sensed his distress and had begun hanging around him and nuzzling close every chance he got.

He was sick of it. Sick of being on edge and anxious every moment of every day. Sick of feeling like a failure for not protecting Charlotte. Sick of waiting for his mother's next bombshell.

And he was sick of the gaping hole in his heart where Charlotte should have been. He missed her so much he physically ached with it. Despite Chris's best efforts, he had little appetite. Every time he closed his eyes, he imagined the pool of blood on the floor where River had been shot, and the gun in Clayton's hand. He worried constantly that Victoria would come after Charlotte again, and he was terrified that, this time, Charlotte wouldn't be able to protect herself. It wasn't like he'd been of any use to her the last time.

Charlotte's words played over and over in his head, haunting him with possibilities that could never be. *No one will understand you better than me. And no one will love you better than me.*

Ben attempted a smile, no doubt to reassure him. "It's okay. Morley will be back in the office soon. He said he had some news. Would you like some coffee while we wait? I can put on a fresh pot."

"Sure."

Damon had no interest in coffee, but it gave Ben something to do. He was truly grateful for his brother's support, for the support from all his family and friends. He just wished he didn't need it.

He joined Ben in the outer office while he made coffee. Carmen's desk was bare, the office eerily quiet without her. As he promised, Morley had escorted Carmen and her husband to the sheriff's office where they made a full confession about the blackmail and the theft that led to it. No decision had been made about Carmen's future employment. Damon knew Ben wanted to fire her, but in deference to Morley and the years he and Carmen had worked together, he was letting his senior partner make the decision.

It was still a mystery as to how Victoria had found out about Carmen's husband's theft from his employer, though Morley had a theory. He believed Victoria had an unscrupulous private investigator, or perhaps a police officer, dig into the lives of everyone surrounding her children, looking for any dirt she could exploit. That had to be the way she'd found out about Clayton Brown, though Damon didn't yet know what she was holding over him.

The outside door opened, and Morley walked in with Peter close behind him.

"Good, you've put on fresh coffee. I could use a cup." Morley lowered himself into one of the chairs in the outer office. "We've had a very interesting discussion with the police."

Ben poured coffee into paper cups, and Damon passed them around. "What have you found out?"

"We went there initially to tell the sheriff about Victoria's assault against Peter. He's ready to talk about it now and lay charges. But they had some things to tell us, too."

"Like what?" Ben stirred powdered creamer into his coffee and sat next to Peter.

"Clayton Brown has been denied bail. However, he made a full confession. As we suspected, Victoria had someone dig into Brown's background. It turns out that three young women made rape allegations against Brown back in college when he was playing for the university hockey team. His grandfather paid the women handsomely to drop all charges and keep quiet. When Victoria's investigator discovered this piece of dirt, she blackmailed Brown, telling him she'd make sure every tabloid and news agency in Minnesota and North Dakota heard about his past. His business and his family's reputation would be ruined. She was especially keen on Brown finding ways to extort money from

Damon. She was the one who suggested it."

A wound that had never fully healed ripped wide open in Damon's heart. Despite knowing what Victoria was, it was painful to hear she hated him so much that she wanted to ruin his life now and into the future. Once more he felt like the frightened eight-year-old boy who'd been betrayed by his mother.

But he couldn't help thinking about Charlotte, too. She wasn't the only young woman Brown had assaulted. She'd want to know.

"The biggest news is that the police have arrested Victoria for extortion and blackmail, and now because of Peter's story they'll add assault as well. I believe they'll also tack on accessory for Charlotte Saunders' kidnapping."

Peter looked directly into Damon's eyes. "She's going away for a long time. You don't have to worry about her any longer, son. None of us do."

Damon nodded, too choked up to speak. It sounded promising, but it was far from a sure thing. He'd been confident he'd been rid of her before, like when he left home to join the military, but somehow she always managed to slither back into his life. Would this time be any different?

He could only pray it would.

****

Charlotte parked her Jeep in front of Morley Walker's law office on Main Street. Leaving her shift at the hospital when it ended at three in the afternoon, she'd checked her phone and seen a text from Damon. *Can you meet me and Ben at his office? There's something important we need to tell you.* She'd texted back, telling him she'd be there as soon as she could.

She almost didn't care what news they wanted to convey. It was likely something to do with the law and Clayton Brown, since Ben was involved. All she cared about was seeing Damon. It had been a week since she'd last spoken to him, and she missed him fiercely. It was like a part of her was lost, her heart misplaced in the confusion that had become her life. He thought he was protecting her by keeping his distance, but Charlotte couldn't help wondering if what she'd told him about having an abortion also kept him away.

She couldn't be ashamed anymore. She'd done what she'd had to do to carry on with her life. Charlotte wished things could have been different, but the self-flagellation had to stop. She'd spoken to the social worker at her hospital, who had referred her to a counselor. Getting the help she needed was long overdue.

Charlotte got out of the Jeep and headed to the office, inhaling deeply before going inside. As soon as she opened the door, she saw Damon. He gave her a hesitant smile, and her body immediately relaxed and her mind calmed. He was her touchstone, her north star, and she loved him. She had to find a way to make him understand they belonged together.

Charlotte reached out her hand, and Damon grasped it. "It's good to see you."

"It's good to see you, too," he said. "I was surprised to hear you've gone back to work already."

"I needed to get back to some sort of normal. It feels good. My neighbor, Mrs. Klein, offered to babysit my dogs while I'm at work, at least until River loses the cone of shame."

Damon's smile disappeared, and Charlotte knew

immediately it had been the wrong thing to say. It only reminded him of the night of the kidnapping. She held onto his hand when he would have pulled away.

"We're getting better every day, Damon. We're going to be fine."

He responded to her whispered words with a brief nod, and she let him go. She and the dogs might be getting better, but she wasn't sure Damon was.

Ben came toward her and enfolded her in a hug. He held her at arm's length. "It's good to see you, Charlotte. You look well."

"Thank you, I feel well. How's Jamie?"

Ben's wide smile told her she'd hit on his favorite subject. "She and the baby are doing great."

"That's wonderful."

"Yeah, it's pretty fantastic. I'm a very lucky man." Ben exchanged a brief look with Damon, and his demeanor sobered. "Before we get started, can I get you anything? Coffee? A bottle of water?"

"Water would be lovely. Thank you."

"Coming right up. Damon, could you take Charlotte to my office?"

"Ben's office is the one on the left," Damon murmured. His hand on the small of her back warmed a path up and down her spine.

Charlotte sat in one of the chairs in front of Ben's desk. "What's this about?"

"Let's wait till Ben gets here."

Ben arrived a moment later and passed her a bottle of water before sitting behind his desk. "Charlotte, we asked you to come here today because there've been some developments that we want to make you aware of."

She opened her water bottle. "Okay. What kind of developments?"

"Since the news of your kidnapping became public, several women have come forward to say that Clayton Brown raped them. One said he held her at gunpoint."

Charlotte put the cap back on the bottle, her hands too shaky to take a drink. It shouldn't have surprised her that she wasn't the only girl Clayton had assaulted, but even so, hearing it shocked her.

"How many?"

"So far, five. That doesn't include the three young women back in his college days. His grandfather paid them off in exchange for their silence." Ben told her about the rapes Victoria had used as leverage to blackmail Clayton. "Brown is singing like a canary. He's telling anyone who'll listen that he'll testify against our mother if it means a reduced sentence for him."

Charlotte glanced at Damon. His head was lowered, and his shoulders slumped. He was taking this all on himself, as if he were somehow responsible. She touched his shoulder, and he jerked around to look at her. The pain in his eyes made her want to cry, but she pushed back her tears. Her eyes locked with Damon's as she spoke.

"I want to tell the police my story. The whole story. Clayton raped me in college, too. When I was out at that campsite, I swore I'd never be his victim again."

"I'm sorry for what you've been through, Charlotte. I can arrange for a meeting with the sheriff's office," Ben said. "Damon and I can come with you, if you like."

She smiled for Damon. "Yes, I'd like that. But

first, I need to tell my family." She swallowed and blew out a breath. "That's going to be a lot harder than telling the police."

Damon reached for her hand. "I'll come with you."

She searched his eyes. "Are you sure you want to do that?"

He nodded. "Yeah. I want to help."

She couldn't help thinking that he offered as a sort of penance for the sin of…what? Being his mother's son? Charlotte didn't know, but she could see it was important to him.

"Okay. Thank you."

Ben cleared his throat. "When you're ready, call me, and I'll make an appointment to speak to the police."

"I will."

"There's something else you should know, Charlotte. Our mother was arrested. She's being held on a number of charges, including accessory to kidnapping."

Charlotte turned back to Damon. His head was bowed again, distress rolling off him in waves. "I see. How do you feel about her being arrested, Damon?"

He lifted his head and looked at her, his eyes bleak. "She got what she deserves. She belongs in jail."

How utterly sad for a son to think that of his mother, Charlotte thought. But if Victoria Greyson did even some of the things she was accused of, she needed to be locked up.

Charlotte sighed and got to her feet. Right now, she had her own issues to worry about.

"I'm going to call my family and see if they can meet me at my house this evening."

Damon rose as well. "Tonight? Already?"

Charlotte put a hand on her stomach and blew out a breath. "I need to do this before I lose my nerve."

"I'll be there."

She smiled. "Thank you."

After thanking Ben, she left the office. Damon walked her to the Jeep and opened the driver's side door for her. Charlotte hesitated before getting inside.

"Are you really sure you want to come tonight?"

"Yes, absolutely." He spoke without hesitation, his expression resolute. "I'll support you any way I can."

Charlotte leaned over to kiss his cheek, her lips lingering against his skin, the stubble of his beard tickling them. "I love you, Damon. You're a good person."

His brow furrowed, and Charlotte wondered if he believed her. "What time do you want me to come to your house?"

"Let's say six-thirty. If that changes, I'll let you know."

He stepped away, breaking contact with her. "I'll be there."

Charlotte climbed into her Jeep with a heavy heart. Damon was determined to put distance between them emotionally and physically. She had to be patient and hope that with time he'd find his way back to her.

****

Damon arrived at Charlotte's house promptly at six-thirty. He knocked on the new front door. The reason it had needed to be replaced reminded him of how close Charlotte had come to being seriously hurt.

Or worse. He couldn't think about it or he'd lose his mind.

Charlotte opened the door with a smile, with Daisy and River at her feet. River wagged his tail enthusiastically, giving Damon a wide doggy smile. Aside from the shaved hair and line of sutures on his hip, no one would guess he'd been shot trying to defend Charlotte.

Another thing he couldn't think about.

He scratched Daisy's ears before giving River a vigorous scratch as well. "I bet he'll be glad to be rid of the cone of shame."

"Yeah, it will be a relief for all three of us. Daisy is terrified of the thing." Charlotte stepped away from the door and called for the dogs. "Come on, guys. Let Damon get in the house."

He followed her into the kitchen. Memories flooded back of mornings spent in this room having coffee with Charlotte after a night of making love with her. The morning light slanting in through the east window would highlight the honey-blonde streaks in her hair. She was so incredibly beautiful—

"Damon? Did you hear me? Would you like something to eat, or maybe coffee?"

He shook himself out of his dream world. He'd come here tonight to help Charlotte, not to take a trip down memory lane. That road was permanently closed.

"Sorry. No, I'm fine, thanks."

"I think I'll put on a pot in case anyone wants some."

He doubted anyone would feel like coffee once she told them about the rape. Charlotte filled the coffeepot with water and poured it in the coffeemaker, then braced her hands against the counter. "I've decided to tell my family about the abortion as well. I've been keeping secrets for too long. Besides, if I testify against Clayton, it could come out, and I'd rather my family hears it from me than be blindsided in court."

He nodded. She was right. It was better to tell them before they found out on their own. When he'd added his name to the list of Victor Campbell's victims, he couldn't find the courage to tell his brother and sister about his abuse. They'd been shocked to hear about it on the news. He knew it wasn't fair, but at the time he simply couldn't look them in the eyes and speak his truth.

But he'd confessed to his grandparents. In fact, they'd encouraged him to speak up and to get help. Without them and their support, he wasn't sure he'd still be alive. By then, his life had become unbearable.

No one knew better than he did the courage it took to speak up about a sexual assault. He admired Charlotte. After all she'd been through, she was thinking of her family and what they needed.

She was amazing, and he'd love her to his dying day. But she deserved better than him.

"Is there anything I can help you with?"

"Can you take the dogs into the back yard before everyone gets here?"

"Sure." He whistled for Daisy and River. "Come on guys, follow me."

By the time he came back into the house with the dogs, Grace and Robert Saunders had arrived, followed closely by Charlotte's sister Lauren. Garrett and Blair were last to appear. Blair gave Damon a warm smile and kissed his cheek.

"Hi! I didn't expect to see you here."

Damon shook Garrett's hand and gave his sister a

hug. "I'm only here for moral support."

"Moral support?" Blair's smile faded. "What do you mean?"

"Let Charlotte tell you."

After helping themselves to coffee, they gathered in Charlotte's living room. Charlotte stood in front of them, clutching her hands together. Damon stood behind her, giving her enough distance to tell her story in her own way, but close enough to support her if she needed it.

"Thank you for coming on such short notice." Charlotte looked down at her feet and blew out a breath before lifting her gaze and continuing. "What I have to tell you isn't easy for me to say, and it won't be easy for you to hear. I'm sorry." She hesitated once again. "Back when I was in college, I was raped."

Grace Saunders inhaled sharply. "Oh, Charlotte!"

Charlotte reached out her hand in a stopping motion when her mother would have come to her. "Let me finish, Mom. Please."

Grace nodded, and Robert put an arm around her shoulders.

"The details aren't important. But something you need to know is that Clayton Brown, the same man who kidnapped me, was the one who raped me in college. I couldn't tell you. I couldn't tell anyone. I was too ashamed, and I blamed myself for a long time. But that's over." She turned to glance at Damon. "Damon helped me see that it wasn't my fault. Rape is never about sex. It's always about control."

Lauren was crying. "I'm so sorry, Charlotte. I knew something had happened to you, but I was too caught up in my own drama to be of any support."

"I'm not telling you this to make any of you feel guilty. No one here needs to feel guilty about anything. I'm telling you now because I'm going to make my statement to the police and tell them about the rape. I'm going to make him take responsibility for what he did last week, and for what he did ten years ago."

She told them about the other women who'd come forward to accuse Clayton. "I know that's a lot to take in, but I'm afraid there's more." She took another deep breath, as if she were marshalling her courage. "After the rape, I discovered I was pregnant. I couldn't imagine having the baby, so I had an abortion."

For a few moments the room was totally silent, so quiet that Damon could hear the clock ticking on the kitchen wall. Finally, Grace rose to her feet, her hands outstretched as she stepped in front of Charlotte.

"I'm so sorry you had to go through that alone, sweetheart. Whatever happens from now on, you have to tell us. Okay? We're here for you, no matter what."

Charlotte nodded, and her mother wrapped her in her arms. Robert put his arms around both of them, and Garrett and Lauren joined them. Together they formed a tight cohesive group.

Blair walked over to Damon and put her arms around his waist. "She's going to be okay. You don't have to worry about her anymore."

Damon closed his eyes and buried his face in Blair's hair. Charlotte had her family now. She didn't need him anymore.

The thought made him want to weep.

Chapter Twenty-Five

"Hello? Anybody home?"

Damon recognized his father's voice calling from the back door of Ben and Jamie's house. His niece Sophie recognized his voice, too, and ran to the door to greet him.

"Grandpa!"

"How's my girl? I think you've grown since I last saw you."

"You mean I grew since yesterday?" Sophie asked, her voice excited.

Peter laughed. "Yes, I think you did, sweetie."

Jamie stepped to the back door. "Hi, Peter. Have you eaten? We've just finished, but we could put together a plate for you."

"Thank you, Jamie. That's very kind of you, but I ate earlier. I was walking in the neighborhood, and I thought I'd stop by."

"Ben and Bella are at her swimming lesson, but the rest of us are here in the kitchen. Why don't you come in?"

Damon sighed. He didn't particularly want to speak to his father. He didn't particularly want to speak to anyone. Ever since Charlotte told her family what had happened to her in college, he'd been adrift. Charlotte didn't need him anymore. She had her family, and she was better off leaning on them. She'd phoned and texted, but he hadn't responded.

But life went on. Peter was working hard on his sobriety and on reconnecting with his family. He went to AA meetings regularly with Ben and was seeing a counselor. Ben and Blair had made tentative connections with him. Ben's daughters had already welcomed him with open arms. It was uncomplicated for children. They simply responded to love.

Unless their trust was broken.

For the last week nightmares had haunted Damon's sleep, the same nightmares he'd had as a child. A faceless man was touching him in places he didn't want to be touched, making him do things he didn't want to do. He woke in the middle of the night in a cold sweat, unable to go back to sleep. For the rest of the night he'd stare at the dark ceiling of his basement bedroom, wondering where his life was going and if anything even mattered anymore. How could he counsel others when he couldn't help himself?

Peter walked up the short staircase between the back door and the kitchen, with five-year-old Sophie following him. He gave Jamie a one-armed hug, his right arm still in its plaster cast and supported by a sling.

"How beautiful you look!" he told Jamie.

Jamie smiled warmly as she laid her hand over her pregnant belly. "Obviously, you're blind. I'm as big as a whale."

Peter took her hand. "There's nothing more important than family, Jamie. Take it from someone who nearly lost his. But I still think you're beautiful."

Jamie nodded and placed her hand over his. "Would you like a cup of tea? I was about to make some."

"Thank you, no. I think I'm going to continue my walk. Maybe Damon would like to join me?"

All Damon wanted was to hide in his basement bedroom. "I don't think so."

"Come on, son. It's a beautiful, sunny evening. Some exercise will do you good."

"I have to help Jamie with the dishes."

"Sophie and I can handle them. Can't we, Soph?"

His niece grinned. "Yes! And I get to wash!"

"See? It's settled," Peter said. "Come walk with me."

Damon met his father's eyes. They were steady and calm on his, their brown depths urging him to step into the light. To live.

He shook his head at the fanciful thought. *I must really be losing it.* "Okay, fine. A short walk."

Peter nodded. "Wonderful. Let's go."

A few minutes later they were walking down the street, neither of them speaking. Damon finally broke the silence.

"Did Ben talk to you about me?"

"Your brother is worried about you. He says you're spending a lot of time alone in his basement when you're not at the farm. He's worried you're depressed."

Damon opened his mouth to deny it, then closed it. As a counselor, he knew all the classic signs of depression—the sleeplessness, lack of energy, self-loathing, and avoidance of others—all symptoms he was exhibiting. He was standing on the edge of a cliff, ready to fall into a pit of despair. It frightened him because he'd been there before and he knew what a deep hole depression was to crawl out of.

"I know I have no right to offer you advice, but I'm going to do it anyway. Don't let Victoria win."

Damon turned to his father, surprised by the vehemence in his voice. "What do you mean?"

"I want you to live your life the way you want, with who you want. Don't give Victoria any more power over your life. If you love Charlotte, be with her."

"Charlotte deserves better than me." She'd found the strength to face her past, but he never had, not really. He'd pushed his feelings down the last few years so he could keep moving forward, but the shame, and the guilt, was always with him. Charlotte's kidnapping had brought it to the forefront of his thoughts.

"You're wrong about that, son. You've been through hell and back, and you've come out whole and strong. Don't let Victoria's sickness ruin your life, your happiness."

"I don't deserve to be happy."

Peter turned to him in surprise. "Why would you say such a thing?"

Damon turned away, his eyes on the sidewalk. "You don't understand."

"No, I truly don't." Peter grasped Damon's shoulder. "Tell me. Help me understand."

Damon simply shook his head. How did he even begin to explain?

"You can tell me," Peter said gently. "There's not much I haven't heard, and God knows there's not much I haven't done. You won't shock me."

As they walked, Damon counted the cracks and blemishes in the concrete. He wanted to free himself from the prison that guilt had kept him in for so long.

But it was frightening to lay bare his inadequacies. The things he should have done but failed to.

He forced out a few words, his voice sounding dry and rusty. "I should have spoken up."

Peter turned to look at him, his brow wrinkled in confusion. "Do you mean about Campbell? But you did. Your testimony helped put him away."

"I was twenty-three before I spoke up. When I heard that three young boys had accused Campbell of sexual abuse, I couldn't hide any longer."

For many years, Campbell had been a volunteer hockey coach, a job that gave him ready access to young boys. Hearing the boys' stories had brought back all the horrible feelings he'd been trying to run away from for years. The feelings of helplessness, powerlessness, and shame. And they also brought a new emotion—guilt. He managed to summon enough courage to go to the police and tell his story. His testimony had added enough weight to the children's stories to put Campbell away. So he couldn't hurt any other little boys.

"But you didn't hide. You told the truth."

"Don't you see? It was too late by then. If I'd said something years earlier, Campbell would have been stopped and those boys wouldn't have had to go through what I did."

"But years earlier, you were a child, Damon. You couldn't be expected to make a decision like that." Peter sighed. "And even if you had, I'm not sure anything would have changed. I was too deep inside a bottle to be of much help to you. And your mother…"

He didn't finish.

"If I'd spoken up years ago, maybe Ben and Blair

wouldn't have gone through the hell they did growing up. And maybe Charlotte wouldn't have been kidnapped."

"I don't understand. How could you have changed any of that?"

"Because she knew!" The words exploded out of him in a shout. Damon forced himself to lower his voice. "It wasn't coincidence. Victoria knew what was happening to me. She made a deal with Campbell. I heard them talking."

Peter stopped walking and turned incredulous eyes to him. "What do you mean?"

"Victoria offered me to Campbell in exchange for membership at the exclusive country club you belonged to. I really hope the golf was worth it."

"Oh, my God." Peter rubbed a hand over his pale face. "I remember we suddenly got a membership to the club after being turned down a couple of times, probably because they knew I was a drunk. Victoria said she'd had another interview with the selection committee and this time they let us in."

"Campbell was the head of the selection committee. She made a deal with the devil. I should have told you or someone at school right away. Maybe if I had, Victoria would have been sent to jail along with Campbell. If she'd been gone, she wouldn't have been able to hurt Ben and Blair anymore."

"I can't believe she went that far. For a stupid country club with a bunch of snooty members. She sacrificed our son." He shook his head. "I…I think I need to sit down for a minute."

"We're not far from the school. We can find a place to rest there."

Damon took Peter's good arm and led him to the schoolyard. They found a park bench adjacent to the playground equipment. Peter slowly lowered himself to the bench, suddenly looking years older than he had a short time ago.

"I've known for a long time that she's ruthless at getting what she wants, but I never imagined..." He shook his head, unable to finish. "I'm so sorry, son. You were a child. If you want to blame someone, blame me. I didn't protect you. I was too consumed with alcohol and with pleasing Victoria, and I didn't see what was right in front of me. Blame the world, blame me, but don't blame yourself."

Damon heard the self-recrimination in his father's voice. Was Peter right?

"As long as the Greyson money kept rolling in, everything was fine. Victoria could live the lifestyle she wanted and hobnob with St. Paul's elite." Peter shook his head. "I'm so sorry, Damon. I can't even begin to tell you how sorry I am."

Damon believed him. Peter was working hard to turn his life around and make amends. He only wished Peter could have been the father he needed when he was a child.

"We can't let her get away with this, Damon. She's a sick, dangerous woman. She needs to be locked up. Permanently."

"Yeah." He had to go to the police and make the confession he should have made a long time ago.

"When you were in your twenties, and you came forward to tell the police about Campbell, why didn't you tell them the whole story, that your mother had given you to that...to that monster?"

It was something he'd been asking himself for a very long time. "I think I was still in denial. I didn't want to believe it was true. I mean, how could a mother do that to her child? So I told myself it hadn't happened."

Peter nodded. "We both deluded ourselves. I wanted to believe she loved me, in her own way. But I know now that Victoria is incapable of love."

They'd all been cheated and damaged because of Victoria. "Are you ready to go back to Ben's house?"

"Sure." Peter rose slowly to his feet, and Damon did the same. "I think I need to call my sponsor."

Damon nodded. His confession had unsettled his father, but there was no helping it.

They walked back to Ben and Jamie's house in silence. When they got there, Damon asked, "Would you like a ride back to Morley's house?"

"No, I think I'd like to walk. It's not far."

"Okay. Goodnight. I'll talk to you soon."

"Goodnight." Peter grasped his hand. "Don't let guilt and blame eat you up, son. You deserve better. Don't wait until you're my age to try to find some peace."

An image of Charlotte's face floated into Damon's head. He wanted to be worthy of her.

And he wanted to be worthy of himself. He wanted to look in a mirror and be proud of the man staring back at him. But how did he accomplish that?

A plan began to form. To get the life he wanted, he'd need to make some bold moves.

He hoped he was brave enough. And strong enough.

****

"Do you have anything you'd like to add to your statement, Ms. Saunders?"

The deputy waited for her response, a pen poised in her hand, and a recording device running. Charlotte glanced at Damon sitting next to her. True to his word, he'd accompanied her to the police station as she made her statement about how Clayton Brown had raped her ten years ago. It had been difficult to talk about the rape, but having Damon close by gave her strength. Ben was also there, acting as her lawyer. He'd interjected a couple of times when he thought the questions the deputy was asking were inappropriate. Like when she asked her what she'd been wearing on the night of the rape.

The Greyson brothers had wide protective streaks.

"No, I think I've told you everything," she told Deputy Muller.

"All right, then. Thank you for your statement. We'll be in touch if we have any further questions."

"Thank you."

Ben rose and offered his hand to Charlotte. "Let's get out of here."

The sunshine felt good on her face as they left the sheriff's office and walked through the parking lot. Ben slipped on a pair of sunglasses.

"I've got to head back to my office." He kissed Charlotte's cheek. "If you think of anything you want to add to your statement, let me know, and we'll speak to the police again together. You don't have to do this alone. Okay?"

"Okay. Thanks for everything, Ben."

"You're welcome. Take care of yourself." He nodded at Damon. "I'll see you later at home."

"See you later."

They watched Ben get into his car and drive away. Charlotte clutched the strap of her purse, not knowing what to say to Damon. She hadn't seen him for nearly a week, not since the night she'd told her family about the rape. As promised, he'd been there to support her, at least physically. But he'd barely spoken to her, either that night or today. Charlotte got the feeling she was an obligation to him, something he needed to take care of before moving on.

Before moving on. Was Damon thinking about leaving Masonville? Her heart lurched at the thought. With all the upset and trauma he'd been through the last few weeks, it wouldn't be a surprise if leaving was on his mind.

But God, she hoped she was wrong.

Damon turned to her, his eyes not quite meeting hers. "I…uh…I wanted to let you know that I'll be out of town for a few days."

So I was right. "Where are you going?" She shook her head, her heart aching. "No, sorry. You don't have to tell me."

She started to move away, but he caught her hand. "No, it's okay. I want to tell you. I'm going to St. Paul. To file charges against my mother."

Charlotte blinked in surprise. "What kind of charges?"

This time Damon's gaze was level with hers. "I'm not sure of the exact name of the crime, but whatever you call it when a mother pimps out her eight-year-old son."

Charlotte couldn't speak. She gripped Damon's hand while he calmly explained how his mother gave him to a pedophile, knowing what the man was and what he'd do to her child.

What kind of mother, what kind of person could do that?

Oh, Damon. My poor, sweet Damon.

She managed to squeak out a few words. "You shouldn't go alone. I could get a few days off."

"I'll be fine."

"Seriously, Greyson. Don't go all Lone Ranger on me. It's a long drive. I could help—"

"Charlotte." Damon placed his hands on either side of her face. "It's all right, really. I know you want to help, but I've got this. And if I'm honest, it would be easier for me if you're not there."

His words hit her like a slap to the face. It hadn't been easy to talk about details of her rape to the police, but having him in the room with her, knowing he supported her, gave her the courage to do what she had to do.

Obviously, Damon didn't feel the same way. She tried not to show how much that hurt.

"Okay."

"Charlotte." His brows knit together as he gently rubbed his thumbs over the delicate skin under her eyes. The tenderness of the small caress made her want to cry. "I'm sorry."

Then he dropped his hands and walked to his truck. As he drove away, she wondered if he'd ever touch her again.

Chapter Twenty-Six

After the group counseling session finished, Damon went back to the house. Blair was on her knees in front of one of the flowerbeds surrounding the house, pulling weeds and stacking them next to the bed.

"Need a hand?"

She looked up at him with a smile. "Sure. Just don't pull any good stuff."

"How do I know what's the good stuff?"

"If I scream at you when you pull it, it was a flower."

"Good to know." Damon found a small plant nestled between two blooming flowers that he believed were geraniums. "How 'bout this thing? Yea or nay?"

Blair leaned over for a look. "Yea. Garrett's mom calls that a sow thistle. It needs to go."

Damon wrapped his fingers around the weed and gave it a tug. He was rewarded by a satisfying length of root coming out of the ground. He shook off the dirt and set it on top of Blair's pile of weeds.

"You've become very close to Grace Saunders, haven't you?"

"I have. She's treated me like one of her daughters since Garrett and I have been together." She smiled as she pulled up another weed. "When we have kids, I hope to be like her. She's a good role model."

They both knew their mother was no role model for

motherhood. He sighed and sat back on his heels.

"I need to tell you something. I'm going to St. Paul."

Blair stopped weeding to look at him, confusion in her eyes. "Why?"

"Because I can't let her win, Blair."

He told her how Victoria had offered him to Campbell in exchange for a membership at the country club. Every time he told the story, it got a little easier, as if it lost some of its power with each telling.

But it was the first time Blair had heard it, and the look on her face spoke to her shock and horror.

"Victoria's done some low things, but this…" She shook her head. "I don't have words."

Damon squeezed her shoulder. "Are you all right?"

"I should be asking you that. Are *you* all right?"

"I'm getting there. Bringing this out into the light helps. So will telling the police."

"I'll come with you."

"No, you won't. I have to do this myself."

"Don't be stupid. You definitely don't have to do this yourself."

"Blair—"

"Have you told Ben?"

"Not yet."

She pulled her phone from the back pocket of her jeans. "Then now seems like a good time. I'm sure he'll want to come, too."

"Blair, don't—"

She lifted a hand to silence him. "Ben, is this a good time to talk? Good. Our brother has something he wants to tell you."

She hit the speaker phone button and held the

phone in front of him. "Go ahead. Tell Ben what you just told me. Tell him what you plan to do."

"Did anyone ever tell you you're a pain in the ass?" Damon grumbled.

"Just you. Now, spill it."

"Come on, you guys." Ben's annoyed voice was crisp over the phone lines. "Will somebody hurry up and tell me what's going on?"

"Fine." With a sigh, Damon repeated the story once again. When he finished, there was complete silence on the phone, and he wondered if they'd been cut off. "Ben? Are you there?"

"I'm here." He cleared his throat. "I just…I'm trying to take it in."

"I'm sorry. This wasn't how I wanted to tell you."

"I'm sorry, too, Ben," Blair said. "But he's talking about going alone to give his statement, and I don't think it's a good idea."

"Blair's right. I'll come with you."

"Good. So will I," Blair said.

Blair gave him a satisfied smirk, and Damon knew this was an argument he wasn't going to win.

"There's something else. I'm planning on seeing Victoria."

"Why?" Blair shook her head in disbelief. "Why would you want to give her even one minute of your time?"

"You owe her nothing, Damon," Ben said.

"It's not about her, it's about me. Like I said, I can't let her win. I need to say some things to her, and she likely won't understand or give a damn, but I have to say them."

Blair silently stared at him. On the phone, Ben was

silent as well. Finally, Damon heard Ben clear his throat again.

"Yeah, I get it. I totally get it."

"So do I," Blair said with a nod. "And it's all the more reason for Ben and me to go with you. This affects us, too. We don't want her to win either."

"Yeah. What Blair said."

Damon stared at the determined set of Blair's chin. His brother and sister had as much right as he did to confront their mother. And if he was honest, he needed their support.

Charlotte had wanted to support him too, but he'd pushed her away. The idea of her hearing details about his sexual abuse and the deep dysfunction in his family shamed him. He didn't want her pity, and he especially didn't want thoughts of his abuse as a child to be on her mind when they made love again.

If they made love again. He'd hurt her by not accepting her help. He had to trust she'd be able to forgive him some day. After he'd done what he needed to do, he'd talk to her and see if there was a chance for them. But he couldn't give his heart to her until he'd exorcised his mother from his life.

"All right, we'll go together."

"We'll take my car," Ben said. "I'll drive."

"I call shotgun," Blair said with a grin.

"Well, then." Damon exhaled a breath. "Looks like we're going on a road trip."

****

The prison guard let them into a visitation room. It was stark, the only furniture a small table in the middle of the space with one chair on one side and two chairs on the other. A guard brought in a third chair while they waited, and Damon sat in it as he glanced around. The room could only be described as bleak. The concrete block walls were painted a sickly green similar to the color of hospital scrubs. There were no signs of human habitation, no magazines strewn about, no empty coffee cups or soda cans. Just a door on the far side of the room where prisoners entered. Damon stared at the door. His mother would soon enter through that door.

Blair and Ben sat on either side of him, neither of them speaking or even moving. This couldn't have been any easier on them than it was on him, and yet they'd insisted on coming. He'd never loved his siblings more than he did right now.

The door on the far side of the room opened, and Victoria walked in wearing an orange prison-issue jumpsuit, followed by a female prison guard. Victoria smiled in triumph as she sat across from them.

"Well, children. Isn't this nice? A family reunion between a mother and her babies. Couldn't stay away from Mommy, could you?"

"Cut the crap, Victoria," Damon said. "This isn't a social call."

Victoria draped one arm over the back of her chair and crossed her legs. "Well, if not to support your mother, what did you come here for? And don't say to gloat, dear. Gloating is so unattractive."

"I don't expect you to understand anything I've come here to say, because I finally realize you have no feelings, no caring for anyone but yourself. Anyone who's done the despicable things you've done is nothing but a monster."

"Do not speak to me with such disrespect," Victoria hissed. "I'm your mother."

"You're not a mother. You may have given birth to us, but you've never been a mother."

Her smug smile widened. "If you're so upset with me, then why are you here?"

"To tell you I've been to the police to inform them that Campbell didn't find me by accident when I was eight. You gave me to him. You gave your own son to a pedophile."

"Don't be ridiculous." Damon heard the sneer in her voice, but he also heard a note of worry.

"I told them everything. How it started when Campbell picked me up after hockey practice instead of you. How I heard the two of you arguing about the country club membership he was supposed to secure for you in return for free access to my body."

"You don't know what you're talking about. No one's going to believe such an outlandish story."

"They've already questioned Campbell, and he confirmed it."

Victoria turned noticeably paler. Even she recognized the danger she was in.

"He's lying."

"No, for once in his life he was telling the truth. And for once in your life, you're going to listen."

"Don't be rid—"

"I said you're going to listen." Damon raised his voice only marginally, but some of the rage inside him must have surfaced because Victoria immediately stopped speaking. "We've danced to your tune for too long, but that's over. You've tried to destroy everyone you've ever come close to—your husband, your children, your parents. You came close to totally destroying me as a child and again now, but I'm stronger than you. I'm not going to let you win. I've never felt so powerful as when I told the police how you gave me to a pedophile. Peter's already told them how you beat him. Clayton Brown and Carmen Miller testified that you blackmailed them. You're going away for a very long time, Victoria. And if you ever get out, don't come looking for any of us, because we never want to see you or hear from you again. As far as we're concerned, you're dead and we're free of you. You don't matter. We win."

With that he turned and headed to the exit, Blair and Ben right behind him. As they left the jail and started across the parking lot to the car, the adrenaline he'd been running on suddenly evaporated, and he began to shake, unable to take another step. Blair looped her arm through his and Ben supported him with an arm around his waist.

"You were magnificent, Damon," Blair said. "I'm so proud of you."

Ben tightened his hold. "She can't hurt any of us, or anyone we love, ever again."

Damon nodded. He closed his eyes and breathed in deeply, then expelled the breath through his mouth. As he breathed over and over, his body supported by his brother and sister, the darkness began to lift. Black thoughts left his body with each exhale. The weight of the world fell from his shoulders, and the chains and shackles that had kept him imprisoned for so long dropped away.

He began to laugh. Blair poked him gently in the chest.

"What are you laughing about?"

He wrapped his arms around their shoulders. "I'm

free. I'm finally free. Let's go home."

"Those are the sweetest words I've heard all day," Ben said.

****

Charlotte arrived home from her evening shift shortly after midnight. As she pulled into her driveway and opened the door of her Jeep, she noticed a beat-up Chevy truck parked in front of her house. Damon's truck. Her breath caught as he opened the truck door and walked across the lawn toward her.

He stopped a couple of feet away from her, his hands in the pockets of his jeans, his eyes downcast.

"So when you said you loved me, did you mean it?" he asked.

"Of course I meant it. I don't throw around words like love if I don't mean them."

He lifted his head. "That's good, because I love you, too."

His monotone delivery annoyed her, even as hope blossomed in her heart. "Try not to sound so enthusiastic about it. You've told me you love ice cream with more gusto."

His sudden grin made her heart beat faster. "There she is. There's my girl with the smart comeback." He reached for her hand. "Do you know the exact moment I fell in love with you?"

She shook her head, concentrating on the loving way Damon caressed her hand.

"I was fourteen that summer, and I got braces on my teeth a couple of months before we came out to the farm. Ben and Garrett teased me mercilessly. You had just turned twelve."

"I remember." Damon had been so shy, so

awkward. She'd been drawn to him, wanting to protect him from their brothers and all the bullies in the world.

"I was the only one in my family who needed braces for my crooked teeth. I always felt different from Ben and Blair because they were so beautiful, and I was so exceedingly ordinary. Being molested by a pedophile made me feel different, too. I felt very much alone in the world."

Charlotte squeezed his hand, afraid to speak and break the spell. He needed to say something to her, and she needed to hear it.

"One day they were teasing me, and you got in between us and gave them hell. I'll never forget what you said. Do you remember?"

She didn't have a clue. "No. What did I say?"

"You told them that big brothers were the dumbest and the meanest. And then you said, and I quote, 'Braces are temporary, but stupid is forever.' I fell in love with you on the spot."

Charlotte burst out laughing. "I didn't realize how profound I was at twelve. Maybe I should cross-stitch that on a pillow."

"Maybe you should." The smile left his face as he stepped closer to her. "It was the first time anyone aside from my grandparents ever stood up for me. You made me feel like I was worth something. If someone as wonderful as you could see something good in me, maybe I could go on."

She couldn't speak. She reached for him and wound her arms around his neck, holding him tight. Damon spoke quietly, his mouth close to her ear.

"When we met again last year, you were as kind and funny and sweet as you were at twelve, and I fell in love all over again."

Charlotte pulled back so she could see his face, and he could see the truth in her words. "First of all, Damon Greyson, you are anything but exceedingly ordinary. You are a remarkable, wonderful man. I may not have fallen in love with you at twelve, but when I did fall, I fell hard and forever. I'm never going to fall out of love with you, because you're the best person I know."

"Right back at you, Charlotte Saunders. You're the best person I know." Damon softly kissed her lips. "Let's go home, sweetheart."

With their arms wrapped around each other's waist, they walked to the front door. Home at last.

Epilogue

The following spring

Damon clasped his hands tightly together as he waited at the altar, his foot tapping silently against the carpeted floor. His brother leaned over and whispered in his ear.

"Relax. She'll be here in a minute."

Damon nodded and unclasped his hands, flexing them to work out the cramps. With everyone in the church staring at him, his insistence on a big wedding no longer seemed like such a great idea. Charlotte had wanted something simple, a wedding at the courthouse with a dinner at her parents' house for family, but he'd talked her into a bigger celebration. He'd told himself he didn't want Charlotte to feel cheated in the future about not having a larger, more elaborate wedding, but maybe he'd been motivated by pride. He wanted to show the world the beautiful woman who'd agreed to marry him.

A panicked thought hit him. Had she changed her mind about marrying him? Was that why she was late?

And then the doors of the church opened, and the organist began playing the wedding march. Sophie and Bella were first to walk up the aisle, wearing matching dresses in pale lilac and carrying small bouquets of lilac sprigs, as befitted a spring wedding. Lauren, Blair, and

Jamie followed, their dresses the same color as that of the girls. The sweet scent of lilacs from their bouquets reached Damon as they approached. He knew he'd forever associate the scent of lilacs with love and happiness.

Finally, Charlotte stepped inside the church, flanked on each side by her parents. She was a vision of beauty in ivory lace. *His angel.* As she walked up the aisle, her eyes locked with his, and she smiled, happiness shining on her beautiful face. Damon smiled back, his body and mind relaxing.

She's here. She's really here. And she loves me.

At last, she reached him at the front of the church. She kissed her parents as they handed her over to Damon and sat in the front pew. He took Charlotte's hand and led her to stand in front of the minister.

Damon barely heard the minister speak. He was only aware of Charlotte standing beside him, and the scent of lilacs from her bouquet swirling around him. Every moment of his life, every trauma and heartache he'd endured had brought him to this point, and to this woman. This was where he belonged. In this community with the people he loved. With Charlotte.

As they exchanged vows and rings, he said a silent prayer of thanks for making him strong enough to be the man Charlotte wanted and needed.

"I now pronounce you husband and wife."

With those words they were married. Charlotte wrapped her arms around his neck and kissed him as their delighted guests clapped and cheered.

Hand in hand, they made their way out of the church, followed by the bridal party. Damon waved at his father in the front pew, and Peter grinned back. He was holding Ben and Jamie's sleeping son Ethan, who'd been born the previous October. Peter was happy and thriving. He regularly attended AA meetings and was now living in the Fletcher Building in the apartment Damon had originally planned for himself. Morley and Ben had been able to recover some of the money Clayton Brown had stolen, and with the help of a new contractor, work on the building had been completed. To Damon's relief and joy, it was now filled with veterans looking to rebuild their lives. Peter acted as a sort of house father in the Fletcher Building and was around whenever someone needed to talk. For the first time in Damon's life, he and his father had an honest, caring relationship.

Outside the church they lined up to greet their guests. Ben and Jamie stood next to them, along with Sophie and Bella. Sophie told anyone who'd listen that it was her second turn at being a flower girl. She and her sister had done the job once before for their parents.

Next to them were Garrett and Blair, and then Cole and Lauren. Blair and Lauren had matching baby bumps beneath their bridesmaid dresses. Their babies were due to arrive within two weeks of each other in about four months. Damon was grateful for his family's happiness.

The guests filed out and shook hands with the bridal party, offering their best wishes. Damon shook Robert Saunders' hand and accepted a kiss from Charlotte's mother, Grace. For one moment he let himself remember his own mother. Her trial over the winter had been difficult, but Damon had come away feeling stronger. She was in prison where she belonged and would likely be there for the rest of her life. Her co-

conspirator, Clayton Brown, was convicted of his many crimes, including kidnapping Charlotte, and for that he was serving hard time. He pushed both of them firmly from his mind.

Morley Walker shook his hand and told him how pleased his grandfather would be to see him so happy. Damon was sure his grandparents, Everett and Anna Branson, were smiling down on him today. They'd wanted nothing more than for Damon and his siblings to be happy, and that wish had come true.

Following Morley was Chris Redwick and his wife Alison and their children. Chris had become one of Damon's closest friends. He was so proud of the great strides Chris had made in battling his PTSD.

After the Redwick family, Charlotte's friends Gina and Michelle from the shelter shook their hands and wished them happiness. They'd all celebrated the previous October when the last hoarder dog went to her forever home. Because of the attention in social media and in the national news, every dog at Branson Farm was adopted. It was an amazing accomplishment Damon had never imagined possible.

As if Blair and Garrett's bold move with the dogs wasn't enough, over the winter they'd rescued three more horses, bringing the number at Branson Farm to seven. Many of the veterans who came to the farm found solace and acceptance working with the horses. Others preferred the company of dogs, so Damon continued to work with Best Friends Haven for Dogs as a satellite shelter, though with fewer dogs than during the crisis. It was a mutually beneficial arrangement for both the shelter and Branson Farm.

It seemed the whole town was at their wedding—

the staff from the veterinary clinic where Jamie and Blair and Cole worked, Isabelle and Jenny from the Homestead Restaurant where Lauren had once waited tables, Charlotte's friends from the hospital, all the veterans currently going through therapy at the Fletcher Building and the farm. Damon was especially pleased that the first five veterans to be treated at Branson Farm—Des, Mike, Trey, Tom, and Ray—had returned to Masonville for the wedding. Damon had kept in touch with them since they'd completed the program. He was pleased that they'd all begun to turn their lives around.

Masonville had opened its arms to him, and its heart. He'd found more friends here than anywhere he'd lived in his entire life. He'd be forever grateful to his grandfather for the legacy that had brought him here.

The limousine pulled up in front of the church, and the bridal party, including Sophie and Bella, got inside. A couple of bottles of sparkling mineral water were waiting inside in an ice bucket. Ben opened a bottle, and he and Garrett filled champagne glasses that they passed around.

"To Charlotte and Damon. May they always be as happy as they are today," Ben said.

Everyone clinked glasses. "Hear, hear."

Damon looked into Charlotte's smiling eyes. "To my beautiful wife. I love you today, tomorrow, and forever, Mrs. Greyson."

Charlotte lifted her glass to him, her eyes shining with happiness and love. "Right back at ya, Mr. Greyson."

A word about the author…

Jana Richards has tried her hand at many writing projects over the years, from magazine articles and short stories to full-length contemporary romance, paranormal suspense, and romantic comedy. She loves to create characters with a sense of humor but also a serious side. She believes there's nothing more interesting than peeling back the layers of a character to see what makes them tick.

When not writing up a storm or dealing with dust bunnies, Jana can be found pursuing hobbies such as golf (which she plays very badly) or reading (which she does much better).

Jana lives in Western Canada with her husband Warren. You can reach her through her website at:
http://www.janarichards.com

Thank you for purchasing
this publication of The Wild Rose Press, Inc.

For questions or more information
contact us at
info@thewildrosepress.com.

The Wild Rose Press, Inc.